The
Reservationist

by

Barbra Porter Coleman

CandleStick Publishing
P.O. Box 394　　　　Cedar Hill, TX 75104-0394

Cover Illustration by Chris Rayson
Cover Designs by Janet Long
Editing by Weis Revise/Ann Fields/Penny Marquez

Visit our Website at www.candlestickpublishing.com
Email at bcoleman33@swbell.net

Printed in the United States
The Reservationist First Edition

ISBN: 0-9774679-0-2
LCCN: 2006901872

ACKNOWLEDGEMENT

Members of Writer's Block Inc, Antionette Coleman, Thelma Frost, Sandra Stevens, Stephanie Morris, Tammy White, Florence Jones, Denise Lewis, Dee Dee Freeman, Delisa Coleman, Vanessa McDaniels, Stephanie Jones, Elizabeth Holman, Joyce Owens, Carmen Jackson, Tammy Hudson, Beverlyn McQueen, Patsy Splawn, Takeyiah Lewis, Lynn Reese, Bonita Willis,Sandra Starnes, Zyronda Higgins, Christine Perkins, Reba Woodson, Linda Newman, Sheila Chandler, Angela Shearry Sneed, Octavia Coleman, Erma Davis and Denise Clayton.

A special thanks to my husband, Alton—for being patient with me. I love you.
A special thanks to Gerri H. Savala for coming up with the airline name and eagerly helping in wanting to see my dream. (I swear you watch too much TV) Ann Fields - Thanks Ann, I couldn't have done it without you. Girl you're a tough editor. Elaine Flowers - Thanks Elaine for always willing to answer my questions. Jose Martinez- Thanks Jose for my website. Robin Brewer- Thanks for always lending an ear. Deborah Coleman- Thanks (Rose) for literally lending a hand.
Cherieka Morgan-Gossett (niece) Thanks for your picture.
To my nieces and nephews—I love you.
To my siblings - Marilyn, John Jr., Delman, Debra and Terissa. I love ya'll.

To my children Jamario, Jarvis (Ivrie), Altonia, Ja'nai, and Alton Jr. Thanks for your contribution.
To my grandchildren Anaya, Amaya, Anajiah and Gavin.

To my pastor Rev. Alfred C. Stapleton thanks for your Inspirational messages.

In Memory Of

This book is dedicated to my late mother and father Rosetta and John Edward Porter, Sr. **Rest In Peace.**

In loving memory of my buddy - Dorothea Flournoy-Evans.

In loving memory of La'Vare D. Ballard (My son) you're not forgotten.

The
Reservationist

Prologue

*E*arly morning dew lay on the Texas grass as Diamond O'Connell, the fictitious name she frequently used, dashed across the front lawn in her teddy. With the sun highlighting her slim body, she hurriedly picked up the newspaper and ran back inside before the neighbors could see her. She sat at the breakfast table, opened the paper, and scanned the want ads.

Suddenly, there it was—her gateway to revenge: JET AWAY AIRWAYS ACCEPTING APPLICATIONS FOR SALES RESERVATIONIST. "The deadline is today!" She jumped up, letting the paper flutter to the floor as she ran to the shower.

Two hours later, she stood in front of the corporate office of Jet Away staring at her reflection in the glass door. A mad woman camouflaged by beauty stared back. She pushed open the door and smiled at the receptionist as she stepped up to the glass case.

"May I help you?" asked the receptionist, sliding back the small glass door.

"Yes, I'm here for the Sales Reservationist's position."

"Your timing is perfect," she said then smiled. "The manager has been hiring on the spot today." She handed Diamond an application on a clipboard. "Can you type?"

"Yes, I can," Diamond lied, aware that it had been years since she'd been near a keyboard.

Pointing to the other end of the room, the receptionist said, "Take a seat over at the table."

As Diamond walked over to the round table, her silky black hair swayed across her shoulders with each step. Forty minutes later, after completing the two-step process, the receptionist escorted her to a large office where six other applicants—four young ladies and two men—eagerly waited to find out if they had the job.

Diamond took her seat. "I've got to get this job; I have to," she muttered to herself, clenching the pencil in her hand until it broke. "Jet Away, you're going to pay for what you did to me." Realizing she was speaking aloud, she looked around, hoping no one had heard the hostility in her voice or the threat, but everybody continued talking and looking at magazines.

The receptionist returned fifteen minutes later with a big smile. "Congratulations, you've all been accepted."

"Oh, thank you!" Diamond said as she stood. *This is the break I need*, she thought, trying hard to suppress a wicked grin.

"Study the airline codes and the other information in your packet and we will see you next Monday for training," said the receptionist as she handed out the packets.

"Thank you. You won't regret it," Diamond said again as she left the office with a vengeful smile. *And God said vengeance is mine,* the voice wailed inside her head. "I know, but you have to take the backseat on this one," Diamond retorted.

The next week, Diamond sat in the intense training session with twenty other new hirees. Determined to complete training, she put her personal life on hold to focus on the class. She knew she had to get inside the operation if she wanted revenge.

After successfully completing four weeks of training, plus another two months on the phone, she began covertly studying ways to get into the administrative office. Each day she would walk by the administrative office getting familiar with its layout, watching the security guard perambulate through the building making his rounds. One afternoon as she headed for her break, she peeked through the glass door of the administration office and noticed a set of keys on the desk. She could hear two women laughing somewhere in the background, but saw no one in the office. She slipped into the office, quickly slid the keys into her jacket, and walked out the opened door.

Later that night, at around midnight, she returned to the dark office and tried one of the keys in the lock. Nothing happened. "Damn." She frowned, glanced around the empty hallway, and tried the second key. The lock clicked softly. Bingo! She slithered through the door like a snake, looking over her shoulder for the frail security guard, who constantly walked the halls. She locked the door and walked a few feet toward the back of the room where there was a beveled glass door labeled 'Archives'.

She opened the door leaving it slightly ajar while she surveyed the small room, which contained several four-foot-tall gray file cabinets. She quietly searched the cabinet closest to the door for ten minutes, but didn't find the information that would set her free from the demons that haunted her. Just as she finished going through the second cabinet the door up front rattled, making her gasp. Her hand went to her chest. She turned off the light, closed the door, and hid behind a file cabinet, removing the switchblade from her jacket. *Must be the security guard making his rounds,* she thought as she felt her heart pounding. Sweat beads began to form. "If he walks in here, this will be the last round he makes," she uttered through her gritted teeth. Apparently, all was well with the guard for after ten minutes she felt secure.

She came out from behind the cabinet, flipped the light switch on, and continued her quest. Tackling the third file cabinet, she began tossing folders on the floor, not caring where they landed. Her anger began to boil at not finding the information she sought.

Finally, she pulled out a file labeled 'Employees' Deaths' and began scanning each page before tossing it aside. Halfway through the folder she ran across what she had been looking for: 'Lacy Brent.' "This is it," she said, gripping the paper. She continued reading the rest of the file. 'He has a wife, Wanda Brent, and daughter, Tia.' "Wanda Brent, you will pay," she spoke with emphasis, "for what your husband did to me."

She placed the folder underneath her arm, stepped over the files, and quickly walked to the glass door. The slight sound of keys jingling caught her attention as she peered through the glass and saw the security guard coming her way. Diamond hid behind a wall while the guard shook the door handle, and then continued down the hall. When she saw the guard walk around the corner and out of sight, she unlocked the door as her hand trembled, swung it open, and fled to the safety of her car.

Diamond drove home like a crazy woman. Heading straight for the phone, she took out the paper and began pressing numbers. "Damn, it's disconnected." She slammed down the receiver and rushed to the computer, pulled up Mapsco, typed in the address, got the directions to the Brents' house, printed them out, grabbed her purse, and headed for her Jeep. Tears of grief welled in her eyes as she pulled up in front of the house and turned off the motor.

Convinced this was the moment, she got out and peeked through a small window at the front of the house. She was overwhelmed with vengeance. Then she saw a shadow moving inside and returned to her vehicle. After scoping out the house for an hour, she decided to leave. "I'll be back early before she goes to work." She began to start the engine, then thought, *I may miss her if I leave.* She coaxed her black Jeep Cherokee a few yards down the street, parked between two cars and camped out for the night.

Exhausted, she didn't feel the chilled air rushing through the cracked window, brushing her face as she slept. The chirping of the birds woke her. *The sun would be out any minute,* she thought as night faded and day broke. She sat for a while then stretched while checking the clock on the dash before opening the glove compartment for her disguise. A piece of paper where she had repeatedly practiced writing her fictitious name fell to the floor. She pulled out a blonde wig styled in a feathered look, tucked her hair underneath as she adjusted the wig on her head, popped a couple of mints into her mouth to disguise her morning breath, put the gear in reverse and backed the Jeep up to the house. She walked boldly up the steps to the beautiful, white, two-story brick house. She cleared her throat and rang the doorbell.

"Coming," she heard from inside the house. Seconds later, the door opened half way. "May I help you?" a woman asked.

Diamond glared at the tall, blonde woman and then extended her sweaty hand. "Hi, I'm Diamond O'Connell with

Secure Security System." She flashed a smile. "I noticed you aren't serviced by a security company." She looked back, "there's not a sign in the yard."

The woman reluctantly eased her hand from behind the door to shake hands. It was obvious that the woman thought seven o'clock in the morning was too early for solicitation.

"Yes," she hesitated. "In fact we do have a security system," the woman replied. "However, it's through my husband's business. The same security company monitors both our home and his business."

"Your husband?" Diamond asked surprisingly as she pretended to look at a list of names on her clipboard. "I have here that this house belongs to a Wanda Brent."

"No, we've lived here for the past ten years. I heard the people that lived here before moved to Dallas."

"Do you know where they moved in Dallas?" Diamond asked, dismayed to learn Wanda had moved, and for the moment, foiled her plan.

"No," answered the woman, a look of curiosity crossing her face.

"I'm sorry to have bothered you," Diamond said flashing a half smile.

"That's quite all right," the woman answered as she quickly shut the door.

Diamond walked back to her Jeep, got in, snatched off her wig, and started beating on the steering wheel. A thrill of ferocity ran through her. "Dammit! She thinks she's gotten away, but that witch is mine!" Sneering wickedly, she grabbed the wig and began pulling out strands of hair. "Dallas, huh? Goodbye, Houston, hello, Dallas!" She threw the wig on the floor. "It's not over, Wanda, it's just beginning," she said. It was a smooth ride home.

One

*T*he December sun peeked through the Venetian blinds, illuminating every angle of Sky Winters's pink-shaded room. She opened the white French doors to her walk-in closet and looked at the top shelf, where a cardboard box had lain untouched for months—until today. Now she was glad she had it. Sky reached for the box and glanced inside, but hurriedly replaced the top. Her hands started to tremble and she dropped the box, which hit the floor with a metallic clunk. Her heart raced like a rabbit chased by a greyhound as she picked up the box and returned the pistol to its tissue paper padding. *What would Mama think of her little girl if she saw this? Sky* thought. She wasn't sure of what she thought of herself, but she did feel a sense of security with it being there. She'd been having second thoughts about getting the gun until last night. She built up her courage and removed the small, black, pearl-handled nine millimeter, feeling its heft in her small hand. The automatic fit snugly, and gave her a feeling of power. "What am I doing? I don't know how to shoot this thing," She said to herself. She made sure the clip was out, aimed at a Picasso print next to the dresser, and pulled the trigger a couple of times. She rubbed the barrel, feeling the smooth hardness of the weapon. "I still should give you back," she said aloud, as if hearing the words echoing in the bedroom might convince her that getting rid of it was the right thing to do. An old boyfriend had given Sky the gun after a couple of murders in the Dallas area. Five months had gone by without a fresh killing until last night, when there had been a murder terrifyingly close—at the airport. Still fighting her anxiety when the telephone rang, she placed the pistol on the bed and answered the phone.

"Sky, turn on the television to CNN!" Thelma Winters shouted.

Sky reached for the remote. It must have been something bad, as her mother rarely spoke much louder than a whisper. "What's going on, Mother? Is everything OK in Houston?"

"Houston's fine," Thelma snapped. "It's you in Dallas that I worry about. They've just discovered another body. This one was in the ladies' restroom at the airport. They're getting ready to show the murderer on a surveillance video from the airport. They think the killings there and the other two here in Houston are connected."

Sky rapidly flipped through the channels like a mobster firing his machine gun, until she located CNN. "I know about the murder already, a co-worker at the airport called last night and told me the police shut down the terminal for four hours. Nobody got in or out."

"Look! They're showing the security video—there's the killer!"

Sky moved closer to the TV. "The background is too fuzzy. I can't make out the picture. All I see is a woman wearing a baseball cap."

"I know. That's her. The detective said the crime lab is in the process of trying to enhance the picture. All the cops will say is that the killer is a woman and is left-handed."

Sky couldn't keep her voice from quivering. "This is scary," she said as she walked out the bedroom to the front door checking the lock with the gun in her hand.

"Baby, just be careful. The only family you have in Dallas is Aunt Cindy, and Lord knows she can't help you."

Sky had transferred from Houston to Dallas to help take care of her Aunt Cindy, who had eventually checked herself into the nursing home.

Securing the phone between her ear and shoulder, Sky said, "Mother, she's OK until her senility gets to creeping upon her. The dementia has her a little confused." Sky rubbed the barrel, and pulled the trigger a couple more times. "Mama, I'll be all right, don't worry. Niki will be here soon. We're commuting this week and it's her turn to drive today."

"I still haven't met your friends, Niki and Pebbles. Maybe they can come up here for Sheila's birthday party." Sheila was Sky's younger sister and was graduating from college the following fall.

"I'll check." Sky walked back in the bedroom, put the gun in the box, and placed it back on the top shelf. "Is Sheila home?"

"No, your sister left early for a job interview."

"Where's Daddy?"

"He's in his study going over his sermon for Sunday's service." Reverend Gabriel Winters was the minister of Second Street Baptist Church in Houston, with a congregation of 1500 people. He's known for his generosity, helping the community, and feeding and housing the homeless.

"OK. Tell him hello. Love you."

"Love you, too, Baby. Be careful. Bye."

****

Nicole Salem, Niki for short, had been working in the reservation center for Jet Away Airways for three years. This was where she met her friends, Sky and Pebbles. With almost a hundred calls handled daily, they found themselves talking to customers all around the world. Niki learned that a reservationist wore many hats. You had to be fast on the computer, patient, comforting, pleasant, and calm. Niki wasn't always calm, and sometimes if the passengers rubbed her the wrong way she would let them know it. She didn't take sarcasm and insults well, but Sky always told her not to take it personally, as she just happened to be the one who answered the phone. Getting cursed out, Niki definitely wouldn't tolerate, releasing the call in a heartbeat.

As Niki headed for Sky's apartment, she slipped into a daydream, thinking about those dreadful words that her father had spoken twenty years ago. Her father had clutched her tightly in his arms and told her that her mother, Debra, wouldn't be coming home ever again. She was dead.

To that point in her young life, Niki had been very happy in the middle-class suburbs of Houston. She spent Saturday afternoons in Elliott Park having picnics, swinging, and playing on the merry-go-round.

After her mom's death, Niki's dad raised her alone for a

year before suddenly dying of colon cancer. Following her dad's death, she went to live with her only living relative, Aunt Helen, who was in her mid-sixties and suffered from Lupus. Within a year, her aunt's health failed and she entered a nursing home. That was the start of Niki's horrible rollercoaster ride in and out of various foster homes where she endured verbal, physical, and sexual abuse until she ran away at seventeen.

Niki went from being part of a happy, caring family, to a childhood full of emotion and pain. She remembered one incident when her foster mother had placed her hand over an open flame at the age of ten.

Her daydreams of the past shattered as she jerked her hand from the steering wheel as if she could still feel the heat. Looking around, she realized she had almost missed the Kennedy Street exit and cut across the morning traffic to the exit, pulling up at Sky's, at eight o'clock sharp. She tapped the horn and waited.

"I'll be right out!" She yelled from the front door. Three minutes later, Sky trotted to the car, with her black, shoulder-length, silky hair bouncing. Her size seven jeans hugged her sexy curves and left nothing to the imagination. Her makeup neatly applied to her mulatto skin, as though it was painted on.

"Girl, if you don't hurry, we're going to be late," Niki said as the car door opened and Sky got in. Niki's beautiful auburn hair streaked with gold, swayed with each word spoken. Her hazel eyes sparkled with a tint of green, which brought a glow to her fuzzy peach color face. "We still have to pick up Pebbles, and I heard on K-104 that traffic on Interstate 35 is bumper to bumper. Donna told me if I'm late again she's going to write me up."

"The Terminator always wants to write up somebody." Sky laughed as she buckled her seatbelt. "You haven't been late in months. We have an hour before we start work and it only takes us thirty minutes to get there—we have plenty of time."

Sky could always calm Niki with her sophisticated southern drawl. Niki drove several blocks down to the Whispering Hollow addition. "I never have to wait on Pebbles," she said with a smile. "She's always on time."

"She only carpools with us once or twice a week," Sky said with a smirk, but she knew it was true. Pebbles and Sky had been best friends for three years, meeting at Jet Away in Houston before transferring to Dallas.

At twenty-nine, Pebbles lived off her mother's small trust fund. Her grandmother, Hanna Stone, had raised her from the age of eight. Forced to play the piano and take music lessons while growing up in Houston, she could have pursued a career in the music industry because she was that good. Pebbles Stone commuted with Niki and Sky for the friendship, and Lord knows she didn't need to save money on gasoline. She worked at Jet Away for the fringe benefits.

Pebbles's slightly olive skin was as smooth as powder on a baby. She was very attractive and didn't need makeup. She visited the tanning salon twice a week to maintain the gorgeous brown color of her five-foot, seven-inch frame.

Niki pulled up to the gate, picked up the black phone, and dialed a couple of numbers.

Pebbles answered, "Hello."

"Hey, I'm at the gate," Niki said.

"OK, I'll let you in."

As the black iron guardrail rolled back, Niki and Sky saw Pebbles at the window. She waved, disappeared from view and seconds later was dashing into the back seat of the car.

Niki turned down the volume of the radio as she and Sky stared in disbelief. "I don't believe you cut off all your thick pretty long hair!" Niki said.

"I like it," Sky told her. "It's very pretty."

Pebbles's long, natural blonde curly hair, which had hung to her waist, was now extremely short and she was wearing it spiked, with plenty of mousse.

"Thank you," Pebbles said with a smile as her blue eyes glistened in the sunlight. "What do you think of this dress? It came from Paris." She spread out her yellow and orange flared A-line dress, and then looked at her matching orange boots. She reached up front for the rearview mirror, turning it in her direction. "Don't you think this dress accentuates my figure and my eyes?" she asked, batting her eyelashes while Niki repositioned the mirror.

"If you say so," Sky replied, admiring her dress. *She's so conceited,* she said to herself, shook her head and smiled.

"Those girls at work dress so dull. They need a class in fashion design," Pebbles said digging in her purse.

"And you would be the prime candidate to teach it," Niki said as she looked in the rearview mirror. *You're just one step up from a hussy,* she thought as a smile spread across her face. It was all about Pebbles when she was around; she was self-centered, but harmless as a pussycat. Her presence always lit up a room.

"Why, of course I would," she boasted. "Hey, we can start up a fashion club and call it the Tall Girls' Designer Club."

"The Tall Girls' Designer Club," Niki repeated.

"Yes, since we're all tall, in our late twenties, and look like models—we could do that," Pebbles said.

"Work on it, Pebbles. I'm sure you'll come up with something," Sky said as she looked out the window at the abandoned oil pumps.

"Did you hear about the murder at the airport last night?" Niki asked, changing the subject.

"Girl, yes," Sky continued. "I've been thinking about it all night. It's all over the news. This morning on CNN they released a copy of the surveillance video. You can't tell if the killer is black or white; her body was covered from head to toe. The police believe she's the left-handed serial killer and think this killing is linked to those in Houston. She looked like she could be black," Sky added, "but she was quite light skinned."

"A black lady serial killer!" Niki shouted. "Girl, please! We don't fit the profile."

"Correction," Pebbles said with emphasis. "Ya'll didn't used to fit the profile, but you can't say that anymore. She could be any race, anybody." Pebbles never had a problem speaking her mind although some considered her forthrightness a little offensive. "She could be your neighbor, even someone in your own family, do—do—do—do—do—do—do—do." Pebbles began singing the theme to *Twilight Zone.* "What I'm afraid of is that if she isn't captured soon there will be more killings."

"Yeah, me too, so I got a gun," Sky said.

"A gun..." Niki looked over at her as she continued driving down the highway.

"Are you crazy?" Pebbles asked.

"I need to protect myself, I live alone."

"You don't need a gun," Pebbles said. "I had a friend who bought a gun and the desire to shoot it was so strong that one day when she and her boyfriend had an argument, she pulled out the gun and accidentally shot him in the foot as he was running from the house. She didn't kill him, but it scared both of them."

They laughed.

"I don't have a desire to shoot it," Sky said, "but I do feel safer with it being there. I've been debating whether I should keep it."

"Girl, just keep it, you may need it," Pebbles told her as she sat back and rested her arms on the backrest. "I can't wait for happy hour. I'm going to need a drink after talking to these fools all day."

"Amen to that," Sky and Niki agreed.

"There isn't going to be anyone interesting at the club. There never is," Sky said. Because of bad relationships, Sky's lack of interest had withdrawn her into a shell of celibacy. "The times that we've gone we just sat around looking. Now, Ms. Thang," she turned to look at Pebbles. "Didn't have a problem finding a guy last month," Sky laughed. "She stayed on the dance floor, and we didn't see her until it was almost time to go."

"Some of us have it like that," Pebbles said, a wide grin covering her face. "Don't hate me—I can't help it if I'm beautiful." Indeed, she was. "Niki, last time you wouldn't dance. You turned down several guys. What's up with that?"

"I don't have time for their bullshit," Niki said. She wasn't ready to get involved with anyone, and didn't feel like discussing the reasons with her friends.

"I know that's right," Sky said, noticing the strained look on Niki's face. She changed the subject. "I hope it's not too busy at work today."

"Well, get ready—thunderstorms are approaching Florida, Chicago, and New York, so the airports will have an off-schedule operation all day today. You know what that means." Pebbles sighed.

"Yes, we're going to be inundated with calls rushing into reservations—it will be nonstop—call after call. No time to breathe," Niki said, sounding tired already. "I couldn't wait for my shift to end yesterday. I was ready to leave at five-thirty when a call came in. I was stuck on that call for an hour, booking a reservation for a man and his dog." She frowned.

Pebbles laughed, "I know how you feel getting stuck on a call when it's past your shift. I hate that too."

"Yeah, especially when you have somewhere important to be after work; this passenger, I wouldn't mind rushing off the phone." Niki looked annoyed as she continued to talk. "He wanted to know if his dog could travel. When I told him yes, he wanted to know if we had a dog menu, and what seat he and his dog would be sitting in."

"Can you see him fastening that dog in a seat belt?" Sky said. They all laughed as Niki whipped into the parking lot.

"The stuff we have to put up with—is it worth it?" Sky asked as she opened her door.

"Yes, it's worth it," said Pebbles. "Think of our flight benefits—London and Paris, *oui oui.*" Pebbles flew to Europe twice a year with her grandmother.

"You're right," Sky said, as they high-fived each other and walked into the busy office.

Two

Detective David Hall sat across from Captain Wineglass's desk, studying the Dallas map of the areas where the serial killer had struck. As the captain spoke, David gazed out the window, *this temporary move is off the chain. I'm glad I decided to take this assignment in Dallas. I need a change,* he thought. The detective continued to think back to his last day at the Houston Police Department. He remembered the voices of the other detectives echoing off the wall like a racquetball. Telephones rang constantly, and detectives paraded nonstop across the room. A thick pile of files lay on each officer's desk.

"Hey, Detective Hall, I heard you're leaving us," a detective called out as David Hall entered the Houston squad room on a surprisingly cool October morning.

"Yeah, man, it's only short term until we catch that serial killer," David replied. He'd stopped by the office to pick up his personal belongings. He walked to his mahogany desk and started packing pictures, his crystal-clear paperweight, and other objects he'd acquired over the last fifteen years. His fellow detectives walked over to congratulate him, give him the high five, and wish him luck. He'd been working on one of the most difficult high-profile cases in the history of the Houston Police Department; now it was taking him to Dallas.

Detective Eddie Smith walked over to Hall's desk, grabbed the crystal paperweight from the box, and began tossing it back and forth with another detective.

"You can't catch one simple killer so they're shipping you

off to Dallas—that's a shame!" Smith said, his voice dripping with contempt. *This is my case. I should be the one going to Dallas, not you,* he thought as he looked at David.

Before Hall could respond, Captain Ron Perkins came out of his office, his strands of brunette hair combed to the side in an attempt to cover the bald spot on top of his head. Smith and the others scattered as the captain cleared his throat.

Perkins's deep baritone voice filled the office. "Hall, here's all of your information." Captain Perkins handed David a manila folder. "Malcolm Wineglass is the manager of Jet Away Airways and he's expecting you. He's the nephew of Captain Ronald Wineglass, your contact in Dallas. The Captain is expecting you at the Dallas Police Department Thursday morning; you can brief him on all the details. He's excited about having you temporarily on his team," Perkins said, pulling up a chair.

Hall tried to contain his excitement as he took a set of keys from the large brown envelope.

"Those are to your new furnished apartment. There's also a gasoline card," Perkins told him.

Dropping the folder on the desk, David said, "The killings in Dallas are so similar to the ones here in Houston that it has to be the same person. It has something to do with the airline. A pair of metal airplane wings about two inches wide was found next to each of the victims here and in Dallas."

"You haven't released the information about the airplane wings to the press yet, have you?"

"No and I won't, I'm leaving that up to the killer."

"This murderer has Texas in an uproar," Perkins said, banging his fist on the desk for emphasis. "If we don't close this case soon, the governor will be calling. We've been working this case for months now and we don't seem any closer than when I took it away from Smith. If anyone can find the killer, you can. When you find her, you'll learn the motive. Catch this son of a bitch," he said with a puckered brow.

"Yes, sir," David said. "I will, and soon."

"For some reason the killer has moved to Dallas, and I need to know why. Keep me posted." The Captain stood.

"Don't worry, Captain Perkins, sooner or later the killer will do something stupid; killers always do. When I crack this case, I'll see that she's behind bars for eternity," Hall promised as the captain turned to leave. David took one last glimpse of the office, picked up the box of belongings, and headed for the door.

"Detective," Captain Wineglass said as David continued his stare out the window. "Detective Hall," Captain Wineglass repeated, as he waved his hand in front of David's face after noticing his blank stare.

David's thoughts quickly scattered when he realized Captain Wineglass was trying to get his attention. "I'm sorry, Captain," he said, embarrassed. "I was just thinking about the serial killer and the strategy I plan to use."

"Now where were we?" The Captain asked, pointing back to the Dallas map where he had circled the hit areas in red.

Three

*W*hen Wanda Brent heard the faint sound of the phone ringing inside, she rushed to the door like a run-away locomotive.

"Hello," she said, panting as she dropped the groceries on the counter and went back to lock the front door.

Her dark ebony skin was smooth as coal and her curly black hair swirled over her head in Shirley Temple-like curls. A tint of orange lipstick covered her thick lips. She was five-feet, three-inches tall and in her late fifties, but she could pass for forty, maybe thirty-something dressed in her jeans and matching jean jacket.

"Hey, Sis, what took you so long?" asked Troy Brent, Wanda's brother-in-law. "I was just getting ready to try your cell phone." Troy and Wanda had kept in touch since Lacy Brent's death nearly twenty years ago.

"I just got back from the Boys and Girls Club," she answered as she placed her purse on the counter.

"I was calling to find out if you're still driving down here to Houston for Lacy's appreciation ceremony." Lacy was one of several people that the NAACP was honoring at its annual gathering in Houston in June. Lacy was finally getting the recognition he deserved for breaking the race barrier among airline pilots.

"Yes. Brittany and I plan to spend the weekend there with you, if it's OK."

"Sure, that's fine. What's that preacher's name that has that big church over on Zion Street?"

"Reverend Gabriel Winters," Wanda answered without a second thought as she began to put the groceries in the pantry. She remembered the pastor's name because her friend Evan was a member of that church, but she didn't dare tell Troy that's how she knew the name.

"He's also being honored for helping with the homeless and cleaning up the neighborhood on Jefferson Street. I hope they also plan to recognize my brother for his contribution to the community. Not only was he a damn good pilot, he also volunteered as a Big Brother for several years."

"You don't have to remind me, Troy. We took many kids to different outings on numerous weekends. It was fun but tiring," she sighed. "We always joked about having a house full, but only had Tia," she said sadly, recalling that awful day exactly eleven years before, when a drunk driver had run into Wanda's car, injuring her and killing her precious ten-year-old daughter.

Wanda took Tia's fifth-grade picture from the kitchen drawer and rubbed her fingers across it. She'd been looking at it the night before and had shoved it in the drawer when Brittany walked into the room. Wanda had conquered her grief some years ago, but still got misty-eyed around the anniversary of her death.

"I remembered today was the anniversary; that's another reason I called. I still don't think that boy stayed in prison long enough, he should have gotten the electric chair." The tension was evident in Troy's voice.

"Leave it alone, Troy. Evan has served his time," Wanda replied in defense of the young man, who had since become her friend.

"Wanda, you're always trying to save someone. You can't save the whole world. I can't believe you went before the parole board with his mother to petition for his early release from prison. And to add insult to injury, you agreed with the board's decision to have him spend one holiday a year with you as part of his punishment. That's just plain crazy."

Because of Wanda's altruistic attitude, she was able to befriend the young man that accidentally killed her daughter. "It's not a punishment, it's part of his therapy, his healing," she said tersely, her annoyance beginning to show. "It has helped him tremendously. It's not crazy." She slammed the can of green beans on the counter. "He needs help now, not punishment."

"Punishment, therapy, whatever you want to call it, it's still just plain crazy," he said. "This sounds like some Oprah shi–"

"Don't swear at me, Troy," she snapped. "It's not an insult. I had to learn to forgive, to make peace with myself. Of course, I was devastated and angry over her death but I've come to terms with it. I've forgiven Evan. From the beginning, he's been remorseful about the whole circumstance. It was tearing him apart. I know this is unusual, but it's what I want to do."

"Unusual! That's an understatement," Troy retorted. "You're out of your mind to sit down at the dinner table with the drunk driver that killed your child. You're a better person than I, because I would never do such a thing."

"Obviously I am," she answered. "Of course I don't condone drinking and driving. It was very wrong, but he was only a teenager, a good boy who got caught up with the wrong group of people—"

"Yes, it was wrong!" Troy interrupted, surprised to see his once angry sister-in-law, friends with the drunken driver.

Wanda continued to speak ignoring Troy's comment. "Some teenagers had gone to a frat party. It was his first year in college and away from home. Unbelievably, it was his first time drinking. It was part of his pledging—some part of initiation. I listened to all the evidence in court. He came from a good family, but he made a big mistake—getting behind the wheel. It may sound strange but once I forgave him, my nightmares stopped. I have bittersweet feelings. His visits will never replace Tia, but he has proven to be a loving and trustworthy young man. I don't expect you to understand. Furthermore, I don't have to apologize for anything I say or do. It's none of your business, so butt out," she said emphatically.

"I wish that I could butt out, Sis, but it's hard."

"Evan is a human resource manager at Skyline Airways there in Houston, and he doesn't look twice at alcohol." She added. "He's doing great. He's married and has a beautiful wife, Kaley, and an adorable young son, Gavin. In fact, you'll get to meet him in June. I've invited him and his family to the appreciation ceremony."

"You did what!" Troy yelled.

"You heard me. I expect you to be on your best behavior."

He sighed. "But, Sis—"

"No buts. I don't want to talk about it anymore Troy," said Wanda as she walked into her bedroom, placing her tennis shoes in the closet.

"I can't make any promises. It's hard forgiving the person who killed my niece."

"I never said it was easy," she snapped. "It's very hard. But we're going to squash it right now."

Silence.

Wanda ignored Troy's silence. "I'll call you when the event gets closer. I told the chairperson not to put any dates on Lacy's plaque, to leave that part blank."

"There you go, trying to protect people again. Brittany is going to find out sooner or later."

Wanda walked back into the kitchen and leaned against the bar stool at the center island. "I'm not ready for Brittany to find out that she's adopted. She's too young. I plan to tell her when she turns eighteen." She sighed. "I feel so guilty at times."

"Wanda, you didn't know that the adoption agency was crooked. Who's to say that Brittany was illegal, only fifty percent of the babies were sold illegally.

"I knew a year later, I could have come forward." She shook her head in shame. "But I didn't want to lose my baby."

"Eighteen is a good year for telling her."

"Yeah, I think so. We'll see you at the ceremony, and remember what I said—this means a lot to me."

"Yeah, yeah, yeah," he muttered. "OK, I'll talk to you later."

Four

As the evening set in and things settled down in the office, David leaned back in his chair with his arms folded behind his head, looking up at the ceiling. The ringing of the telephone interrupted his thoughts.

"Dallas Police Department, Detective Hall speaking, how can I help you?" he asked, adjusting the phone to his ear.

"Hey, man, this is Malc—"

"What's going on, man?" David interrupted.

"A lot of work and no play," said Malcolm as he laughed. "Am I interrupting something?"

"No, actually I was uh... daydreaming."

"You have too much time on your hands. I'm going to have to tell my uncle to give you more work." Malcolm laughed. "What are you doing this evening?"

"I plan to work around here, trying to get caught up," David answered as he shuffled through the papers on his desk.

Malcolm knew David had been working around the clock on the serial killer case since he had moved from Houston to Dallas some months earlier. Malcolm kept his uncle, Captain Wineglass, and David abreast of the situation at the airport. Malcolm was a skycap supervisor at Jet Away. He was single with no children and enjoyed every bit of it.

"You're working on a Thursday night?" Malcolm shouted.

"Yes, I have a ton of work," David answered, thinking about the challenge he faced. He knew the killer was leaving a set of wings from an airline that served both Dallas and Houston. So far, that was the only concrete information he had and ten airlines service both Dallas and Houston.

"Club Elite is having happy hour this evening for airline employees. There's going to be a lot of honeys there. So I'm not taking no for an answer," Malcolm told him.

David's mind wasn't on the honeys but he knew there was a connection between the left-handed serial killer and one of the airlines and saw this as a chance to, perhaps, get some leads in the case. He also realized it had been a few years since he'd stepped inside a club for pleasure; maybe it was time he relaxed a little.

"OK, I'll come, but I'll meet you there."

"Good. The club is located on the corner of Wilson and Peak, I'm leaving now. Meet you in the lobby."

"I'm walking out the door as soon as I hang up the phone," David said as he shrugged into his suit coat. "Good bye."

****

Niki looked at the square wall clock with large Roman numerals. "I won't get stuck on a call today," she said pressing the unavailable button on the phone pad to inhibit calls from coming in on her line. She gathered her belongings and met Sky and Pebbles in the break room.

They exchanged smiles and said in unison, "Happy hour," and headed out the door.

"You wouldn't believe the calls I had today," Pebbles said as they got into the car.

"Try me," Sky said, always amused with the different types of calls received.

"A woman called to ask if the airline put your physical description on your bag so they would know whose luggage belongs to whom. I told her no. She explained that when she checked in, they put a tag on her luggage that said 'FAT.' She said she was a little overweight and wanted to know if there was a connection. I briefly covered the mouthpiece, took a deep breath to keep from laughing, and then explained that FAT is the airline city code for Fresno, California; the airline was just putting a destination tag on her luggage. I guess she must have felt embarrassed, because she started to laugh."

Sky laughed. "I was assigning this lady a seat and she said to put her by the window just in case she got hot and wanted some fresh air."

They laughed.

Talk of work stopped as Niki pulled into the lot at the club. "There are a lot of people here tonight," Niki said.

They got out the car and walked through the door of the mixed club where the band played *Rock Steady* by the Whispers. A tall, well-built man dressed in a stylish navy blue suit approached Sky. She couldn't help noticing how handsome he looked with those sexy bedroom eyes.

"Would you like to dance?" he asked.

Sky accepted and took his hand and followed him to the dance floor. Just before he started guiding her smoothly across the floor, Sky looked at Niki, winked and mouthed, "Find us a table." Someone grabbed Pebbles and led her to the dance floor, leaving Niki to search for an empty table.

Sky and her partner moved across the huge dance floor, getting lost in the crowd. After the fourth dance when Sky turned to leave, he grabbed her and gazed into her eyes. "This is my favorite song. May I have one more dance?" he asked, as the band began to play the Michael Jackson song *Rock with You.*

He reached for her hand but Sky slowly pulled it away. "I left my girlfriends and I know they're looking for me. I better not."

He pointed across the dance floor. "Is that your friend over there?"

Sky looked to her left and saw Pebbles with a drink in one hand and twirling the other hand high in the air shouting, "Party over here!"

Sky laughed. "Yes, that's one of them."

"Doesn't look like she's missing you to me," he said, looking at Sky with puppy dog eyes.

Sky looked around for Niki, but couldn't spot her. She assumed she was dancing and turned her attention back to her dance partner. His hair was cut close to his head, short on top, and faded on the sides. *How can I turn him down? He's been a gentleman, he's tall, and handsome, and it's been a long time since I've genuinely felt some sparks immediately after meeting a man*, she thought as she looked into his eyes. People had begun to dance around them and she really didn't want to stop. She smiled then started moving her shoulders. "What are you waiting on?"

Embracing the moment, he pulled her closer to his chest, and captured by his enticing cologne, she felt weightless, as if she was gliding slowly across the dance floor. His six-foot, five-inch frame towered over her sultry five-foot, eight-inch body like the Eiffel Tower.

"What's your name?" he finally asked.

"Sky, Sky Winters."

"Sky? What a beautiful name and you are as beautiful as the sky."

"Thank you, and what's your name?"

"David Hall," he spoke proudly.

"Nice to meet you David Hall," she replied as she lifted her head to look into his eyes.

David's green eyes were cat-like in the dark. A warm smile covered his face, and when he laughed, he leaned his head back.

"Nice to meet you Sky Winters," David said as he dipped her toward the floor. When the song ended, they stood holding each other. Neither wanted to let go but David reluctantly removed his arms from around Sky's waist.

"Will you excuse me while I look for my friend?"

"Sure," he said, moving to the side. "May I buy you and your girlfriends a drink?"

"Yes, I would like that, thank you."

"What would you like?"

"An amaretto sour for me and an apple martini for my friend, Nicole."

"What about your other friend?"

Sky glanced at Pebbles, who was still on the dance floor. By the look on her face, she had no plans to sit down anytime soon. "She's holding a glass right now; she doesn't need one."

"My friend, Malcolm, is with me; he's somewhere in here." David looked around. "Do you mind if we join you?" he asked, hoping she'd say yes.

"It'll be great to have you guys join us," Sky answered,

trying to sound nonchalant, even while she was jumping with excitement inside.

"I'll give you a moment to locate her, and then I'll be right over," David said as he moved toward the bar.

Sky squeezed through the crowd until she found Niki in the back next to the buffet table, nibbling on a chicken wing.

"Who was that fine guy you were dancing with?" Niki asked as she licked her fingers.

"His name is David. He'll be over in a minute; he's buying us a drink." She winked. "I ordered you an apple martini."

"Thanks. I signaled for the waitress to come over, but she hasn't made it yet."

As the music grew louder, Sky raised her voice. "Niki, I don't believe in love at first sight, but my body shook like an earthquake 6.0 on the Richter scale when he held me. He is so fine. He has a friend named Malcolm. I hope you don't mind, I told him that they could join us."

Sky hoped perhaps Malcolm would be someone that Niki might be interested in dating, but she knew she was wrong when she saw the look on Niki's face. Since she had been hurt a couple of times in bad relationships, Niki put up her defense mechanism as strong as a brick wall.

"I guess that'll be OK. But you know I'm not interested, at least not right now."

"I'm not asking you to marry the guy!" Sky picked up a hot wing from Niki's plate and started eating. "They're just coming over to talk, don't get so uptight." She wiped the napkin across her lips.

Before Niki could respond, David and his friend appeared, carrying drinks. "Ladies, these are for you." David handed Sky her drink.

"Thank you," Sky said. "That was nice of you." She reached for her drink with her left hand and David made a mental note.

"No problem." He winked then straddled a chair, not taking his eyes off Sky, admiring her beauty.

Malcolm handed Niki her drink. "Thank you," she said as she smiled.

"David, this is my friend Niki." Sky looked at Niki. "Niki,

this is David."

"Hi there, nice to meet you, David," Niki said, stirring her drink.

"Nice to meet you too Niki and this is my friend, Malcolm." David tapped Malcolm's shoulder.

Malcolm smiled, licked his lips, and extended his hand.

"Nice to meet you, Malcolm," Niki replied, as she shook his hand.

"Same here, Malcolm," Sky said as she sipped her drink from the straw.

Malcolm was sporting a pair of well-filled 501 jeans and the brown silk shirt he was wearing was partially unbuttoned, showing off his sexy hairy chest. He topped his look off with a small gold serpentine chain, blinging around his neck. This was an indication to the ladies that he was ready for whatever the night had to offer. He reminded Niki of the rapper LL Cool J. Malcolm also straddled the chair with his hands on the backrest. "What brings you two beautiful young ladies out tonight?" Malcolm asked.

"We had a rough day at the office so we decided to have a drink before going home," Niki told him as she looked around the room, observing the atmosphere.

"What line of work are you in?" David asked.

"We answer questions all day long," Sky said, trying to suppress a chuckle as she mimicked some of her customers. "'How much does it cost to fly to Los Angeles?', 'May I order a child's meal?', 'May I upgrade to first class?', 'You changed my flight,' 'I wanted a window, not an aisle,' 'You lost my suitcase.'"

"Oh, you must work for the airline." David's eyebrows rose as he sipped on his Southern Comfort. *Airline employees, huh?* he thought.

"Yes, we do," Niki said as she looked around for Pebbles. "We average between eighty to one hundred calls a day. By the end of the day, we don't want to see a telephone. My mouth gets so dry from talking to passengers sometimes I feel myself talking but no words come out."

They all laughed.

David noticed that deep dimples pierced both of Sky's cheeks. When she smiled, she glowed. Her eyes were big, round and as black as the La Brea tar pits, and accentuated with naturally curved long eyelashes top and bottom.

"What airline do you work for?" Malcolm asked.

"Jet Away Airways," Sky answered, and then turned her attention to her dance partner. "So, David, what line of work are you in?"

David was mesmerized by Sky's beauty and didn't hear her. It had been two years since David had been in a serious relationship. He wasn't looking for one now, but he felt a strong attraction to Sky that had him spellbound until Sky snapped her fingers. "I'm sorry, what did you say?" he asked with an embarrassed smile.

"What line of work are you in?" she repeated.

He had to make a split–second decision—then lied. "I'm a skycap for Jet Away."

Intrigued by Sky's beauty, David was distracted from his primary objective, getting information from the airline employees.

"We're both employed there. I'm the skycap manager," Malcolm added.

"I've never seen you there," Sky said as she looked at David.

"He transferred from Houston, where he worked for a few years," Malcolm said, before turning to Niki. "Are you from Dallas?"

"No we're from Houston, too," Niki answered, running her finger around the rim of the glass.

"Niki, that reminds me—my sister is celebrating her twenty-first birthday in May. It's on a Saturday and Mother wants to know if you and Pebbles would like to come."

"I would love to. I'm sure Pebbles would, too."

"I'd guess that's Pebbles on the dance floor." They all turned their attention towards the illuminated dance floor. "She certainly knows how to party, doesn't she?" David commented, as they all looked at Pebbles.

"Right on both counts," Sky told him.

"Speaking of the dance floor, Niki, would you like to dance?" Malcolm asked.

Her voice dropped. "No, thank you, I just want to listen to the music." She turned her face away and continued to tap her feet to the beat of the music.

"Oh, go on Niki," Sky said, gently nudging her out of the chair.

Niki reluctantly stood and felt Malcolm gently grab her soft hand. He placed his hands around her waist. She squirmed to free herself from the uncomfortable feeling.

"Niki, I haven't seen you in here before," Malcolm said as they moved around on the dance floor.

"I've been here a couple of times." She looked around, avoiding eye contact with Malcolm. They danced one fast dance. A slow song followed and Malcolm gently pulled Niki close to him. She slapped him, turned, and walked off the dance floor and into the restroom. *I don't want him to touch me. He didn't ask! He just grabbed like an octopus. That'll teach him,* she thought as she stared at her reflection in the mirror.

She left the restroom and was headed for the table when she noticed that Malcolm was also walking toward the table. She evaded Sky, David, and Malcolm and walked to the bar.

Malcolm pulled David to the side. "Man, what's wrong with your friend? She acts like I'm a mass murderer or something." Malcolm shouted over the loud music.

"Who?" David looked confused.

"Niki."

"Niki!" David repeated, "A mass murderer? What are you talking about?"

"She's crazy," Malcolm said, as he rubbed his jaw.

"What happened?"

"When I tried to put my arms around her, she knocked them down, and then slapped me. Damn, that hurt!" Malcolm wiggled his jaw. "Somebody must have done a number on her. It will take an act of Congress to get her to loosen up," he added.

"She seemed OK at the table."

"Yeah, seemed like it, but while we were fast dancing, she danced so far away from me she might as well have been dancing with the guy next to her. So, the next dance I gently pulled her close to me." He paused. "Niki has baggage. I can't deal with that."

David laughed. "Man, their other friend is in here somewhere," he said jokingly.

"If she's anything like Niki, I'm not interested. Anyway, I saw her friend leave with a guy. I'll be on the dance floor." He turned and walked away, still rubbing his jaw.

"Good idea." David returned to the table. "How about it, Sky, want to dance?" He stood snapping his fingers to the music.

"Sure," she answered, offering him her hand.

Niki was content just enjoying the atmosphere from the bar. At one point, Sky spotted Niki through the crowd, went and got her and pulled her onto the dance floor to do the Macarena.

"Hey, look at me, I got it!" Sky yelled over the thundering music. "Move to the side, Niki."

"You know I can't do this dance," Niki said as she tried to keep up with the beat.

"You got it."

"I slapped Malcolm," Niki blurted as she extended her hands, placed them on her butt, and shimmied to the floor.

"You did what?" Sky stopped dancing and stared at her friend.

"I'll tell you later," Niki said. When the dance ended, Niki began to tell Sky what had happened but David interrupted, not letting Sky leave the dance floor. He pulled her to him when '*If Only You Knew*' by Patty Labelle came through the speakers.

Sky raised her hands in the air as if to apologize and danced away with David.

Niki crossed the dance floor and sat down at their table, hoping she wouldn't run into Malcolm, when a man stumbled over to her table, reeking of alcohol.

Niki looked up at him thinking, *What a loser!*

"Do you want to dance?" He belched as he placed his glass on the table, spilling his drink.

"No, thanks." She frowned.

"Oh, come on," he said, as he pulled her arm.

"Excuse me. If you don't get your hands—"

"Hey! Don't I know you?" Before Niki could respond, he asked, "Didn't you live with us?" He spat as he spoke.

Niki focused on his handsome face as she wiped spit from her jaw. "I don't know you and I never lived with you," she said with deadly authority. "My boyfriend will be back in a minute. You don't want to be here if you know what's good for you."

"All right. But I'm Charles. Don't you remember me?" He moved closer to her face.

Using the light from the strobe streaming from the ceiling, she searched his face. *Does he know me?* she wondered. Not wanting to remember anything about her past, she glared at the man. "Like I said," she answered in a measured voice, "I do not know you, and you have one second to get away from this table."

"Come on, dance with me." He pulled her again.

Niki discreetly grabbed him between the legs and squeezed as hard as she could, "I said get away from my table, jerk." She bit her bottom lip.

"Ouch! Ouch! OK, Ma'am."

She released him. Her flesh crawled as the man picked up his glass and stumbled to the next table. She walked quickly to the restroom, hoping he would stay away.

Sky and David finally decided on a breather and zig-zagged their way to the table.

"What do you think happened between Niki and Malcolm?" asked David as he pulled out the chair for Sky.

"I don't know. I haven't talked to her yet," Sky answered, looking around for Niki. "She looked upset."

"So did he," David said as he sipped on his watered-down drink. "I'll be right back." He pushed his chair up to the table, letting Sky think he had gone in search of Malcolm. It was a good chance for him to check out the club and the patrons without Sky suspecting anything. He knew he was looking for a left-handed tall woman, possibly white with brown skin, maybe a tan, or a light-skinned black woman, possibly with Halle Berry's skin color. He'd noticed that a few women in the club fit that profile—including Sky and Pebbles. He pulled out a small pad and pen and began scribbling. He kept an eagle eye on Sky as he stood in a half-lit corner across the room. *Everyone is a suspect until proven innocent,* he reminded himself.

He hoped he would be able to befriend Sky to get information that was more tangible. He hoped this was a connection to the airline.

Soon the DJ announced, "Last dance of the night, so grab your lady for a little bump and grind!"

That was David's cue to return to the table. "May I have

this dance?" he asked quietly as he walked up behind Sky. Niki returned to the table and took a seat, as David escorted Sky to the dance floor.

He began to sing in Sky's ear, "*Don't you remember you told me you love me, Baby*," a rendition of Carol King, sung by Luther.

She stopped dancing and took a quick look at him. "You have a beautiful voice, David."

"Thank you. I used to sing in the church choir as a young boy."

"So did I," Sky said. "I'm a preacher's kid."

"You're a preacher's kid, huh? Let me hear you sing."

She pulled back. "You don't want me to do that. When Mama sent my sister Sheila to music lessons, she sent me to PE."

David laughed and pulled her closer. He whispered in her ear, "I had a wonderful time tonight. May I see you again?"

He had captivated Sky. "I would love that," she answered as she laid her head on his chest.

David smiled as they continued to slow dance.

Niki noticed Pebbles rushing in the door and making her way toward the restroom. She pulled Pebbles to the table. "Where have you been? I've been looking for you all evening."

Pebbles began to speak, slurring her words. "I've been right here." She banged her fist on the table.

"Sit down. You're drunk."

"No, I'm not. I just had a couple of drinks," she said, holding up three fingers.

"You've had more than that. And you haven't been here. I walked this whole building, inside and out."

Pebbles began to wipe sweat beads from her face. "Just say that I was around. Where is Sky?" She asked taking a seat.

Niki pointed to the dance floor just in time to see David put his arm around Sky's waist and walk her off the dance floor.

"Well, there you are!" said Sky as she walked up to Pebbles. "Where have you been?"

"I've been right here."

"David, this is Pebbles Stone."

"Nice to meet you, Pebbles." David could smell the alcohol. He whispered to Sky, "You better get your friend home and into bed."

Sky smiled and nodded in agreement.

"Nice to meet you too," said Pebbles as she stood. "Damn, you're tall." She looked at David from head to toe.

He laughed as they walked toward the door.

A man ran up to them and unexpectedly snapped a picture of the foursome as they made their way out of the building. That'll be $10.00," the photographer said quickly over the loud chatter as he handed David the picture.

David sneered then handed the man a ten-dollar bill. "What people would do for money," commented David as he observed the young man continuing to snap unexpected pictures of other patrons.

They all looked at the photo.

"I keep this," David said to Sky, "If you don't mind then I can see your pretty face when I want to."

Sky blushed as she and David continued to walk to the car holding hands. David took out an ink pen and wrote his name and number on a piece of paper then handed it to Sky. Sky handed David a business card. After they had exchanged telephone numbers David kissed Sky on her forehead, and thanked her for a lovely evening.

"Niki, I apologize for monopolizing all of Sky's time."

Niki smiled, "Oh, that's perfectly OK. Normally when we come, we pretty much sit and talk. We don't dance much. That's Pebbles's thing."

"Ladies, lock your doors. I don't want anything to happen to you. Good night," he said, realizing that tonight had been one of the happiest times he'd had since breaking up with his girlfriend two years earlier. He smiled as he pointed at Niki. "See you later, Muhammad Ali." Then he walked away.

Confused, Pebbles blurted, "Muhammad Ali? That's not her name."

That sent a ripple of laughter through the others, which only confused Pebbles more as she flopped back in the seat.

"I had so much fun tonight. It's been a long time since I partied like this," Sky said, as she adjusted her seat and lowered the backrest to a comfortable position as Niki pulled into traffic.

"And you stayed on the dance floor," Sky told Pebbles.

"She disappeared for quite a while but you didn't notice, because you were preoccupied with Mr. Jet Away," Niki told her.

"His name is David, thank you," Sky proudly corrected.

"Niki, I looked around and you were gone too," Sky said. "After you slapped Malcolm—"

"Who?" Pebbles interrupted.

"The man with David," Sky said, letting down her window to let in some fresh air.

"Why?" asked Pebbles.

"He grabbed me around my waist and he didn't ask me to slow dance. He just assumed that I wanted to, and pulled me close to him. I couldn't breathe. He was squeezing me so tight and wouldn't let me go." She quivered as she thought about it.

"Girl, what is wrong with you? Are you gay or something?" Pebbles asked, not caring about Niki's feelings.

"Pebbles!" Sky snapped.

"What?" asked Pebbles, oblivious to the effect of her comment.

"I'm more of a woman than you'll ever be," Niki said with a smirk. She had had several drinks herself. "I've had a child!" she blurted out in anger, and then looked around knowing that she had made a mistake, revealing a secret that she had suppressed for sixteen years.

Sky looked surprised but didn't respond because of the look on Niki's face.

"I've had one too," Pebbles bragged, sending the smell of alcohol wafting through the car as she moved. "My grandmother didn't want me to shame the family so I gave her up for adoption. I was only fifteen when I became pregnant," she confessed, not caring that she had revealed her most precious secret. "You should've seen my parents' face when the baby came out." She laughed, slapping her leg. "My grandmother fainted and my dad turned just in time to catch her. They were stunned. I never told them that the baby's dad was black. They made me sign the adoption papers and the baby was out of my life just like that." Pebbles changed from a happy drunk to a sad drunk as she talked, remembering her precious daughter's face.

"Have you tried to locate her?" Sky asked.

"Nope," Pebbles answered, trying to focus her eyes. "I

figure she'll find me when she's ready." She sighed. "I'll be happy one day to get the big call." She hiccupped. "I'll welcome her with open arms. But I'm not afraid of men," she teased, pointing her finger at Niki before passing out.

"You know she didn't mean what she said earlier," Sky told Niki.

"I know." Niki forced a smile. "She won't remember any of this tomorrow."

They both let out a short chuckle.

"I didn't mean to blow up. It's just sometimes Pebbles..." Niki's voice trailed off.

"Pebbles can be rude when she wants to, especially when she drinks too much, but she's as harmless as a kitten," Sky said.

"I know."

"Where's your baby?" Sky asked.

"I'd rather not say." Niki turned on the radio.

Sky didn't push the issue, and they rode home listening to jazz.

Five

*N*ervousness ate away at David as he sat holding the phone in his hand wondering if he should call Sky this early in the morning. He looked at his watch and said, "What the hell, I'll take a chance."

Sky had only been home fifteen minutes after leaving Club Elite when the telephone rang. She wondered who could be calling at this hour and answered the phone. "Hello."

"Hey, this is David. I'm checking to see if you made it home safely, and to tell you that I had a wonderful evening."

"Aren't you sweet? Yes, I did, and I really enjoyed partying with you, too." He released a sigh of relief glad that she was receptive. Usually the lady would give out the wrong phone number purposely when meeting guys at the club because those types of relationships hardly ever worked.

His phone beeped, indicating that he had another call. "Hold on one second, it's probably Malcolm."

"Hello."

"Detective Hall, this is Captain Wineglass, there's been another murder. This time at a club in North Dallas."

Caught off guard, he jumped to his feet. "What club?"

"Club Elite."

"Club Elite! I just left there. Is it the left-handed serial killer?"

"I don't know but his throat was slashed. I know it's late but will you check it out please?"

"I'm on my way!" He started to put the phone down and

then remembered he had a call on the other line. He quickly switched back to Sky. "I'm sorry. Something has come up. I have to go. I'll explain later."

David abruptly hung up the phone, without saying goodbye.

"Well, OK. Goodnight." Sky said as if she was still speaking to David. "I hope she's worth it."

I had better not jump to any conclusions until I talk to him tomorrow, but two in the morning sounds like a booty call to me, she thought.

When David arrived at the crime scene, police officers had already canvassed and sectioned off the area with yellow tape. He walked over to a black Infiniti where a man sat slumped in his seat, his throat slashed.

"Fill me in," David told a nearby officer.

"The police department received a call from the club owner reporting a man slumped over in the front seat of a parked car. When we got here, we found him like this." The man smelled of alcohol; his throat was slit from ear to ear. His white silk shirt was completely unbuttoned and saturated in blood; his belt was unbuckled with his pants unzipped and pulled partially down his legs.

"Looks like he was going to get busy, but she got to him first," the officer said.

David bent over and picked up a stray strand of hair from the man's hairy chest. This hair was a different texture and a different color from those he had collected from previous murders. He placed it in an evidence bag, then walked over to the passenger side and scraped a sample of blood from the seat. He handed the evidence packets to Detective Mike Samuel. "I need to get a composite on these hair and blood samples."

"I'll have someone do it right away, Detective Hall." Samuel called to an officer guarding the back of the car. "McDaniels, get this to the lab, NOW!"

"Samuel! Call the officer back here," David ordered as he pulled a set of bloody airplane wings from between the seats. "I want this checked for fingerprints." He dropped it in the plastic bag, thinking, *the left-handed serial killer strikes again.* He was pissed. He slammed the car door.

The Reservationist

I knew this was happy hour for the airline employees but I never suspected the killer would be bold enough to kill someone at this crowded club. I was preoccupied; I should've been more focused, David thought as he walked around the car searching for more evidence, before turning his attention to the club staff.

After questioning the staff, David walked back to his unmarked patrol car. He had let Sky distract him from his job, something no other woman had been able to do in a very long time. Women often shied away when they learned he was a detective, fearing he'd be killed in the line of duty, or that he would always be on a case and not with them. His job required him to be on stakeouts for long periods, break dinner dates, turn down party engagements, and change his plans at the last minute.

That's what had broken up his two-year engagement to April. She had complained that he was always working and never had time for her. When they did spend time together, he would often fall asleep from exhaustion. He tried to make it work with April but his job always seemed to get in the way. Serious dating wasn't compatible with his line of work.

David thought back to his conversation with April regarding the night he had missed dinner. The sound of a police siren woke her. She glanced at the clock on the microwave, 11:30 p.m. She knew it couldn't be David. He wouldn't use his siren to get home, no matter how late he was. It was illegal. However, she couldn't keep herself from running to the window.

All she saw were the streetlights—no David.

"Two and a half hours late! I can't take this anymore," she said to the empty room. She sat at the table, resting her head in the palms of her hands. She could feel the tears start to well in her eyes. She stood up and yanked open the kitchen drawers until she found a pen and paper, not caring what else fell out. She began writing fiercely.

Dear David,
I'm sick and tired of being stood up, or coming second to your job. I've had enough. You can't even commit to me for one evening. It's Friday, the weekend, and I wanted to spend some time with my man. But you are nowhere around. I can't take this anymore.

April was pressing down so hard, she cracked the tip of the pen. She began reading the unfinished letter and tore it up. She found a new pen, and started over, this time with her thoughts calm and collected.

Dear David,

I know you meant to show up for dinner tonight, and I do respect your line of work, however, I can't take the disappointments anymore. I can't stand not knowing if you're going to return home after a day's work or if one of your fellow officers will show up at the door some night to tell me you won't be home—ever. I can't take the butterflies in my heart as it sputters every time I hear police sirens.

I know you've tried, but I'm looking for more in a relationship than you can offer. You have to get your priorities straight. I feel I'm at the bottom of your list.

It's not only you. I let the relationship continue, hoping for a change. I hate to end this but I believe it's for the best. I know you enjoy your job and love your undercover work. I don't want to destroy that by giving you an ultimatum—your job or me.

Good luck with your career.

Love, April

David had been working late on a missing person's case when the chimes on the clock struck midnight. He'd jumped from the chair and immediately started collecting his papers. "Damn! April!" He felt bad because he inadvertently took advantage of her, always thinking she would be around.

He picked up the phone and dialed his home. No answer. He hurriedly moved toward his car and sped home.

As David approached his house, he noticed that April's car wasn't in the driveway. He walked in and immediately went to the kitchen. A crystal vase holding six large red roses sat in the center of the table; filled wine glasses sat by two plates. The ring he had given April the previous Christmas lay next to a letter propped against the vase. He picked up the letter and began reading, feeling a sense of inevitability.

David picked up a glass of wine and emptied it in a single swallow, then reached for the second glass and did the same with that, before reaching for the phone. He started dialing but stopped midway and hung up. He sat back at the table with his face buried in his hands.

In a burst of fury, he swept his arm across the table and knocked the wine glasses on the floor, sending glass shards in all directions. He walked over to the kitchen counter, picked up the bottle of Chablis, and began drinking from it.

He swore he would never tell another woman what line of work he was in because it caused too much conflict, especially, if the relationship wasn't serious—why bother?

David snapped back to the presence as he thought of the left-handed serial killer; and how he may have seen her at the club never realizing it was she.

He cranked up his engine, leaving Club Elite on his way to the police department to complete his police report. David walked into the building, completed his report, and headed back home for a few hours of sleep before another busy day started. He'd explain to Sky that Malcolm had had a flat tire.

Six

*T*he brisk morning air hovered over Dallas as Sky drove along in heavy traffic, her thoughts on the night before. She had been celibate for the past three years and was adamant about staying that way until she married. Meeting David brought a spark back into her life, a spark that had vanished a few years ago. One minute she was singing, the next she was wondering why she was getting so excited about the guy she'd just met.

Sky pulled up in front of Niki's apartment and Niki immediately headed down the sidewalk. "I can see that you really enjoyed yourself last night—you're glowing," Niki said as she climbed into the BMW and shut the door.

Sky's eyes fluttered. "David was such a gentleman and so genuine. You can tell when guys are phony but there was something about him. He's caring and concerned; he called me last night when I got home to make sure I made it home safely." She spoke like a young girl in love. "But he did hang up abruptly after receiving a call last night."

"Um, after two in the morning, sounds like a booty call to me." Niki smiled.

"At first I thought that, but he said he would explain everything today, and I trust him."

"Girl, don't fall so fast—take your time. You don't even know him talking about trust. I was in love once, but that didn't last long. He was not only dating me, but he was also dating half of Houston. I have trust issues but I was actually giving that relationship an opportunity to grow."

Sky raised her chin. "You have a problem with trust?"

"Yes, I just never said anything." Niki tried to remember her last date, which happened to be six years ago.

"Is that why you gave Malcolm the cold shoulder?" she asked as she stopped at the stop light.

"I didn't mean to be rude, but..." Her raspy voice faded and she turned her head away. She knew she had been melodramatic.

"But what? What, Niki?" Sky knew by the look on her face that whatever it was, it had Niki very upset.

Niki sat quietly. She tried not to think about the horrible conditions that she had encountered in multiple foster homes, but her past haunted her daily. She sighed, and then spoke slowly. "My background..." she started to tell Sky, but quickly changed her mind. "Oh, it doesn't matter. It was a long time ago."

As Sky pulled into the parking lot at work, Niki jumped out and began walking toward the building. The tapping of Niki's heels on the pavement grew harder, then faster with each step. Her long strides left Sky behind.

"Hey, wait up—I didn't mean to upset you," Sky said, hurrying to catch up with her friend. She turned Niki toward her. "It does matter. I see that it's hurting you."

"It was a long time ago." She waved her hand nonchalantly. "I'm OK."

Sky gently rubbed Niki's arm. She'd never seen this side of Niki. "You're not OK. What is it that has you so upset? We have a few minutes—let's go over there and sit down," Sky said, pointing to the marble bench along the walkway to the entrance.

Niki sat on the edge of the bench and looked off into the distance. "Remember when I told you that I had lived with my aunt?"

"Yes."

"Well, after she went to live in the nursing home, I was forced to go to a foster home. I was nine. I can remember the first day vividly. I was so frightened. I can still see the face of Mrs. Little, my caseworker. She took my hand and we walked up the sidewalk to a yellow house. She introduced me to Rita Johnson, my first foster mom. The first of many," Niki said as her lower lip slightly hung with a look of innocent—from sucking her thumb as a child. "She was a short, round woman with her right front tooth missing. She said, 'Oh, you made it.' Mrs. Little said, 'This is Niki Salem.' My new foster mom spoke to me as we walked inside, and then yelled out the door at two boys wrestling in the dirt. I saw toys in the yard and children running around the house chasing each other, playing tag. I was frightened and hid behind the caseworker. She said, 'It's OK, Sweetie, you're going to stay here with Mrs. Johnson for a while.' I started to cry, begging Mrs. Little to take me home with her. While I clawed at her legs, she told me that she couldn't take me home, but I was going to be fine and she would be back the next week to check on me."

"Did she?"

"Not then." Niki gritted her teeth as she hugged her purse tightly in her lap. "She pried herself away from me and handed my suitcase to my new mom. I sat on the floor crying, afraid. Mrs. Johnson looked at me and said, 'Hush up, now, nobody going to hurt you. You go on outside and play with the rest of the kids until dinner's ready.' A little girl about my age sat down next to me and handed me her doll and I finally stopped crying."

Sky looked at her watch as employees came and went around them.

Niki sighed and laid her head back, letting her eyes close as she continued to tell her story. "Eight of us lived in a three-bedroom house. I cried every night for a month. I just wasn't comfortable in that overcrowded house. Before long, the other children were complaining about my crying. Our foster mom would yell at me from the next room, telling me to hush up or she was going to give me a reason to cry. Then she started making me stay in the bedroom alone while the other children went outside to play. She started calling me for dinner after everyone else had eaten, leaving me at the table by myself. She was mean and hateful to me. I often wondered why. I didn't do anything." As Niki blinked her eyes, a tear rolled down her cheek.

Sky rubbed Niki's arm, "I'm sorry."

"But at nine, what could I do except accept it? I wanted to run and run far away but my feet wouldn't move. They felt like heavy steel." Her hazel eyes sparkled in the sun as she continued to speak. "On this one particular night, I was missing my parents more than usual and began to cry. I was screaming as loudly as I could. Ms. Johnson got out of bed, pulled me by my pigtails, and threw me in this dark stuffy closet. I kicked and screamed all the way to the closet, saying, 'I want my mommy!' Ms. Johnson screamed, 'Your damn mama isn't coming back! When you shut up, you can get your ass out of that closet.' When I woke the next morning, I was lying on the floor of that closet. I had cried myself to sleep. She opened the door and told me to get dressed. I remember washing my face, not knowing where the tears ended and the water began. The more I wiped, the more the tears ran." She pulled her coat tighter to brush off the chill. "That was the start of a routine. Every night Rita would put me in the closet, even if I wasn't crying. Every morning my eyes would be as red as an apple from rubbing them all night—frightened. One day my teacher noticed that I had been coming to school with red eyes. I told her that I had been sleeping in the closet."

Sky sat there in disbelief taking in the information like a juror in the courtroom. "Bless your heart."

"I guess my teacher reported Rita because after school that day, Mrs. Little picked me up and placed me in another home. This started the roller-coaster ride in and out of multiple foster homes. I never saw Ms. Johnson again but I'll never forget her face," Niki said, clenching her teeth.

Sky, amazed at Niki's openness and hurt, hugged her. "Oh, Niki, I'm sorry, I didn't realize that you had experienced such trauma—you always seem to have yourself together."

"And I do," Niki said, uncomfortable with praise.

"But why were you so rude to Malcolm? Why did you slap him? He hadn't done anything to you."

"I don't think rude is the right word," Niki said with a scowl, avoiding the real issue. "Maybe," she paused, "extreme reluctance."

"Reluctance," Sky repeated, rubbing Niki's shoulder.

"Yes, I didn't want to tell you this, but…" she hesitated, "I was molested." Tears welled in her eyes, "Twice, in fact." She wrinkled one brow as she looked away. "It was once by a foster brother and another time by my foster father—a different family."

Niki felt a little comfort confiding in Sky. "I moved in with this family and thought I had finally found a good home. The Clarks were the perfect family. I really felt at home with them until Mr. Clark came into my bedroom one night, saying he was tucking me in. The next thing I knew he had ripped open my pajamas and forced himself on top of me—I became pregnant and had a baby girl," she said, lowering her head. "I was only fourteen."

"What?" Said Sky, stunned at what her friend had just told her. "Why, those bastards!" She frowned. "I'm so sorry." A tear slowly ran down Sky's cheek. "Did you seek any kind of counseling? You were so young for so much misery and pain."

"I went to counseling on and off, but it didn't help."

"I can see why you didn't want to talk about this last night."

Niki looked away, glancing at the squirrel that was running up a tree.

"Where's the baby?"

"She died." Thinking she had revealed too much information to Sky, Niki looked down at her watch and jumped up. "It's time to go in. We're going to be late." She hurried toward the building. "Tell Malcolm I'm sorry I didn't mean to hurt his feelings. It's just that when Malcolm grabbed me last night, everything I've tried so hard to forget came flooding back."

Sky knew that Niki was upset, but she thought she needed to warn her friend that when you stew in anger, it affects your relationships. She rubbed Niki's back as they walked into the building. Hesitantly, she told her friend, "If you don't let go of your past, you'll poison your future."

"I know, but it's tough," Niki replied as they walked into the horseshoe-clustered office where three-hundred-fifty positions occupied the entire fourth floor of the Jet Away Airways building. Each cluster had eight chairs with noisy mini-workstations. Agents were talking as if they were traders on the floor of the Wall Street Stock Exchange. Pebbles saw Niki and Sky and waved to get their attention.

As they walked over to Pebbles's workstation, Niki whispered, "Please don't tell anybody about what happened to me. I'm trying to forget my past."

"It's forgotten," Sky replied, as they approached Pebbles.

"I saved two seats," Pebbles whispered, pointing to the chairs before turning back to the computer screen and completing her call with the passenger. They each got comfortable in the leather chairs.

Sky scanned the newspaper while waiting for her first call. She pointed to an article in the *Dallas Morning News,* showing Pebbles the headline.

Pebbles's eyes bulged as she stared at his face and read— MAN FOUND MURDERED AT CLUB ELITE.

"We were just there last night!" Sky said. "Do you recognize him?"

"No," Niki replied. "What's his name?"

"Charles Scott," said Sky, reading from the paper.

Pebbles grabbed the paper from Sky and clamped her hand over her mouth as she stared at his picture. She practically threw the paper at Sky.

Niki picked up the paper. "Do you know him?" she asked Pebbles, but an incoming call kept Niki from hearing the answer. A passenger wanted the fare traveling from Los Angeles to Dallas. Reluctantly, Niki turned from the newspaper and retrieved the information from the computer.

"Can you hurry up with the information? I have somewhere to go," the woman said impatiently.

Niki politely answered, "I'm hurrying. One minute please." She could hear the sound of children playing in the background.

She could also hear the woman screaming at them. "You damn kids are getting on my last nerve. I said shut up!" Suddenly she was back in Niki's ear. "Do you have the information yet?" she snapped.

What a bitch, Niki thought. "It will cost you $241, including all fees and taxes."

"What time are the flights?"

"I have a flight departing Los Angeles at 12:48 p.m. and arriving—"

"That time is fine. I have a foster care conference to attend the following morning and I want to be well rested."

"Oh, how many foster children do you have?"

"I don't have time for idle chit-chat." The lady snapped. "Just book me on the flight."

The half smile that had appeared on Niki's face suddenly turned into a frown. "How many are traveling?" she asked, thinking again, *What a bitch.*

The woman sighed. "One adult."

"Do you prefer morning or afternoon on your return flight?" Niki rambled off.

"Just book me on a flight, I don't care. Can you type any faster? I have to go."

Niki rolled her eyes. "I'm typing as fast as I can. One moment, please." She let out a silent sigh, pissed at the woman's behavior.

She heard a noise that sounded like a slap. Then a child began to cry. A muffled sound, sounded and then Niki heard the woman screamed, "See what you made me do, you little bastard? Shut up!"

The slap triggered memories of those awful days when Niki's foster parents had slapped her and yelled obscenities at her for no reason. Niki knew those children didn't deserve that treatment, just like she didn't. She thought about reporting the woman to Child Protective Services, but figured no one would listen to her. They had never listened when she was a child. Still she wondered how she could get those children out of that environment.

"Are you there?" the woman asked rudely, cutting Niki's thoughts short.

"Yes," answered Niki. "On your return you will depart at 1 p.m. and arrive in Los Angeles at 2:23 p.m."

"Well, what are you waiting on? Book me on those flights."

"What's your name?" Niki asked, rolling her eyes in frustration.

"Leslie Turner. My frequent traveler number is F329T6."

"Mrs. Turner, may I have your phone number?"

"(555) 6-7-5-2-9-1-1. Did you get it?" she asked sarcastically.

"Yes," Niki answered, managing to keep her cool, even though she was boiling inside. Going off on a customer would just get her another reprimand and she didn't need that on her record. "What credit card are you using?"

"Don't you have my credit card number on file?" she yelled. "It should be in my profile."

"No, I don't," Niki said, frustration simmering just below the surface.

The woman sighed deeply and spit out her Visa number and expiration date. "I guess you need my address as well," she said sarcastically.

"Yes, I do," Niki answered, flipping off the phone with her middle finger, taking about all she could take, but still trying remain professional. Another minute and Niki would snap. Niki had just begun recapping her itinerary when the dial tone buzzed in her ear. She turned to Sky. "Damn, she was hateful! She just hung up on me!"

"There are a lot of jerks out there. Let it roll off your shoulders and add her to the rest of the fools," Sky said as she continued to scan the paper, waiting on her next call.

"Let it roll off my shoulders," repeated Niki, sounding perturbed. "I started to let some words roll off my tongue. If I wasn't sure that I was being monitored I would have given her a piece of my mind." She rolled her eyes, unplugged her headset, and was about to get up when a thought struck her. She wrote down Mrs. Turner's itinerary and quickly stuffed it into her purse with a self-satisfied smirk. She walked up to Pebbles, "You know him, the dead guy—don't you?"

"I just met him last night. I was with him briefly but I swear I didn't kill him." She defended herself. "We just sat in his car and talked. The next time I saw him, he was inside the club drunk and stumbling over people."

****

The stars glistened in the sky as the cool brisk air hung in the calm night. Sky lay across her bed talking to David on the phone about the good time she had had the night before at the club. "I really enjoyed myself. You're a lot of fun," Sky said as she snuggled under her covers.

"I did, too. I'm sorry I had to cut our conversation short last night. I got a call from Malcolm; he had a flat tire on the busy highway. I put out flares to alert the other drivers and helped him change the flat."

"Aren't you sweet?" she said, relieved with his answer.

"Enough about last night, let's get back to something more

pleasant. You're another Beyonce," he said with a soft laugh.

"I wish," she said as she reached to turn off the white porcelain lamp that sat on the nightstand. As she lay in the dark room listening to David's soothing voice, it seemed like she was lying next to him; she cuddled her pillow. "I'm surprised that I've never seen you at the airport."

David cleared his throat. "I'm busy checking the passengers' bags." Then he quickly changed the subject. "How is it working in reservations?" he asked, prying.

Sky didn't notice how quickly David had changed the subject. "I love talking to the customers; each call is different. It's fun most of the time, but sometimes customers can be a challenge. Sometimes they don't know where and when they want to travel."

"I bet you work with all kinds of people."

"Yeah, they're some weirdoes working there, but most of the people are pretty cool."

"How do you like working with the other employees?"

"I don't have many friends, except my best friend, Pebbles and Niki. I pretty much keep to myself. With the office being extremely large you don't get to see your friends, except maybe at break time."

"What's Niki's last name?"

"It's Salem, like the cigarette."

"How many employees are there?" he continued to pry.

"We have about two thousand in reservations."

"Jet Away is a big organization," he said, before steering the conversation back to more personal topics. He needed to find someone from the airline that could help his investigation but first he needed to be sure that that person wasn't involved in the killings. He thought Sky might be that person.

"Well, I could talk to you all night but I have to be up early to take care of some business. I really called to see if you would like to go out tomorrow." David really did want to get to know Sky on a more personal level.

"I would love to."

"Good bring your work ID."

"What?" she asked in surprise.

"I'll explain tomorrow. Goodnight."

"Good night," Sky replied, still wondering why she

needed her ID as she held the phone close to her chest for a brief moment before hanging up.

Seven

Saturday was usually Sky's day to sleep in, but not this Saturday. She went to sleep the night before thinking about David and woke with a smile in her heart and questions on her mind. "Where is David taking me?" she asked herself. She didn't know of anywhere other than the airport that would require a Jet Away ID. *Are we taking a short flight somewhere?* She wondered.

She stretched and looked at the clock. She couldn't believe it was only 6 a.m. and she was wide-awake. She rolled over and tried to go back to sleep, but after looking at the clock every five minutes for the next hour, she decided she might as well get up. If she was awake, she might as well be doing something rather than just lounging in bed. Her mother had always told her time drags when you've got nothing to do, but flies when you're busy. Today, Sky definitely wanted the time to fly—well at least until it was time to get ready for her date with David.

That thought made her smile and then frown. She was excited about their first real date, but if she didn't know where she was going, how would she know what to wear? She knew David was probably at the airport by now, so she decided there was no sense in calling him; she would probably just get his voicemail. Instead, she started cleaning her house and washing clothes, moving like a dust devil on the Texas plains.

By early afternoon, she had finished her chores. It was time to call David and see if he would give her a hint about where they were going. She tried the work number he had given her, which was Malcolm's number, and his voicemail came on. She tried to read, but she was too excited. She tried to nap, but she wasn't tired. At about 3 p.m., she decided she'd get ready, since she didn't even know when David planned to pick her up. And she certainly didn't want to keep the man waiting on their first date. She washed her hair, took a leisurely bubble bath, and did her nails—both toes and fingers.

She didn't hear the phone ring while she was in the bathroom. When she came out and saw the light blinking, she quickly redialed her number to retrieve her messages.

"Hi, Sky. Everything is working out great here. See you around six, and oh, by the way—don't ask where we are going, it's a surprise. Look forward to seeing you. Goodbye."

"Well, I guess it's best to play it safe," she said as she looked through her closet, discarding one outfit after the other as either too dressy or not dressy enough. Finally, she settled on a sexy light blue skirt and a jacket trimmed in white. She added blue pumps and a purse, silver earrings and bracelet. "Perfect," she said as she checked her profile in the mirror.

Then she remembered her ID and dug around in her work purse until she found it, tucking it into her blue bag. She checked her watch and the clock on the television, both said it was only 5 p.m. "What am I supposed to do for an hour?" she said.

She called Pebbles and Niki but neither was home, so she flipped on the news. Nothing new there.

She decided she'd put on some soothing music and try to relax. It worked. Suddenly someone was at her door.

Sky ran to the door and looked out the peephole. There stood David, even more handsome than she'd remembered him. She opened the door. "Hi, David, come on in," she said, stepping aside.

"Actually, Sky, if you're ready we should be going. I hope you're hungry."

She grabbed her purse and locked the door. "I'm starved." She rubbed her stomach. "Do I look OK?"

"You look just fine. In fact, you look stunning," he said as he walked her to the car and opened the door for her.

David headed for the Interstate as he talked about his make-believe day and asked about hers. David had already sent in for a background check on all of the three ladies and was waiting on the results. About twenty minutes later, he took an exit in a part of Dallas that Sky knew little about. Suddenly they came to a building sitting off by itself—nothing glamorous, but not your run-of-the-mill restaurant, either, Sky decided. "David, where are we?" she asked as he parked the car.

"Just wait," he said as he got out and went around, opening her door.

As they neared the building, Sky heard faint music and smelled a delicious Texas barbecue. "It smells and sounds wonderful," she told David.

"Wait until we get inside," he answered with a grin.

As they walked to the door, a doorman opened the door for them.

"Yes, reservations for David Hall," said David as they stepped up to the podium.

The host checked their names on the guest list. "May I see your Jet Away IDs, please?"

David pulled his out of his jacket pocket and Sky took hers out of her purse. The host took the cards, looked at them, then at David and Sky, and handed the cards back. "Welcome to Jet to the Stars, the exclusive club for our special Jet Away employees. Enjoy your evening." She waved for a host to seat them.

A host greeted them and led them to their table on the edge of the dance floor. A few people were dancing to the smooth music, but most were eating and talking. The decor was elegant, with just a hint of Texas here and there.

As they sat down, the waiter delivered shrimp cocktails and a bottle of wine. "Compliments of the house, folks. Enjoy and I'll be back to get your order."

Alone at last, Sky finally had a chance to ask David about the place. "How did you find this place? Why haven't I heard about it?"

"It's a private club, reserved for management and guests. Malcolm is a member; he called ahead and told them we were his guests tonight. The food is excellent, the music is easy, the atmosphere relaxed. I thought it would be a perfect place to spend the evening, enjoy a good meal and a bottle of wine, and get to know each other. I hope you aren't disappointed that we're not at some fancy, noisy club downtown."

"Oh, David, this is absolutely perfect," Sky replied,

reaching across the table to take his hand.

An hour later, they had finished one of the best meals Sky had had since moving to Dallas. They danced to a couple of slow numbers, with David pulling her ever closer until she was resting her cheek against his chest. It was wonderful, but a little difficult to talk that way. Pulling back slightly at the end of the third song, Sky had a suggestion. "David, let's go back to the table so we can talk and get to know more about each other."

"I thought you'd never ask," David replied, leading Sky off the dance floor.

"Who goes first?" Sky asked.

"The lady, of course," he gestured his hand toward her.

Sky started to tell David about her life and soon she found herself sharing things with him she'd never told a man before. And she was perfectly comfortable doing it. "OK, David, now you know all about me, it's your turn," she said a half an hour later.

"I doubt I know everything, but I can wait to learn the rest," David told her as he reached over, took her hands and began to tell his story—part the truth, part his cover. When he stopped talking and looked at his watch, it was nearly midnight. "Sky, I've had a lovely time tonight, but I think it's time we head back. What about you?"

"You're right, David. I didn't realize how long we'd been talking," she said as she stood and stretched to get the circulation going again in her legs.

David saw a detective walking toward him and he quickly left the table. "I'll be right back."

"Hey, Hall, how did you get in here?" asked the detective, shaking David's hand.

"I'm undercover with the left-handed serial killer case." He looked over his shoulder at Sky. "She doesn't know that I'm a detective so keep it on the down low."

"Yeah, right, right." The detective gave him dap. "I'll catch you later," he said and then walked away.

That was close. He walked back over to Sky and escorted her out the door with a brief explanation.

David was quiet on the walk to the car and on the drive back to Sky's place. He was still thinking about the killing last night at the club.

"I didn't say something that upset you, did I, David?" Sky asked as he drove down the highway.

"Heavens no—girl, tonight has been just perfect. Just being able to ride in comfortable silence says a lot to me. It seems like I've known you for years."

"I know, I feel the same way too," she said as he pulled up in front of her house.

David got out, went around the car, opened Sky's door, and waited for her to step out. He walked her to the door with his hand around her waist.

When Sky pulled her key out of her purse, David took her hand. "Sky, tonight has been one of the best nights of my life. Do you think we can do it again soon?"

"How soon?" she asked.

"Would tomorrow be too soon?" he asked.

She laughed. "Let me check my schedule," she said, drumming her fingers lightly against her temple. "It's your lucky day, my man, my schedule is free."

He smiled. "I'll call you and let you know what time I'll pick you up. And thanks again for a wonderful evening, Sky." David turned to kiss Sky's cheek, but she had quickly turned to get a glimpse of a neighbor coming home and their lips met. Surprisingly they began to kiss, after two minutes; she dropped her purse, breaking the rhythm. He picked up her purse, took the key from her hand, and opened the door. She stepped inside and he handed her, her purse. "I had a good time. I'll see you tomorrow. Good night."

"Good night."

"I want you to lock that door. OK?" he said. "I'll stand here until I hear the lock turn."

"Yes, David," Sky said as she shut the door. She turned the bolt and heard a muffled "Good night." She leaned against the door and smiled. Then she heard David's car door shut.

"This man is a keeper," she said as she kicked off her shoes and made her way slowly to the bedroom.

David whistled quietly as he started his engine and headed home. *This lady has definite possibilities*, he thought as he drove down the street. *Definite possibilities.*

Eight

*W*anda Brent sat in her big spacious living room early on a Monday morning watching the fire dance around in the fireplace. Her head rested on the armrest of the sofa as she waited for Brittany to finish dressing so she could take her to school. Although Wanda didn't want to expose the secret that had been gnawing at her for almost sixteen years, she knew she couldn't keep it forever. It looked like that day had arrived—all because Brittany had enrolled in her high school's driver education summer program. That had prompted Brittany to ask for her birth certificate, for which she kept asking and asking.

Summer would begin in a few months, which left Wanda little time to obtain it. She got up from the sofa and yelled down the hall, "Brittany, I'm headed for the car. Come on, before you're late." She walked out to her circular driveway to her white convertible Mercedes.

Brittany grew more independent every year. Like many girls her age, Brittany began to wear makeup and lived to go to the mall and other places with her friends. Wanda studied her budding beauty as she made her way to the car, opened the door, and flopped down in the passenger seat, still upset because Wanda continued to ignore her request.

"Did you lock the door and set the alarm?" Wanda asked.

"Yes, Mother." Brittany glanced at her mother, a frown clouding her face. "You're so paranoid." She rolled her eyes.

"I'm not paranoid. The left-handed serial killer struck

close to our area, at Club Elite." Wanda said with a smirk. "I'm just cautious, there's too much going on in the world."

Brittany ignoring her mother, pulled down the sun visor, looked into the mirror, and began applying makeup to the discolored spot on her face.

"Brittany, you don't need makeup. Your face is beautiful without it."

"How can you say that with this ugly mark on my face?" She raised her hand in front of her face. "And this widow's peak, I look like Eddie the monster."

"Eddie the monster." Wanda glanced at her daughter smiling as she pulled out of the driveway. "Brittany, it's a beautiful mark in the shape of a butterfly," she said, trying to allay Brittany's concern. "Eddie only wished he looked this good." Wanda laughed playfully, putting her hand to Brittany's chin.

"But where did it come from?" she asked with great concern. "No one else in our family has anything like this."

Wanda avoided the question because she didn't have the answer. She knew very little about Brittany's biological mother and even less about the father.

"Be proud of who you are. Don't ever be ashamed of those marks. They're your beauty marks." Wanda was never one to let Brittany dwell on her imperfections.

Brittany frowned. Over the years, she had developed vitiligo a skin pigmentation that discolors the skin. Just below Brittany's eye was a discolored mark and her hands had begun to loose its color too. "I don't want to wake up one morning and find my whole body white." She looked serious.

"White!" Wanda replied, flashing a wry smile. "Girl, I think you're far from that."

"So Mom do you think you can have my birth certificate before class start this summer."

"I'll do my best."

"That's all I hear you say Mother." Brittany snapped, frowning at Wanda. "I'll do my best." She said mimicking her mother, her head swaying from side to side.

"I'm trying. It should be here soon." Wanda knew the birth certificate was already there, safely locked away in her file cabinet, where it had always been since bringing Brittany home.

The Reservationist

Brittany sat straight up in her seat, her eyes locked on her mother; her two thick sandy red wavy braids hung past her brown shoulders. She released her hair from the braids and ran her fingers through the soft wavy curls. The change was dramatic; now she could easily pass for a model or beauty queen. Satisfied with her makeup and hair, she turned up the volume of the radio, sat back with her eyes closed, and bobbed her head to the music.

Once, she gets that birth certificate she'll know I'm not her mother. And all hell is going to break loose. I'm not ready for that, thought Wanda. She looked over at Brittany as she drove down the street.

Nine

*W*inter had come and gone as the sun hid behind the April clouds, radiating a warm shadow over Dallas, in the late afternoon. Four and a half months had past since the murder at Club Elite. *The left-handed serial killer must be on a sabbatical,* thought David. There hadn't been another murder committed by the left-handed serial killer since at the club. David's arduous effort to the find the killer was wearing thin. Captain Wineglass continuously questioned David about his investigation. He's so close but still far away, all of his leads ended up a dead end. It was a long, busy day for David but it wasn't over. He stepped into Lucas Trophy Store where an older gray-haired woman greeted him. "May I help you?"

He flashed his badge. "Yes, I'm Detective Hall with the Dallas Police Department. I'd like to ask you a few questions if I may."

"Certainly, Detective," the old woman said as she moved closer to the counter to get a better look at David.

He pulled out the of airplane wings. "Did this come from your store?"

She took the wings, held it to the light, and inspected it from every angle. "Yes, this came from my store. Is there a problem?"

"Yes! He shouted." After visiting the airports and literally thirty stores, he finally struck gold. "No there's not problem, but can you tell me which airline ordered it?"

She pulled a book from the shelf, put on her glasses, and

began running her finger down the page, line by line. "Sunset Airline received a batch last year." Then she readjusted her glasses. "Oh, wait a minute—it wasn't Sunset it was Jet Away. The airline purchased a limited number two years ago as a special order."

"Ma'am, are you sure?"

"Yes, I remember the young man who came in and picked them up," she said as she looked at David. "This has a special design, for reservations." She handed the wings back to him. "Look in the corner on the left side. Do you see the squiggly engraved line?"

He held the wing up to the light. "Yes, ma'am, I do."

"That's how I know which airline received which type of wings." She turned the book around so David could read the entries. "See, Ron Williams signed for the order," she said with a smile. "They only ordered two thousand of them."

He looked down at the signature, then back at her, and said, "Thank you." He kissed her on the forehead and the old lady blushed. "You've just made my day." He dashed out the door headed to his car to make his way to Jet Away. He had visited Reservations a couple of times, but came up emptied handed. Today he may get lucky. He contacted the office manager Stanley Duncan, who welcomed the invite.

He dialed Sky's cell phone making sure she had left work for the day, she answered on the second ring, "Hello."

"Hey Sky, how was work today?"

"It was busy, but I'm glad I'm out of that place. Pebbles and I commuted to work today. We're on our way home."

David's curiosity had been answered, "Well they have me working overtime, the airport is extremely busy. I just wanted to let you know that I was thinking about you."

"Am I going to see you tonight I'm looking forward to the weekend?" David could hear the music playing in the background.

"I don't think so."

"Ahh," Sky moaned.

"I'll make it up to you—how about dinner tomorrow night, your place. I'll buy?"

"That'll work. Will you call me later?"

"Of course I will."

David could hear Pebbles shouting in the background, "Hi David."

"Tell Pebbles hello. Goodbye." David hated lying to Sky and had contemplating on telling her the truth. For four months, he had managed to keep his undercover work a secret. He knew that he had to tell her and soon if he wanted to continue their relationship. His background check on Sky and her friends came back with a clean record. Therefore, he pursued the relationship with Sky never thinking it would blossom into something so meaningful and so quickly.

Twenty minutes later David arrived at Jet Away and met Stanley in the lobby. David flashed his badge. "Hello, I'm Detective Hall."

"Yes, Detective, I've been waiting for you." Stanley shook David's hand.

"As I explained on the phone, I would like to speak with one of your employees."

"Sure, who is it?"

"Is there somewhere we can talk?"

"Yes," replied Stanley as he led David back to his office.

"I don't want to alarm you but I think the left-handed serial killer may work for this airline." Stanley took a seat after hearing the shocking news.

"Please take a seat." Stanley gestured. As David sat, he took the airplane wings from his pocket. "These wings were made by Lucas Trophy Company; Ron Williams signed for them."

"Ron? He's in the purchasing department, just down the hall. He's a good guy, he isn't involved, is he?"

"No, I just have a couple of questions to ask him."

Stanley stood, "Follow me." David pushed out of his chair and Stanley led him to Ron's office.

"I should warn you that this is confidential. If it gets out, this office will be in an uproar," David told Stanley as they walked down the hall.

"I understand. Do you suspect that the person works here in reservations?"

"It's a possibility, especially since the wings came from the reservation department. I'm not one hundred percent sure yet. But I want to set up a couple of decoys."

"You got it, just say when," agreed Stanley, knocking on Ron's door. He walked in without waiting for an answer.

"Hey, Stanley, may I help you with something?" The tall slender man asked, getting to his feet.

"Yes, this is Detective Hall."

"Detective?" He looked surprised, and rubbed his hand on his jeans before extending it to David. "Hello, how can I help you?"

David shook Ron's hand then pulled out the airplane wings and laid them on Ron's desk. "I want to know if you signed for these wings."

"Yes, I remember these specifically. I ordered them for a promotion we had advertising our new service to Lubbock, Texas. We didn't order that many, maybe two-thousand. We distributed them between here and Houston. I got a call almost two years ago from Houston reporting that someone broke into the supply room and stole a box. Hell, we would have given them some had they asked."

David realized this was when the killings started. "Thank you," David said as he turned to leave. "Please not a word of this to anyone."

"Is everything OK, Detective?" Ron asked.

"Yes, just don't mention this to anyone."

"Sure, I won't," he assured David.

"Thank you, Ron," Stanley said as he and David walked back to his office. "Donna Morris, one of the head supervisors, will be back in the office in a few minutes. Give her a call and set up the undercover officers with her." He handed David her business card."

Once back in Stanley's office David once again warned Stanley to keep it quiet. "It's important that no one knows about the undercover cops. They will be watching and listening for anything suspicious. I'd like you to do the same. You can reach me at this number." He handed Stanley his business card.

"You've got it, Detective Hall. No one will know."

"I'll be in touch. Thank you." David turned and walked out the office.

David headed back to the office he had already phoned ahead for the two female undercover police officers to meet at his desk. When he arrived, Donna Morris from Jet Away was conferenced in on the phone, giving them instructions of their new job duties. David took his seat. "There are two thousand agents employed here, and I don't know how many of them are left-handed." Donna spoke. "We're open 24 hours a day, 7 days a week. Our shifts are from 12 midnight to 12 midnight." Donna continued to give instructions over the phone for an hour.

After the call ended, David stayed another two hours with the decoys making sure everything was in order for there new assignment. He finally finished his work for the night and decided it was probably too late to call Sky so he headed home. He would ask the Captain for a permanent spot in the Dallas Police Department; knowing he would probably get it made solving the case all the more urgent. Sky would understand why he lied when she heard the whole story. He planned to tell her tomorrow night at dinner.

Ten

David splashed cologne on his face, rubbing his shaped, close-trimmed beard. He tugged on his goatee a couple of times then took one last glance in the mirror before heading for the door. He was dressed in a pair of 501 Levi jeans that hugged his round bottom and covered the top portion of his beige and brown snakeskin boots. His short-sleeve, beige silk shirt completed the picture, making him irresistible; he looked like a true cowboy.

He had been right that night four and a half months ago. This relationship definitely had possibilities. He cared deeply for Sky, but he was getting tired of having to juggle his lies. *Tonight I'll tell Sky the truth and hope she'll understand. If I wait much longer, I could lose her. It's time I stop the deception.* David grabbed his jacket from the sofa and dashed in the rain to his car. He pulled out his cell phone, and hit speed dial.

"Hello?"

"Hey, Baby, I'll be there in thirty minutes. I just have to pick up the food."

"What are we eating tonight?" Sky asked.

"It's a surprise."

She sighed and smiled. "You're spoiling me, David Hall. Do you know that we have spent practically every weekend together since we met? We've only been apart the evenings you had to work late." David knew those were the nights he'd worked late at the police station.

"I know," he said, feeling guilty because his arduous efforts to keep the truth from Sky, was taking its toil on him. He was reluctant to tell her the truth because he couldn't risk doing anything to jeopardize the job he'd come here to do—catch the left-handed serial killer.

"Are you there?"

"Yes, sorry. I was watching this fool swerve in and out of traffic, on the slick road. I'm glad you're happy. You haven't seen anything yet."

"Don't start something you can't finish," she teased.

Suddenly David turned serious. "Make sure your door is locked. They still haven't caught the serial killer."

"It is. See you shortly."

I'm going to tell her tonight, he thought as he pulled up at Merk's Fish Market.

Sky walked around dusting her already polished furniture, and then walked toward the window. She was wearing a pair of hip-hugger, wide-leg jeans. Every curve on her size seven body was perfectly emphasized, especially her hippy bottom. Her silky smooth, shoulder-length hair bounced with every step. The clingy red, low-cut V-neck blouse showed a hint of cleavage.

As she watched, the raindrops hit the window and slid slowly down in tiny rivers. She daydreamed about hers and David's relationship, and how it had blossomed over the months. The burning desire she had for David covered her body like a cocoon. She was sure that David could see it when he looked at her but Sky was determined not to give in to temptation, holding onto her celibacy.

Headlights flashed on the window and Sky smiled. She closed the vertical blinds and ran to the front door. "Hey, Baby," she said, brushing the rain from David's jacket.

David was carrying two Styrofoam containers in a clear plastic bag. He pecked her on the lips, and then brushed past her to the bar that divided the dining room from the kitchen. He placed the bag on the counter and hooked his wet coat on the gold coat rack in a corner of the kitchen. Then he grabbed Sky, and swung her around like a rag doll. He brushed the hair out of her face and kissed her passionately, thrusting his tongue deep into her mouth. He could feel the passion building between them. They could hear the pounding and feel the beating of each other's hearts.

Sky reluctantly broke away. "We better eat before the food gets cold." It was getting harder for Sky to pull away when what she really wanted was for David to take her to the bedroom and make passionate love to her, all night. "What did you get for us to eat?" she asked as she peeked into the bag. Before he could answer, she took a deep breath, taking in the aroma. "Ah, my favorite—fried catfish from Merk's. Thank you, Baby."

"Fried just like you like it," he said as he pulled out the barstool for her.

She sat, took a bite, and smiled. "This is so good." She picked up a hush puppy and popped it into her mouth.

"That's my girl—loves to eat." David laughed as he put a couple of French fries in his mouth.

After dinner, they sat on the sofa, drinking the champagne Sky had chilled earlier. Sky picked up the remote, channel surfing for something interesting. She settled on the news, on which an anchor was giving a meager update on the serial killer. "Do you think they'll ever find that woman?" she asked David, turning to look into his eyes.

"It's just a matter of time," David said confidently.

"It's creepy knowing that woman is still out there. I'm so glad I have you around to protect me." She placed his hand in hers, wiggling her fingers until they were intertwined.

"You don't have anything to worry about," he said, kissing her forehead. "I'm right here or always close by." He made regular trips past her house, being careful she didn't see him. She laid her head on his chest as he stroked her hair. David sat with his eyes closed, envisioning Sky and him as a family. He looked serious and thought, *I have to tell her, I must.* "Baby, sit up," David began, his voice suddenly all business. "I have something to tell you." He knew that he had to warn her about someone killing in the reservation call center and the only way to do it was to expose his secret. He wanted her to be safe.

"Sure what is it?" Sky asked, seeing the seriousness in his eyes.

A loud knock on the door interrupted the moment. "Who could that be?" Sky asked as she walked to the front door. "Hold that thought."

David was happy for the interruption; it gave him more time to collect his thoughts. She looked through the peephole. "It's Pebbles." She opened the door.

"Girl, I figured you'll need this," Pebbles said as she waltzed in handing Sky her wallet.

"My wallet! Where did you get this?"

"You left it in my car yesterday," she replied as she flopped down on the barstool, and poured herself a glass of champagne. "Hey, David," she said as she made herself comfortable.

"Hi, Pebbles. It's Saturday night—you don't have a date?"

"Actually, I'm on my way to the club," she said, sipping her champagne.

"Who are you going with?" Sky asked.

"I'm meeting a couple of girls from the office there."

"Be careful, the serial killer is still at large," David reminded her.

Pebbles laughed. "I know, but she doesn't want me." She gulped her drink, slid off the barstool, and headed for the door. "I'll see you at work on Monday." She told Sky. "David, it's always a pleasure. Good night," she called over her shoulder as she let herself out.

Sky walked over to the front door and locked it. "Now where were we?" she said as she returned to the sofa.

David ignored her question. He had lost his momentum when Pebbles had burst in. "I got *Jackie Brown* from Blockbuster."

"Oh, good," Sky said, taking the DVD from David.

He looked at the cover. "Pam Grier is fine," he said, latching onto anything to take his mind off the real problem.

"She's all right." Sky laughed.

David grabbed Sky's hand and pulled her toward him, his playful attitude turning serious. Looking into the eyes, the highlight of her picture-perfect face, he told her, "You're so pretty." He brushed the hair from her face. *I can't tell you the truth, not just yet. You will get the wrong idea...I'm not ready for this to end*, he thought as he began to kiss her forehead, and then moved down to her nose, and lightly brushed his lips across her shapely, round lips.

Sky closed her eyes and fought to control her own mounting passion, but a pleasant moan escaped. She knew these soft kisses would lead to something else; once again, she reluctantly pulled back. "We'd better quit." She was pleased with her new relationship. David had been the perfect gentleman, but the more time they spent together, the more they were physically drawn together like iron to a magnet. "I hope you don't think I'm leading you on."

"I don't think that at all. I haven't felt this good in a long time. It's something about that smile and those deep dimples. It's contagious." He gently shook her chin.

Suddenly he turned somber again. Mixed emotions were jumping around in his head like grasshoppers. *It's time.* "Sit up, I want to tell you something," he said in a slow, deliberate tone, gently taking her hand.

"David, don't look so serious."

"Remember, when we first met at the club?"

"Yes." She looked with anxious eyes.

"And I told you that I worked at the—"

The telephone suddenly rang. "Damn," he mumbled, hating that he had been interrupted again. *This is an omen. It must not be meant for me to tell.*

"I'm sorry." She flashed an apologetic smile then reached for the phone. "Hello."

"Hey, Sky, what are you doing? Do you want to grab a movie tonight or are you tied up with Mr. Jet Away again?" Niki asked, facetiously.

"As a matter of fact David is here." She looked at him and smiled as he placed the CD inside the player. "I'm sorry, I have to pass tonight. Are you still going to the nursing home with me tomorrow?"

"Yes. Give me a wake-up call in the morning."

"OK, good night." Sky turned back to David, who was deep in thought. Looking into his hazel eyes, she smiled. "What did you want to tell me that was so important? I'm all ears." She reached for his hand.

David was still unsure of what he was going to say. He hesitated as his mind drifted back to that night when April had broken up with him. He looked into Sky's eyes and second thoughts won again. "I just wanted to say that I'm...I'm." He stumbled over his words like an unrehearsed play.

"Yes David."

"I'm falling in love with you." It was true. He had quickly fallen in love, quicker than in any other relationship.

"You're what!" Her eyes fixed on David, surprised because she had the same feelings.

He hadn't planned to tell her this way but he would rather admit his feelings than face the fear of what might happen if he told her the truth about his profession. *Not if, David—when*, he told himself.

He gently rubbed her hands. "I love you." He spoke passionately.

She looked into his eyes. "Say those words again." She hadn't heard those words from him before.

"You heard me, I love you," he said proudly.

"Oh, David, I love you too. It's not too soon, is it?"

"It's almost five months."

"Five months isn't long at all."

"Baby, I know exactly what I want. Don't you?" He looked into her eyes. "Who said it has to be a year—two years?"

"Yes, I want you too Baby."

David slowly kissed her on the lips and she sat with her head leaned back embracing the warmth of his body as he lowered her to the sofa in a relaxed position as they continued their steamy kiss. His kisses were hot, deep, and passionate. After fifteen minutes of deep passion, Sky could feel David's manhood rise and she immediately rose. "David just be patient with me. You know I'm celibate and intend to stay that way until I get married. I hope you can honor that."

"I'm not going to lie and say that I don't think about what it would be like to have you in my bed, but it's not a priority on my list. It's been a long time since I've been with a woman. I've learned to be patient." He gave her a quick kiss, put his arm around her, and hit the play button on the DVD player.

Three hours later, David yawned and stretched. "What time is it?"

"Twelve o'clock," she said, lying cozy in his lap.

He gently removed his arms and stood. "I better get

going...unless you want me to stay," he said, grinning.
She stood, giving him a slight push. "No, you better get some rest. I'll call you tomorrow."
As they shared a long, deep goodnight kiss, David's nature began to rise.
Sky looked up. "David." She spoke softly.
"I'm sorry, I'm trying to control it." His eyebrow was raised.
"David, please, you're making it hard. You know I'm just as weak." She smiled bashfully. "You'd better go," she said, gently pushing him out the door.
"Goodnight." He walked out and stood there until he heard the sound of the door lock.

Eleven

*T*he morning sun glared on Sky and Niki's faces through the open sunroof as Sky drove down the highway to the other side of Ft. Worth. Traffic was generally slow around ten on Sunday mornings but today the three-lane highway was packed. "Thanks for coming with me," Sky said as she signaled and changed lanes. "Normally the drive takes forty minutes but it's going to take a little longer today."

"I didn't have anything else to do, and I've been anxious to meet your Aunt Cindy."

"Sometimes I wonder why she's in that nursing home. She seems like she's in her right mind every time I visit her."

"Sky, you said that she has dementia. Sometimes people with that disease have periods when their minds are clear, especially about things in the past, while their short-term memory fades. Like the time she ended up on your doorstep at midnight with her pajamas on."

Sky laughed. "She knew who I was; I was surprised that she remembered how to get to the house. I guess if you lived there for thirty years like she had you would know."

Cindy Winters had checked herself into the Summit Retirement Home two years earlier when she had started showing early signs of dementia.

One morning she was driving to IHOP for breakfast and ended up in a Kmart parking lot. She couldn't remember where she was going. Other times, she could go to the store without any problem. Her personality changed from jovial to docile and introverted. At times, her mind would be clear and lucid; other times she couldn't tell you who she was. Over the past two years, her mind had deteriorated rapidly, but she always knew Sky.

Sky and Sheila had spent their childhood summers in Dallas with Aunt Cindy. They had often helped her in the neighborhood garden. Sky remembered crawling on her knees in the dirt, picking mustard and collard greens, and the biggest, juiciest tomatoes she'd ever tasted. She'd sneak a bite when her aunt wasn't looking.

The three of them picked and ate persimmons from the tree. Once finished it was always a treat to crack open the seed because the insides would have a shape of an eating utensil—a fork, spoon, or knife.

Aunt Cindy entertained the girls with stories of the old days while shelling peas or doing the dinner dishes, in the very same house that Sky lived in today.

Sky often teased Aunt Cindy about having ESP because whenever someone was picking on the girls, she would show up. Because she never married, she took great interest in Sky and Sheila and enjoyed the summer and winter breaks from school just as much as her nieces did.

Sky said, letting out a deep sigh, "I just hate seeing her in the nursing home. If I was in a better position to take care of her, I would. But I know she's getting good care at the home." She glanced over at Niki. "I can still see that lively glint in her eyes when she turned up on my doorstep. We talked about my mother and father, and reminisced about Sheila and me as kids. I could tell she really hated going back to the nursing home. I did all I could do to keep from fighting back the tears. She must have noticed because she placed my chin between her thumb and index finger, looked in my eyes, and said, 'I'll be all right. You just take extra care of yourself and watch your back.' She's always been overprotective of Sheila and me."

"That has to be difficult."

"At times it is," Sky told her. "I can't wait for you to meet her. At sixty-five, she still has plenty of spunk." That brought a smile to Sky's face. "When I talked to her this morning she was lucid and anxious to see us. Just don't expect too much," Sky warned her. "A lot could have changed by the time we get there. She could be confused. Don't let it throw you."

"I won't," Niki said, as she rested comfortably in the

leather seat.

****

Staring out the window where the April showers had blossomed the first day of May's beautiful Day Lilies, Aunt Cindy sat waiting for Sky. She gazed down the long sidewalk each time a figure appeared, thinking it was her niece. She waited in a brown leather chair, in the lobby glaring at the television one moment, and then staring out the large picture window the next.

Each time the door opened, she turned and smiled to see if it was her favorite niece.

"Miss Winters, would you like a glass of lemonade?" a nurse asked as she pushed a small metal cart of water, lemonade, and various different fruits.

"Don't mind if I do. Thank you, Hon," Aunt Cindy said in her feisty tone as she moved her chair closer to the door so she could see her niece as soon as she arrived.

"Your niece will be here soon," the nurse said as she handed Aunt Cindy the glass.

"I know. She's coming to braid my hair." She patted her head, calling attention to the thick mass of salt and pepper strands.

A geriatric exercise class was in session in the next room. "Cindy, come join us," an older man called out.

"No, my daughter, Sky is coming today and I'm waiting on her." She sipped on her drink, placed the glass on the table, and turned back to the window. She sat up in her chair when she saw Sky walking up the sidewalk. She stretched her hands toward the door as Sky and Niki walked in.

"Aunt Cindy, how are you?" Sky asked as she wrapped her arms around her aunt and kissed her on each cheek. Aunt Cindy's apricot-color skin was slightly wrinkled and she wore her long, wavy hair pinned up in a bun. Even with her rounded shoulders, which gave her back a slightly humped look, she stood five-feet, five-inches tall, a trait in the Winters family.

Aunt Cindy pulled back. "I'm doing well. Girl, you need to put some meat on those bones. I need to fatten you up."

Sky laughed as she looked at Niki and back at her aunt. "Aunt Cindy, this is my friend Niki."

"Nice to meet you, Aunt Cindy," Niki said, grabbing her hand.

Aunt Cindy snatched her hand back as she stared angrily at Niki. "Who are you?" She frowned.

"It's OK, Aunt Cindy." Sky took Niki by the arm. "This is my friend," she repeated slowly.

Niki tried again. "Hi, Aunt Cindy."

"You get away from me!" She turned to Sky and told her, "She's the devil."

Niki stepped back, not knowing exactly how to respond.

"No, Aunt Cindy," Sky said as she gently stroked Aunt Cindy's hair. "She's with me. This is my friend."

Aunt Cindy asked, "She's with you? She's your friend? Are you sure?"

"Yes, I'm very sure." Sky rubbed Niki's shoulder. "This is my friend." Sensing that Aunt Cindy was making Niki uncomfortable, Sky changed the subject. "We're going to see Daddy, your brother, next weekend."

"Gabe, my brother," Aunt Cindy said, slowly seeming to come around.

"Yes, Gabe."

Aunt Cindy looked over at Niki, who had taken a chair across the room. "No! I've seen her before. Look in her eyes," she said adamantly.

Sky raised her eyebrows. "Niki won't hurt a flea," she said, rubbing her aunt's arm to calm her. It was obvious that Sky couldn't convince her aunt that Niki wasn't the devil.

Hearing Cindy's apparent discomfort, a nurse walked over to Sky and asked in a low voice, "May I speak with you for a moment?"

"Auntie, I'm stepping over here, I'll be right back."

Aunt Cindy nodded but didn't take her eyes off Niki, who was sitting quietly across the room, thumbing through an old magazine.

Sky and the nurse walked over a couple of steps so her aunt couldn't hear their conversation. "What triggered that?" asked the nurse.

Sky put her hands in the air. "I don't know. She took one look at my friend and became upset."

"She hasn't had an episode in months," the nurse said.

"I don't know why she doesn't like my friend; she

wouldn't hurt a flea." Sky looked over at Niki. "Have my aunt's habits changed any?"

"Well, thinking back she did have one episode three weeks ago. A lady came to visit her mother and your aunt blurted out, 'She's dangerous'. She always liked to watch the news, but she seems to be following the news even more since this left-handed serial killer story has been on the air. I think it may be affecting her."

"Why wasn't I notified? I've visited several times since the story broke," Sky said with a frown. "Maybe I should just move her from this nursing home."

"I'm sorry, I thought you were notified."

"Well, you were wrong," Sky replied, clearly upset. "Don't let her watch the news. And call the doctor and have him to prescribe her something for anxiety."

The nurse nodded and Sky walked back over to her aunt.

"Aunt Cindy, who am I?" asked Sky.

"Chile, I know who you are—you're Sky."

"How old are you?"

"I'm twenty-five," she said with a frown. "I'm not stupid."

Sky laughed softly. She reached in her big black bag and pulled out a comb and brush. "Are you ready for me to French braid your hair?"

Aunt Cindy nodded and seemed to be the person that Sky remembered from her childhood.

When Sky reached for her hand, Aunt Cindy told her, "I'm not an invalid, I can walk," and stood up to prove her point.

"Niki, would you like to come with us and see Aunt Cindy's room?" Sky spoke above the loud voices all around them.

"I don't want that devil in my room," Aunt Cindy said, sucking her bottom lip. "It's in her eyes, can't you see it. You better watch her."

"It's OK, Sky," Niki said. "It's such a beautiful day, I think I'll go walk around the grounds. I'll be back here in about an hour, if that's OK with you."

Sky looked from her aunt to Niki, torn between two of her favorite people. She asked Aunt Cindy to excuse her for just a moment and walked over to Niki. "I'm really sorry about all of this. I'm sure Aunt Cindy didn't mean what she said, but it's probably best if I don't upset her anymore by trying again to convince her that you are my friend and certainly not the devil."

"Don't worry about it, Sky." Niki laughed. "I know she doesn't mean it. You told me her brain doesn't always function right because of the dementia. I'll be OK, really. The grounds look inviting. You go and take care of your aunt. Get her hair fixed the way she likes it."

Sky reluctantly turned and walked back to her aunt, trying to hide her disappointment behind a fake smile. She really wanted Aunt Cindy to like Niki. "OK, Aunt Cindy, let's see what I can do with your hair," she said, extending her hand again.

This time Aunt Cindy reached out and took it, but not before darting a deadly look in Niki's direction. "Good. I don't like her. You shouldn't trust her. I tell you, she's the devil," Aunt Cindy told Sky as they walked hand in hand to Aunt Cindy's room.

"Turn to the news," Aunt Cindy said as soon as they got to her room.

"Don't you think you're watching too much news?" Sky asked as she discreetly moved the remote out of sight.

"No, this is my way of staying up with what's going on in the world."

"Aunt Cindy, who's the president?"

"Why, honey, it's John F. Kennedy."

Sky laughed, "Just what I thought," then began to comb her aunt's hair.

The day was fading as Sky and Niki headed back to Dallas. Niki sat quietly during most of the ride.

"Niki, I'm so sorry Aunt Cindy treated you that way."

"That's OK. I understand her condition," Niki told her even though she was having trouble getting Aunt Cindy's words out of her mind.

"The nurse said she's watching too much news, particularly about the left-handed serial killer. I told the nurse not to let her watch the news."

"The serial killer?" repeated Niki.

Sky nodded her head. "Why would she insist that you're dangerous? That puzzles me."

"What does the serial killer have to do with her thinking

I'm dangerous?"

"For some reason when she saw you, she thought she recognized you."

"Recognized me," Niki said, lacing her fingers across her chest, looking confused.

"Yes, isn't that funny?" Sky said, trying to lighten the mood.

Niki's hands shook as she saw her reflection in the window, a look of distress showing in her eyes.

Sky noticed Niki's look of confusion and asked, "Are you all right?"

Niki didn't answer; she was deep in thought. *Could she know?*

Sky raised her voice and tried again. "Niki?"

Niki jumped. "Oh, I'm sorry," she said, flustered. "What did you say?"

"Were you saying something?" asked Sky.

"No, I was just thinking," Niki answered, trying to hide her true feelings.

"Like I said, sometimes Aunt Cindy isn't in her right mind. Tomorrow she'll ask me what happened to that nice girl that I brought by." Sky laughed.

"I know." Niki forced a smile. *She knows*, Niki said silently as she continued to stare at her reflection in the window. *But she can't,* she told herself. *That old lady better not get in my way, or she's dead.*

As soon as Sky pulled into the driveway next to Niki's car, Niki got out and jumped into her Jeep, waving goodbye. Once she got down the street away from the house, she stopped and covered her ears. "It's happening to me again!" she screamed, frantically searching her purse, tossing papers and other items to the floor. "The voices, they're coming back again!"

****

Niki's tires squealed as she pulled into her parking spot. She slammed on the brakes, shifted into park, and ran inside her apartment, almost knocking over the small green and beige ceramic flowerpot next to the door. She headed straight for the bathroom, where she fiercely searched for the small brown bottle with the label that read, 'Take one pill twice a day.' Niki removed the top and shook the bottle. The last pill fell into her trembling hand. She swallowed the pill then cupped her hands under the running water, throwing water into her mouth.

As she covered both ears with her hands, she leaned limped against the wall. "I can't control these voices." They had returned when Aunt Cindy had accused her of being the devil. She stared into the mirror with tears in her eyes. "Why! Why me! I can't, I can't stop this demon inside of me."

Crying uncontrollably, Niki slid to the floor. *Why did you take my parents away from me? We were such a happy family. Now I have nobody, nobody but these voices inside my head!*

She attempted to calm the turbulence that was destroying her mind. One minute she was pacing the floor, the next sitting on the edge of the tub taking long, deep breaths, waiting for the medication to take effect. Her mind continued to bounce back and forth; one moment filled with evil, deadly thoughts, the next moment with things more rational.

Suddenly she stood still and stared at the newspaper clippings she had pasted on the wall. *She knows. Dammit, that old lady knows. She'd better stay away from me if she wants to live.*

She walked over to her bed, picked up her purse, and removed the wrinkled paper. As she straightened the paper she thought, *Mrs. Turner, we have some unfinished business. You thought I forgot, but I didn't. I can't forget how hateful you were to me. I've been waiting on you.* She stared at Mrs. Turner's itinerary, LAX to DFW. With a glimmer in her eye, she dialed Sky.

"Hello," answered Sky.

"Hey, I just wanted to remind you that I have plans after work and won't be carpooling tomorrow."

"I didn't forget. You jumped in your car so quick. I was just going to call you to see if everything was OK, you flew out of here."

"I just have a lot on my mind." She lay flat on her back, staring at the ceiling, feeling calm.

"I hope you're not still thinking about Aunt Cindy. She is harmless, so forget about what she said."

"It's forgotten," Niki said with a bogus laugh, hoping to

convince her friend.

"Pebbles reneged on me, too. She's going out after work, so I'll be driving alone."

Niki sat up on the bed and put the itinerary back in her purse. "OK, I'll see you tomorrow. Good night."

"Good night."

Twelve

*N*iki arrived at work early Monday morning, before her friends, and immediately sat down at the computer. She removed the wrinkled paper from her purse, typed in a few letters, and Mrs. Turner's reservation appeared on the screen. *I have to pay that bitch back for being hateful to me when she made her reservation and for abusing her children.* Niki thought.

"Good, her reservation is still intact," she mumbled. "I'll check the flight manifest after lunch to see if she's checked in."

Lunch came quickly after a few hours of making reservations. Niki and Pebbles walked toward Sky and as they past her, Pebbles tapped Sky on the shoulder to let her know it was lunchtime. Sky nodded as she finished up with her customer, she removed her headset, then walked past the supervisor's door. Donna called her. "Sky, do you have a minute? I just finished monitoring your last ten calls."

The others contained a grimace, and kept moving toward the cafeteria. Pebbles mouthed, "We'll hold a seat for you."

Sky turned back to Donna. "Sure, I hope I sounded OK."

"You always do. You made one-hundred percent. I really enjoy listening to you, and the way you engage in conversation with your customer—that's an acquired skill. You're one of the best."

"Thank you. I'll come hear them after lunch," Sky said, resuming her walk to the busy cafeteria. There she grabbed her lunch and walked over to Pebbles as she watched other agents eating, talking, and watching television. "Where is Niki?" Sky asked as Pebbles removed her food from the microwave.

"I think she's using the telephone." Pebbles looked over in the direction of the payphones on the wall.

"That reminds me..." Sky pulled out her cell phone and dialed David. She waited impatiently while it rang three times before he answered.

"Hey there," Sky said when she heard David's voice.

"What's up Baby, I was just thinking about you."

"I was thinking about you too, that's why I called. I'm excited about tonight." She walked over to the table with her food.

"Good, I'll pick you up at eight. We have reservations at Antares, the revolving restaurant at the Hyatt."

"Ooh, I can't wait. I've always wanted to go inside that flashy big ball," she said as she took a bite of food.

"Well, tonight is all yours but right now I have to get back to work. See you at eight," he said quickly, breaking the connection.

Sky saw Niki on the payphone and motioned for her to join Pebbles and her when she finished.

When Niki joined her friends, she seemed to be miles away. She was fidgety, tapping the table with her hand, glancing around as if she were looking for someone.

Niki had been calling Mrs. Turner and harassing her for a couple of days. Every time she answered the phone Niki told her, "Your day is coming."

"Are you OK?" Sky asked, noticing Niki's blank stare.

"Yes, I'm just a little jittery because I haven't eaten all day. That's all." She took a couple of bites from her sandwich, ate a couple of chips, threw the remaining food back in her lunch bag, and excused herself.

"Hey, where are you going?" Pebbles asked. "We still have twenty minutes left."

"I have to finish up a reservation before I sign back in," Niki answered as she left.

Niki sat down at the computer and retrieved Mrs. Turner's reservation information once again. She smiled and whispered excitedly. "Yes! She's checked in. Flight 285 gets in at five-forty this evening. She's sitting in seat 7B, which means she will deplane the aircraft quickly. I'll have to leave here by five since it's right in the middle of rush hour, I can get there by five-thirty." Niki had a gleam in her eye. *Mrs. Turner, we have some unfinished business, but not for long,* she thought.

As other agents returned from lunch, Niki quickly cleared her screen, but she'd check Mrs. Turner's flight every hour until the end of her shift.

Her last phone call of the day was a man checking on a flight arrival time. "Can you tell me what time flight 4 gets into New York today?"

Niki quickly hit a couple of keys on the computer. "It arrives at eight this evening," she answered. "Thank you for calling Jet—"

"What gate?" the man interrupted.

"Gate five," she answered annoyed as she disconnected the call and reached for her purse. Niki swiftly removed her headset, turned off the computer, and brushed past the security guard as she dashed out the door.

Sky and Pebbles looked up just in time to see their friend leaving without saying goodbye. Sky remembered that Niki had made several calls from the break room during the day, which was unusual. Normally, they would sit and talk during break. *Niki just isn't herself today,* Sky thought. *I sure hope she isn't still thinking about what Aunt Cindy said yesterday.*

****

Niki switched from lane to lane in and out of the heavy traffic, wondering how she would recognize Mrs. Turner. The plane had just taxied to the gate when she pulled into the airport parking lot. She jumped out of her Jeep, flashed her badge to security, and rushed inside to the gate. Cleverly, she asked the gate agent to page Mrs. Turner then propped her body against a pole next to the red paging telephone and eagerly waited. Once the passengers had begun to deplane—Mrs. Turner heard her name and walked to the red phone.

"Hello, this is Leslie Turner." She looked around the airport.

Niki turned toward Mrs. Turner, watching her as she

spoke. "What the hell do you mean my party will meet me at baggage claim?"

Niki quickly walked away when she noticed Mrs. Turner staring at her. "I'm not meeting anybody. I'm picking up a car, idiot." She looked around the airport again to see who could have paged her, then slammed down the receiver.

Niki waited for Leslie Turner to leave and discreetly trailed her out the door down the escalator to Luxury Rental Car. She watched her pick up the keys and walk to a red Grand AM. Niki dashed to her Jeep, pulled in between two parked cars and put on a feathered blonde wig. When Mrs. Turner pulled out of the parking lot, Niki quickly moved a couple of car lengths behind her and followed. Fifteen minutes later Mrs. Turner pulled into the Sierra Grand Hotel parking lot.

Niki slowly continued down the street. "I'll give her time to check in and I'll be back. I'll show her about mistreating foster children," she told herself.

An hour later Niki drove to the hotel and circled the parking lot until she found the red Grand AM. She parked in the back of the building, went in, and took a seat in the darkest corner of the lobby. She sat anxiously, pretending to read the newspaper. She stole a guarded look at the elevator each time the door opened. Finally, she saw Mrs. Turner emerge with a crowd of people and head to the bar.

Still in disguised, Niki walked nonchalantly into the bar and took a seat next to Mrs. Turner.

"Let me have a Jack Daniels on the rocks," Mrs. Turner said.

"And what are you having, ma'am?" the bartender asked Niki as she handed Mrs. Turner her drink.

Niki hesitated and then answered, "I'll just have a bottled water."

Before Niki could drink her water, Mrs. Turner had finished her drink and headed toward the elevator. Niki quickly threw some money on the bar and ran out, yelling for Mrs. Turner to hold the elevator. Once inside, Niki saw that the light for the third floor was illuminated.

"What floor?" Mrs. Turner asked.

"Three please," Niki said as she looked away.

When the door opened on three, she waited for Mrs. Turner to leave before walking out. She pretended trying to decide which way led to her room. She saw Mrs. Turner stop at 301. Niki moved to 304 and fiddled with the lock.

Once Mrs. Turner was inside, Niki rushed back to the first floor. While she had been waiting for Mrs. Turner, she had spotted an employees' closet behind the spiral staircase. She stepped in and quickly grabbed a maroon and gold uniform a couple sizes too big so she could slip it on over her clothes. She pulled a knife out of her pants pocket, placed it in the uniform pocket, and rolled up her pants legs. Confident she wouldn't be noticed, she left the closet, walked over to a nearby table, shoved it into the service elevator, and pressed the button for the third floor. As the door opened soundlessly on the third floor, Niki walked out and down the empty hall toward room 301. She knocked and cheerfully called out, "Room service."

"I didn't order room service," Mrs. Turner screamed angrily.

"Compliments of the house," Niki replied, silently patting herself on the back for thinking so fast on her feet.

When Mrs. Turner opened the door, Niki charged ahead and rolled the cart into Mrs. Turner, knocking her down. "Are you crazy?" Mrs. Turner asked as she started to get up.

Niki swung her leg back, kicked the door shut, turned, and shoved Mrs. Turner back down. "Shut up! Shut the hell up," she ordered in a hushed but deadly voice. "Do you remember those words?" Niki pulled the six-inch switchblade from her pocket, pushed the button, and placed the shiny silver tip at Mrs. Turner's neck.

Stunned by what was happening, Mrs. Turner screamed, "What do you want?" hoping someone, anyone, would walk by and hear her.

"Get up. We have some unfinished business, Mrs. Turner," Niki shouted as she walked Mrs. Turner over to the bed.

Mrs. Turner gasped for air and gagged. "What are you talking about? I don't know you." She managed to get out. "Please let me go," the woman strained.

Niki let out a sick, demented laugh then twisted the knife backward and forward until it pierced Mrs. Turner's skin. A trickle of blood ran slowly down her neck.

Mrs. Turner grabbed her neck and started to shake. "What do you want with me?"

The monster that Niki tried so hard to suppress at times had surfaced. A moment of intense excitement washed over Niki; she was enjoying every minute. "You should be more careful who you yell at," she spoke coldly as she thought back to the day she had made Mrs. Turner's reservation.

Mrs. Turner screamed, "What are you talking about, lady?" She looked in fear as the blood slowly dripped from her hand.

Niki continued to toy with her. "I'll tell you what I'm talking about. I made your airline reservation to come to Dallas. You were just plain rude and nasty to me," Niki said, pulling Mrs. Turner to her feet as she spoke.

Mrs. Turner's eyes popped as she stumbled backward into the corner. "Look, I didn't mean anything personal. I have a tendency to snap when I'm stressed," she said, choking on the words. "Really, I didn't mean any harm, please let me go." She couldn't believe that this lunatic holding her hostage was the same person who had made her reservation. *This is some twisted shit,* she thought.

"Shut up," Niki said in a deadly quiet, controlled voice. "I heard you yelling and cursing at those kids in your home while you made your reservation. I even heard a slap." Niki slapped the woman so hard she thought she heard cowbells. It sent her sprawling to the floor. "How does it feel?" She bent down, pointing the knife closer to Mrs. Turner's throat. "I started to turn you in to the authorities but I decided that wouldn't solve anything so I'm going to fix it so those children will never fear you again." She hit the wall with her fist to prove a point.

Mrs. Turner jumped, still clutching her neck. "You're mistaken! I'm not like that. My children are well provided for," she said, looking at Niki. "You can call them. Please," she begged.

"I'm not mistaken. You're a low-life asshole preying on innocent kids. You see, I was a foster child and was slapped around and beaten most of my young life. You name it and it happened."

"Help!" Mrs. Turner screamed, praying someone would

hear her. "Please, don't hurt me."

Niki dragged her to the corner of the bedroom and covered her mouth with her right hand to muffle her voice. She quickly slid the knife across her neck then jabbed Mrs. Turner in the chest sending the fatal stab into her heart, causing dark red blood to gush out as her lifeless body fell to the floor.

Niki took off the bloody uniform and tossed it under the bed. "That'll teach you," she said, placing a set of airplane wings next to her body before she left the room.

She walked quickly and silently, dodging behind a tall flower plant when she heard people approaching. In the clear again, she turned and tiptoed quietly to the exit door and eased it open, then she fugaciously ran down three flights of stairs. As she approached her car, she glanced around for possible witnesses. None was there. Once in the security of her car, she removed the wig, stashed it away, and took a deep breath before starting the engine. *Home free again*, she thought as she exhaled and headed out of the parking lot.

She was so wrapped up in getting away that she didn't see Pebbles pull up in the hotel parking lot.

"Hey, Niki!" Pebbles screamed through her open car window scrambling out of her car when she saw Niki flying over the speed bumps as she drove out of the parking lot the wrong way.

Niki looked in her rearview mirror and saw Pebbles frantically jumping up and down and waving. *What is she doing here?* she wondered. *If she gets in my way, I'll have to kill her, too.*

Pebbles took her cell phone from her purse and began dialing. No answer. She dialed another number and Sky answered.

"Sky, I just saw Niki driving out of here like a bat out of hell."

"Out of where?"

"The Sierra Grand Hotel."

"Are you sure it was Niki?"

"I know Niki when I see her, and I certainly know her Jeep. I called her on her cell but she didn't answer."

"What's the big deal about her being there?"

"She was speeding out of the parking lot the wrong way

and almost hit me. She didn't stop when I called to her and I know she saw me. That's not like Niki," she said as she walked up to the entrance. "I tell you—she's been acting weird lately."

"Yes, I know. Maybe she didn't see you. What are you doing there?"

"I'm going to happy hour, gotta go. Tootles." She hung up without giving Sky a chance to reply.

****

Afraid that Pebbles had seen her Niki thought, *I shouldn't have driven my car. I'll tell her that I stopped by for happy hour. Yeah, yeah.* Her emotions were swarming like African bees searching for honey as she headed for home.

Her thoughts returned to the late Mrs. Turner. She repeatedly beat the steering wheel. "She deserved it! Yeah, yeah, she deserved it," she said aloud, as if saying the words would make it right. "I wouldn't have killed her, but she was mistreating those kids. I know how it feels to be abused." That seemed to calm her.

The next moment rage enveloped Niki's body; the demon she had tried so hard to suppress was loose again—her other personality ruled. "She deserved it, just like Wanda Brent does."

Wanda Brent, you're going to pay for what your husband did to me. You're going to pay. When she reached her apartment, she rushed inside, turned on the shower, and stared at the mirror. The face of the demon stared back. She stepped into the shower with her clothes on and ripped open her blouse, scattering buttons to the floor. She beat the wall and screamed, "Why? Why did my parents have to leave me? Since they left, I've been on a roller-coaster ride to hell and back."

Niki cried uncontrollably because she just couldn't defeat the monster that had taken over her life. Her emotions raged through her body like a forest fire out of control.

"I didn't ask to be born into a world of abuse. Why did you choose me? I did everything you asked me to do but still I was beaten, abused, and mistreated," she said, looking up toward the sky. "Please forgive me, God, for I can't control what I do." She sunk to the floor, letting the water beat down on her slender body, as she lay in a fetal position.

After fifteen minutes, she reached for the towel and began drying her body. The telephone rang. "Hello," she answered calmly.

Sky immediately started firing questions. "Girl, what happened to you this evening? You ran out of the office as if the building was on fire. I know that you told me you had business to take care of after work but I didn't think it would take all evening. I've been calling and calling. You have your cell turned off and Pebbles said she saw you tonight flying out of a hotel parking lot."

"She saw me?" Niki repeated, wondering what actually she saw.

"Yes, at the Sierra Grand."

"I wasn't there tonight." She wrapped the towel around her nude body.

"You weren't?"

"No."

"She was adamant that it was you." Sky spoke slowly, beginning to wonder if Pebbles had been mistaken.

Niki was silent, lost in her thoughts.

"Are you OK?" Sky asked.

"Uh, yes, I'm fine. I just had some important business to take care of, that's all," Niki replied, choosing her words carefully.

"Are we still on for carpooling tomorrow?"

"Yes," she said as she continued to think about her blemished soul. "I'll be at your house eight o'clock sharp."

"Are you OK?" Sky asked again. "Sound like you've been crying."

Niki was thinking about the real reason she was in Dallas to kill Wanda Brent. "I told you, I'm fine," she snapped. Realizing she was getting annoyed, she reassured Sky that she was OK. "My sinuses are acting up. That's all, I'm fine."

"Are you still going to Houston with me this weekend?"

"Yes, with bells on," Niki replied.

"OK, girlfriend, I'll see you in the morning. David's on his way over, we're going Antares."

"OK, have fun. Good night."

After Niki hung up, she focused all her attention on her dilemma. *I can't continue doing this. All the woman had to do was be nice. It doesn't take a lot of effort to be nice. The sound of her cursing and screaming at those kids triggered me. I thought I had this under control but it's obvious that I can't help myself. The voices keep telling me to get revenge. I can't stop! I can't stop!*

Niki wanted to lead a normal life, but the hurt and outrage was taking over; some days all she wanted was for someone to catch her so all of the madness would end. She sank to the floor, sobbing.

Then she remembered that Pebbles had seen her. *What had she seen?* Fear washed over her, for a brief moment. *What if they find out about me? I can't go to jail. I'll have to deal with Pebbles.* She picked up the phone and dialed Pebbles's cell number.

Pebbles answered, talking above the pleasant brassy music that played in the background, "Hello."

"Hey, Pebbles, what are you doing?"

"I'm at the hotel." She shouted. "Girl what's up with you?"

"Can you stop by tonight so we can talk?" Niki thought if she could talk to her, she could find out how much she knew, or if she had heard anything about the murder.

"Tonight?" Pebbles asked in surprise. "Not tonight, I'm at the club getting my drink on. I'm on the dance floor." She yelled over the music. "I'll see you at work tomorrow. Bye."

At first, because of Pebbles blasé attitude, Niki thought maybe Pebbles hadn't seen or heard anything. It wasn't long, however, before Niki began to worry again. *Damn, I wonder what she actually saw. Did she tell police anything? I'll see tomorrow,* Niki thought, as she lay in bed thinking about the murder, all night.

****

Mrs. Turner's neighbors heard a rumbling sound and voices escalating. Not wanting to complain, they blew it off at first, but when it suddenly got deathly quiet in the next room, the woman peeked out her door and saw someone running down the hall. Something didn't seem right; she decided to call the front desk and ask them to check on the people in the next room.

"Front desk, Jarvis speaking. May I help you?"

"Yes, I'm in room 303 and I heard a lady screaming in the next room and a loud thump that made the picture on my wall shake and fall. It sounded like two women arguing—then it was a quiet hush. Will you please check on them? It's room 301. Thank you."

Jarvis dialed room 301 but there was no answer. He yelled into the back room where the bellhops were on break, "Would someone go up to room 301 and make sure everything is OK?" He looked at the roster. "The room is registered to a Mrs. Leslie Turner. It's probably a lover's spat."

"I'll go," Lawrence the young bellhop said. Reaching the third floor, he walked toward the room, bobbing his head to the soft music piping through the speakers in the ceiling. He looked at the numbers on the door, and then stopped in front of room 301. He knocked once, no answer; he knocked again, harder, but still no answer. "Mrs. Turner, I'm from the front desk. Are you in there?" Still no answer, so he yelled out, "Mrs. Turner, I'm coming in." He stuck the cardkey into the lock and slowly walked into the suite. "Mrs. Turner?" he called out, looking around. No answer. He noticed a shoe print on the floor. He bent down to inspect it. "This is blood," he said, not quite believing it himself. He walked slowly into the bedroom.

As soon as he stepped into the room, he froze. A woman he assumed was Mrs. Turner lay on the floor covered in blood. He backed out of the room, slammed the door, and ran fast to the elevator as if he was running the 200 meter in the Olympics. He looked up, noticing the elevator was up on the tenth floor, and decided it would be faster to take the stairs.

He couldn't speak when he reached the front desk panting, then barked breathlessly at Jarvis, "Call the police." Getting no reaction from Jarvis, he said it louder, but not loudly enough for people in the lobby to hear him. "Please call the police."

"What are you babbling about?" Jarvis asked, preoccupied with his work. Lawrence pointed upstairs and spoke very deliberately. "Call the po-lice! There's been a murder! A woman is lying on the floor in a pool of blood."

"There's been a what?" Jarvis asked, not believing what he had heard.

"A murder...room 301...she's dead. Did you hear me?" He pulled on Jarvis's jacket. "Man, she's dead!" Lawrence said again, trying desperately to get his breath.

"Sit here." Jarvis grabbed a chair. "Quick, somebody bring me some water." Jarvis picked up the phone and dialed security.

"Security, Joe speaking."

"Joe can you come to the front desk, ASAP?" Jarvis asked, nearly choking on his words. "This is an emergency, hurry."

"Sure, I'm on my way." Joe had never heard the normally staid Jarvis sound even the least bit excited before. He quickened his pace, reaching the front desk in a short time. "What's the problem?"

"There's been a murder in room 301." Jarvis spoke softly so that guests milling around in the lobby wouldn't hear him.

"A what?" Joe asked.

"A murder," Jarvis whispered emphatically, his face ghostly white.

"Call the police," Joe ordered as he headed toward the elevator.

****

On the drive to the Sierra Grand, David pulled out his cell phone to cancel his date with Sky.

"Hello." Sky answered.

"Hey, Baby."

"Where are you, you're late."

"I'm sorry but I'm not going to make it tonight."

"How come?" Sky asked, disappointed.

"I have to work late. One of the guys had a family emergency; I said I'd cover his shift."

"David, this is the third time in the past three weeks something has kept you at work. You know I was looking forward to going to Antares."

"I'm sorry. I promise I'll make it up to you."

"Can someone else cover that shift?"

"I'm afraid not. Will you call them and cancel our reservation? I'll call you later. Love you."

She sighed, "OK, love you too, goodbye."

I can't keep breaking her heart with these frivolous lies, he thought as he drove to the hotel.

David had planned to tell Sky about his line of work at

dinner tonight. The call from the hotel banished all such thoughts. When he arrived at the hotel, two police officers met him at the front desk. "Detective Hall," David said, flashing his badge. "What have we got here?"

"Come with us, Detective. We'll tell you what we know on the way up," one of the officers told him.

An officer guarded the door. *That's a good sign; nothing should have been disturbed,* David thought.

David and the others entered the room and began a methodical search. David pulled out his tape recorder and began speaking, "White female, five feet, mid forties, a hundred and ten pounds approximately, and short wavy brunette hair." He picked up a strand of medium-length blonde hair from the carpet and placed it in a small plastic bag. He scraped blood from the floor and placed it on a piece of paper, then placed the paper into a plastic bag.

Just then, forensic arrived and began their ritual of taking pictures of the body from various angles, checking body temperature, and collecting evidence from around the body to send to the lab. They walked around taking pictures of the shoe print from different angles, alerting David before cutting it out and bagging it to take back to the lab. Finished, they turned the body and the crime scene over to David and the other law enforcement people. David spotted the pair of airplane wings next to the body. He picked it up, bagged it, and asked the police officer at the door to get the wings to the lab as soon as possible.

Forty minutes later, David went next door to talk to the woman who had called the front desk. A thin, confused woman opened the door.

David politely flashed his badge. "I'm Detective Hall. I have a few questions to ask you. May I come in?"

A man walked up behind the woman. They looked at each other, and then he spoke. "Sure, come in."

"I understand you heard a noise tonight," David said, opening his notepad and grabbing his pen from his shirt pocket.

The woman suddenly started pouring out information as if she were pouring tea. "Yes. We heard two ladies. It sounded like they were arguing."

"Could you make out what they were saying?"

"No, I couldn't hear their entire conversation. It was more of a mumbling or muffled sound."

"Can you tell me if the voices where high pitched, low pitched?"

"It was low at first, and then one of the ladies screamed, 'What do you want?'" She looked at her husband for confirmation. "I also saw someone running down the hall. I think she stepped behind something in the hall to let someone pass, but my eyes aren't so good, so maybe I just thought she stepped to the side."

"Was the person coming from the room next to yours?"

"I don't know. Maybe. She was already a few doors down when I got up the nerve to peep out of the door. Is everything all right, Officer? I see the police officer standing outside the door."

"No, ma'am, a lady has been murdered," David said reluctantly.

"Oh my God!" she screamed as she grabbed her husband's arm. "What happened?"

"That's what I'm trying to find out. Can you remember anything else?" he asked as he put his pen down.

"Yes, we heard a knock on the door between seven and seven-thirty this evening."

"Did you hear anything else?"

"There was a hard thump against the wall. The painting on our wall shook and fell on the floor," the woman said, still visibly shaken, knowing that someone had been murdered right next door. "That's when I put my ear to the wall to see if I could hear anything."

"Could you?"

"I'm afraid not," she said as she took a cigarette from the package and lit it.

David put his notepad back in his pocket and pulled out his business card. "How long are you going to be in Dallas?"

"Just one more day," her husband said. "Even with the security around here we don't feel safe." Knowing it was useless to continue pushing the couple, David shook their hands and handed the man his card. "Thank you for your help. If you think of anything else, please give me a call."

"We will." They both replied.

David returned to Mrs. Turner's room and did one last

search. *Why would the killer be at this hotel? And what connection did she and Mrs. Turner have?* David's inability to find the serial killer made him angry. He hit the wall with his fist.

He walked over to an open suitcase and looked inside. "This woman is from California," he said to no one in particular. *What does she have to do with Jet Away?* Then he pulled out an itinerary from Jet Away. He noticed a program for a meeting the following day open on the dresser. There was a foster parent conference in town and she was to speak at the function. *Does this have something to do with foster children or foster parents?* he wondered. As he continued to methodically search the room, he walked over to the nightstand, bent down, and picked up a book of matches that had fallen to the floor. *A smudge of lipstick. That's strange; she wasn't wearing any lipstick.* "Ramsey," David called, heading to the door. "I'll be at the bar." He told forensics and the other officers.

David took the stairs rather than wait for the elevator. He'd just made it down the first flight of stairs when one of the officers hollered at him. "Hey, Detective, come back here. We found something you'll want to see."

Wondering what he could have missed, David turned and headed back up the steps two at a time. Walking into the room, he asked, "What is it?"

An officer walked out of the bedroom holding a bloody uniform. "We found this under the bed," forensic told him. "I guess in all the excitement, someone must have kicked it without realizing what it was."

"This is a hotel uniform. Add it to the rest of the evidence," David said and turned to resume his trip downstairs. When David reached the lobby, it was evident that word of the murder had spread throughout the hotel like wildfire; guests had begun checking out.

David looked at the young man's badge. "Jarvis, I need a list of your employees working here tonight."

"Sure, it will take just a moment."

"I'll be in the club," he said, pointing at the fancy red neon sign for Ramsey's. He stepped into the hotel's posh club and spotted Pebbles almost immediately, and headed her way.

"Hey, David, what are you doing here?" she asked as he

walked up to her.

"I had some time to kill before I pick up Sky and I didn't feel like sitting in an empty apartment so I decided to stop for a quick drink," he lied.

"What would you like to drink, sir?" asked the bartender.

He started to say, "Let me have a gin." But he was on duty and he didn't drink on the clock. "I'll just have orange juice." Then he quickly changed his order thinking tonight has been a hell of a night, "Let me have a gin and juice."

"First time you've been here?" Pebbles asked.

He stumbled over his words, "Yes. I heard Ramsey's was a good bar."

"Yeah, it must be. You're the second person I know that's been here tonight."

"Oh really, who else was here?"

"Niki."

"What was she do—"

"When I saw her she was leaving, driving fast," Pebbles broke in before David could finish asking the question.

"Um. He made a mental note."

The bartender, overhearing their conversation said, "Yes, this is a good club but I'm ready to get out of here tonight." She wiped the counter as she spoke. "Guess you heard about the murder."

"What murder?" Pebbles coughed, almost choking on her drink. "What happened?"

"A woman was killed here tonight."

"That's all you have to say, I'm out of here." She grabbed her clutch bag from the counter and other people began to scatter.

David quickly grabbed her arm and whispered, "Do me a favor—don't tell Sky that you saw me."

"Sky is my best friend. I can't keep a secret from her."

"I have my reason, please."

She looked at him quizzically and answered, "Whatever," then made a beeline for the door.

David turned to the bartender and flashed his badge. "The woman that was killed tonight had this book of matches." He pulled them from his pocket and placed them on the counter.

The bartender looked at the matches then at the end of the

counter. "There's a whole box down there. Anyone can pick them up. They're free."

"Do you have a tab for room 301?" David asked as he gulped down his drink and got up from the bar.

The bartender pulled a list of receipts from behind the counter. "Yes, for $5.50, it was signed by Leslie Turner."

"Do you remember the woman?"

The bartender smirked as she continued to wipe the counter with a towel. "If I could remember everybody that walks through those doors, believe me I wouldn't be working here."

"She was a white female."

"That's about half the women that come in here."

David continued, "Five feet, mid-forties, a hundred and ten pounds, with very short wavy brunette hair."

"Hey, wait a minute—I do remember a lady with short wavy hair. She ordered a Jack Daniels on the rocks and guzzled it so fast that by the time I turned from serving another guest, she was gone."

"Was anybody with her?"

"The woman came in alone, shortly afterwards another woman sat down next to her."

David leaned over the counter. "Did you get a look at this other woman?"

"Kinda hard to forget. She was black like your color with blonde hair, very attractive. I think they left at the same time because she ordered water and didn't even drink it. When I turned around she was gone too."

"Anything else?" asked David.

"That's it."

"Thank you. You may not remember everybody that comes through that door, but you did remember the most important ones."

The bartender smiled and raised the towel as David walked out the door.

Thirteen

*N*iki woke up shaking and in a cold sweat. She sat straight up in bed, rocking back and forth. "The voices, I hear them again. They're coming back," she said in desperation. "Please, God, help me. They're telling me to kill her, kill her." She grabbed the pillow, hoping to drown out the sound. "I can't do that, Pebbles is my friend." She spoke back to the voices as she tossed and turned all night. She lay awake consumed with fear, guilt, and anger.

After not being able to take restlessness any more Niki jumped out of bed, went online, and did a search for the hotel murder.

"Here it is." She tensed. 'Serial Killer Strikes Again.'

She picked up the phone and called in sick. Her call went immediately to Donna's voicemail. Then she called Sky to tell her that she had called in sick. She grabbed the pillow ran to the sofa and covered her ears. Niki was on edge all day, without her medication, her thinking was illogical and just plain insane. She lounged all morning up to the evening until the pounding on the door made her jump. Niki stared through the peephole as Pebbles pounded once more. Niki cracked the door. "Pebbles, I'm not feeling well. Go away. I'll call you later." Niki had been having second thoughts all day about harming Pebbles and didn't want to talk to her now. She knew Pebbles hadn't done any harm to her. However, the voices were telling her differently.

"I know. You missed work. That's why I'm here—to check on you before I go on vacation." Pebbles pushed the door open and walked past Niki. "I'm on vacation this week. Damn, you look like you've been hit by a bus!" Pebbles frowned. "Does your calling in sick have something to do with last night?"

"Why? What happened last night?" Niki asked, with all the innocence she could muster. She hoped Pebbles hadn't seen anything; she wanted her to leave before she hurt her, too.

"You know I saw you last night at the Sierra Grand."

"No you didn't. I was out running errands," she replied defensively.

"Girl, stop playing. I know you when I see you. Is that why you called in sick today? What happened?"

"No," she answered. "Let it go."

"There was a murder last night at the hotel."

Niki began to shake.

"Are you OK?" Pebbles asked, seeing the fear in her red eyes.

"No, I'm not. I'm feeling a little faint." The voices had started again. *Kill her! She's in the way.* They sent her into a panic attack.

"No, I can't!" Niki shouted, as she covered her ears with her hands. "Pebbles, please leave."

"You can't what? What's wrong? Why are you turning around in circles? This is some crazy shit! Girl, what's happening to you?" Pebbles stood and watched in amazement.

Several voices were echoing louder and louder in Niki's head. *Kill her. Kill her. Don't let her get away. She's going straight to the police.* Niki had no way of knowing if Pebbles knew anything and she couldn't take any chances.

"I can't," she blurted, running through the bedroom to the bathroom. She reached for the brown bottle with the little pills that helped calm her down. It was empty. She screamed, "Pebbles, get out of here!" as she knocked the pill bottles on the floor.

Ignoring her request, Pebbles started to follow her to the bedroom, but suddenly stopped to read the newspaper clippings plastered on the wall. 'Jet Away Flight 222 from Los Angeles to Houston crashed upon landing due to wind shears. All two hundred passengers on board, including six crewmembers, perished.' The article went on to name everybody on the passenger list. Niki had circled the names Debra Salem and Captain Lacy Brent, in red ink.

"Your mother was in this crash." She pointed at the article, surprised. Niki had never disclosed how her mother died. Suddenly Pebbles' eyes widened and her mouth dropped as she scanned the other clippings on the wall; they were about the murders committed by the left-handed serial killer, including the most recent one of the hotel murder she had printed from her computer hours earlier.

Niki sat on the floor Indian-style, rocking back and forth, ignoring Pebbles. She put her hands over her ears again, trying to drown out the voices. So over powered by the voices, Niki was oblivious to the fact that Pebbles had become disturbed.

"Niki, what's going on?" Pebbles asked as she watched her friend crawl around on the floor searching frantically through the empty pill bottles scattered on the floor. Pebbles stood in disbelief when she glanced into the bathroom. There it was: a blonde feathered wig resting on the counter, a damp, partially bloody white blouse tossed into a corner, and a switchblade partially covered in blood in the sink. Pebbles began slowly backing out of the room, eyeing Niki with every step. "I-I guess I'll be going now," she stuttered.

"What's your hurry?" Niki stood and seized the blonde wig, plopping it onto her head, and picked up the knife.

Pebbles turned and ran toward the front door. "This is some sick shit!" she said as she tried to get away.

"Not so fast, *Sista*." Niki caught her by the neck and pointed the knife to her throat. "I told you to leave."

"Niki, what is wrong with you?" She was frighten knowing Niki was the left-handed killer and that she may be her next victim. "Please let me go." She struggled to break free.

"I just can't do that," Niki said in a villainous voice. "It's too late." She had a stronghold on Pebbles.

"Let me leave," she begged. "I won't say anything."

"It's too late." Niki twirled the knife around on Pebbles's neck. "You should have minded your own business. Now it's out of my control—the voices are chanting, 'Kill her, kill her.'"

"The voices," Pebbles looked confused. "Why, Niki? Why are you doing this?" Pebbles asked, as the tears streamed down her face—still wondering what voices.

"I vowed that I would even the score with the pilot's

family."

"Niki, I didn't have anything to do with that," she pleaded, but she knew there was no reasoning with this mad woman. She witnessed the transformation from Dr. Jekyll to Ms. Hyde. She squirmed to get away from Niki and the knife. Niki had a death grip on her. "It's too late. You know that I'm the serial killer. I can't let you go," she said, as a wicked smile covered her face and something strange gleamed in her eyes. Pebbles' life flashed in front of her as she thought of her grandmother and her child she will never get to meet.

The voices had overpowered Niki once again—they were in control. Niki raised her left hand and plunged the knife into Pebbles's chest as quickly as a lightning bolt. One stab to the heart ended her agonized cry. Then there was silence.

"I can't let you destroy me," Niki said to Pebbles's lifeless body as she moved quickly rolling the body up in the Oriental rug. Blood soon saturated the rug and left a smeared trail across the once shiny hardwood floor as Niki pulled Pebbles's dead weight into the kitchen.

"Keys, keys, where are her keys?" Niki ran back to the living room and checked Pebbles's purse, removed the keys, went outside. She put Pebbles's car on the other side of the apartment building. When night fell, she dumped the body and purse into the trunk of Pebbles's car and drove to the outskirts of town.

Fourteen

*D*avid had made up for Monday's night cancellation by taking Sky to Antares on Tuesday night. Once again, he failed to tell Sky the truth. *What's the big deal if she knows I'm a cop. What's the big deal about keeping it a secret. I'll just let her know that I had to wait to see where the relationship was going. No big deal,* David thought. The next three days were very busy for David, no time for Sky as he tried to solve the hotel murder. Friday flew by and David turned in early Friday night, as he had to drive Sky and Niki to Houston the following morning. He arrived promptly at Sky's place at ten o'clock on a beautiful Saturday morning. When Sky opened the door, David stood with a dozen of red roses.

"David thank you what are these for?" She asked reaching for the crystal vase.

"I love you and couldn't wait to see you." He kissed her on the lips. "I just bought them just to show that I love you."

"Oh David, I love you too." She turned and placed the glass vase on the kitchen table.

"Are you ready for this five-hour trip?" He asked. He wore a white short set, Nike tennis shoes, a Texas Rangers baseball cap, and a pair of Peepers sunglasses. He hoped no one would recognize him with Sky on his home turf, and blow his cover.

"Yes, I'm ready. I just need to get my bag."

As David walked into the living room, he glanced at the certificate Sky had received from Jet Away, which recognized her for displaying courtesy and friendliness and for providing complete and accurate information to the passengers. Beside it was another certificate—the one in which she took the most pride. It was a commendation for five years of perfect attendance printed on beautiful ivory paper and displayed in an ornate frame trimmed in gold. "Very impressive awards." He looked at her as she handed him her garment bag.

"Thanks, they didn't come easy." She smiled. "We just need to swing by Niki's place." She locked the door and they walked to the car. "I'm glad you decided to drive to Houston. It's so much cozier than on the plane," Sky said as David placed her garment bag in the trunk. They engaged in small talk all the way to Niki's apartment.

When they reached Niki's, Sky got out of the car and met her in the breezeway. "What's wrong with you? Look like you got run over by a truck," Sky said. Niki had been out sick for the week still confused with hearing voices.

"Thanks a lot. I didn't get any sleep last night." She said holding a pillow and small suitcase.

"Look like you haven't gotten any for a week." Sky said as she looked upside Niki's head and they walked to the car.

Niki handed David her small suitcase.

He noticed a cut on her hand. "Your hand is cut," David said, gently taking hold of it.

She jerked her hand away. "Oh, it's just a little cut. I'm a klutz in the kitchen." She was far from being a klutz; she had cut herself in the midst of her rage. Niki had climbed in the back of David's car and immediately lay down in the back seat, hoping to go to sleep, but her mind kept going back to Mrs. Turner and Pebbles's murders. She had an overwhelming feeling of emptiness and sadness, trouble concentrating, and thoughts of suicide. She snuggled inconspicuously in the pillow to cover her ears, hoping the voices she heard would cease.

David looked in his rearview mirror with a furrowed brow. "Niki, are you OK?" he asked after seeing the distress look on her face.

"Yes, I'm just a little restless. That's all." She squirmed into a comfortable fetal position.

"You weren't up all night thinking about the serial killer,

were you?" David asked, trying to lighten the mood. He knew Niki had been at the hotel, and was trying discreetly to get information without alerting her or Sky. But his words had just the opposite effect. Niki's palms began sweating and she started to hyperventilate, wheezing uncontrollably.

"Take deep breaths, Niki, in and out." Sky handed her a bottle of water.

David said, "I'm sorry. I didn't mean to upset you."

Niki tried to divert the attention from her behavior. "You didn't upset me. I'm out of my allergy medication. I'll be OK when I get the prescription refilled. I should have done it yesterday, but I didn't realize it was gone until I opened the bottle this morning. I'm sure I can get it refilled at a pharmacy in Houston." She took a few sips of water and repositioned her body in the backseat of David's 525I.

Sky and David talked all the way there; five hours later, he was pulling up in front of her parents' house. Thelma Winters stood on the porch talking to her neighbor Lydia Grayson. "You made it," Thelma said with a smile when she saw her daughter get out of the car.

"We decided to ride with my boyfriend, David instead of flying," said Sky as she walked up to her mother giving her a big hug.

"David? I thought you were just friends. When did that change?" asked her mother, smiling.

"I'll tell you all about it," Sky said as she winked and brushed past her mother to hug Mrs. Grayson.

"Is that Niki getting out of the car?" her mother asked.

"The one and only."

"Oh, I'm glad she made it! I want to meet your friends."

"Where's Pebbles?"

"She's on vacation," Niki answered quickly, flashing a smile as she stepped up on the porch.

"Hello, Niki," Thelma said as she smiled and placed her pleasantly plump arms around the young woman. Niki felt that motherly warmth that she'd longed for all her life. For a moment, Niki put her problems on the back burner. "You're very pretty with those adorable eyes."

"Thank you," Niki said, as Mrs. Winters continued to hold

her hand.

"Mother, this is David," Sky said as he walked up the steps and placed the bags on the porch.

"I see where Sky got her piercing dimples," he said as he hugged Sky's mother, and then shook the neighbor's hand.

Thelma blushed. "David, have I seen you somewhere before?" she asked as she looked up at him.

He adjusted his sunglasses. "No, ma'am, I don't think so. I guess I must have one of those faces." *I had better leave before she recognizes me.* "Well, I better get moving. It was nice meeting you, Mrs. Winters," David said. He tipped his hat to Ms. Grayson.

"What's your hurry?" Thelma asked.

"My mother is probably waiting for me," he lied, knowing he was headed to the police department.

"Well, nice to meet you, David. Don't be a stranger."

"Thank you. I won't." Sky slipped her arm in his and they walked to the car.

Niki and Thelma went inside the house and Mrs.Grayson walked across the yard back over to her place. "Well, Niki, I finally get to meet you. Sky has told me so much about you."

"I hope it was all good," she said, admiring the angel collection that was positioned in a row on the fireplace mantel.

"Yes, it was. Where are you from?"

"I grew up in Houston."

"Who is your family? I may know them."

"I doubt it. Both of my parents died before I was eight years old. I was raised by my aunt." Niki decided not to go into her life story.

Thelma's smile disappeared. "Bless your heart. Well, you are welcome here anytime," she said, rubbing Niki's back. Niki felt the nurturing, the genuine concern that Sky had received and that she longed for. "Thanks for carpooling with Sky. She enjoys the company and you both save on gas and parking expenses. I hope she doesn't talk your ears off," Thelma said with a soft chuckle.

"Oh, no. We help each other out," Niki replied, surveying the decorative dining room.

"Mother, I hope you aren't interrogating Niki," Sky said as she entered the house.

"She isn't," Niki answered quickly. "I'm enjoying your mother's company. In fact, she told me that I'm welcome anytime. Sky, I see where you get your kindness." Niki hungered for the love she had lost. She hadn't been hugged or welcomed so warmly anywhere since her mother and father had died. She'd forgotten what that motherly warmth and love felt like. All she had received was hated stares and abuse.

"Girl, Mother is worse than I am. She's the one that doesn't meet any strangers."

Thelma smiled. "I'm afraid Sky's right."

Niki's smile quickly disappeared when the vision of the murders she had committed quickly surfaced, and how Pebbles inadvertently became one of her victims.

"Are you all right, Sweetie? You look like you've just seen a ghost," Thelma said as she looked into Niki's scared eyes.

"Yes, ma'am, I...I...was just thinking, I'm out of sinus medication. I need to run to the pharmacy. I'll call for a taxi."

"You'll do no such thing. I don't need my car for a few hours. Take it," Thelma offered.

"I can't do that."

"Oh, go ahead, take it," Thelma insisted. "I really don't mind. Any friend of my daughter is a friend of mine."

"Niki, I can drive you if you like," Sky said, reaching for her purse.

"No!" Niki quickly interrupted. "You have to help your mother get ready for the party tonight. I'll be fine."

Thelma walked over to the fireplace mantel, picked up a set of keys with a Cadillac emblem, handed them to Niki, and gave her a hug. "Honey, you're shaking all over. You're not OK." Thelma rubbed Niki's shoulders and felt her forehead.

"Niki," Sky said, grabbing her purse and heading for the door, "I'll drive."

"I'm fine. I promise. I'll be back in no time," Niki said with more confidence than she felt. She brushed past Sky and headed out the door. She definitely wasn't OK. She was confused and scared. She had never killed a friend. The voices were getting the better of her again as she ran to the car.

Once Niki got into the car, she grabbed her cell phone from her purse and began dialing. "Please be there," she whispered. When the party on the other end picked up, not waiting for a voice, she said frantically, "I must see you."

"Who is this?" a man replied.

"Please, I have to see you. This is Niki."

"Nicole?"

"Yes."

"Where have you been? It's been months since I've seen you."

"I moved to Dallas. I really need to talk to you."

"You're lucky you caught me. I usually don't work on Saturdays, but I'm here catching up on some paperwork. I'll be waiting for you."

"I'm fifteen minutes away. Thank you, Doctor Blair."

Reaching his office, Niki opened the door and ran inside. She was sure she had been waiting in the lobby for an eternity but had only been there a matter of seconds when a short bald man with black-framed glasses came out and greeted her. She followed him into his office.

Settling at his desk, he turned on the tape recorder before talking. "Well, Nicole, what seems to be the problem?"

"I'm sorry to barge in on you like this, Doctor Blair."

"That's quite all right. I was just documenting some files before I leave for the weekend."

Doctor Blair had been Niki's therapist for the past nine years, but she hadn't visited him in months—closer to two years. He was treating her for schizophrenia. "So, how have you been since you relocated to Dallas?" he asked.

"I was doing OK until I started hearing voices again." She looked at him for some support.

"Are you getting plenty of rest, Nicole?" He scribbled on his notepad, 'hearing voices.'

"No, I haven't been sleeping lately."

"When was the last time you slept?" The doctor looked into her eyes, noticing the dark rings underneath them.

Niki thought back to the murders, especially Pebbles's murder, which had had the biggest impact on her. She hadn't wanted to kill her but had been coerced by the voices.

"About four days ago," she spoke up. "I've been sleeping on and off."

His eyes widened. Then he wrote on the pad 'sleep deprivation.' "Are you taking the medication that I prescribed?"

"Occasionally."

"Don't sound like it to me. What are the voices telling you?" he asked, checking the recorder to see if it was still recording.

"They're telling me to hurt other people, seriously hurt them." She grabbed a Kleenex from the box and wiped her eyes, feeling slightly remorseful as she thought about Pebbles. The other murders had been justifiable; Pebbles had just gotten in the way.

"Do you know these people?" Doctor Blair asked.

"No, not really." She quickly retracted her statement. "I guess you can say I know them indirectly. But I have this rage built up inside that I can't control." She looked down at the floor, "And the rape visions are still haunting me."

"Niki, you know that you must take your medication to help manage the voices. The abuse you suffered growing up has enabled your predisposition to this illness to get the better of you. It's imperative that you take your medicine if you want to get better. Your desire to hurt other people will go away. The rape visions will also go away."

Niki ignored the doctor and admitted another truth. "I have this strong urge to visit my daughter's grave."

"Why don't you?" he said, studying her body language. She wasn't looking her best. She would usually dress like a model for her appointments, but today she had dressed down. "This would help you achieve closure regarding her death."

"I want to, but I don't know if I'm ready yet."

"I think after sixteen years of tormenting yourself, you should be ready. Why don't you plan to visit her grave soon?"

"I feel guilty because I was sick in the hospital when she died. I didn't attend her graveside service." She put her head down on her knees envisioning her baby's face, then raised her head. "My only memory of her is of her widow's peak and the small spot of discoloration under her left eye about the size of a dime. I called it a butterfly; it was her beauty mark. It's the Salems' trait." She smiled as she talked about her baby. "My mother had the same mark on her neck." She hung her head. It was hard to talk about her mother even after all these years. "Doctor, I think it's hopeless—I've lost everyone I've ever loved."

Doctor Blair had never been able to get Niki to open up about the rape and the death of her baby before, but today she was finally releasing that anger that had built up inside of her since a child. He wondered what had compelled her to do so, but was happy to see a breakthrough. "You shouldn't feel guilty." He tapped the desk with his pen, trying to get her attention. "Remember you were just a child yourself. I truly think you'll get better when you face your problems firsthand. Your life isn't hopeless; you just need to follow my instructions."

The next minute Niki was more self-controlled and her tears had stopped. She dropped her head again, thinking about all the murders she had committed. How many was it now—five or six? She wished she could tell him.

Suddenly Niki blurted, "I'm crazy. I'm losing my mind."

"I don't think you're crazy, Nicole," the doctor stared as he looked over his glasses. "I know that the medication will control the voices if you take it regularly, but you can't miss a single dose. You absolutely must take your medication daily," he said slowly and emphatically. As he thought about what he had just witnessed, he decided that something more than just medicine was needed. "Niki, you need to be hospitalized," he said sternly. "I think your schizophrenia is out of control. You're in a manic depression state."

"Hospitalized!" she said, jumping up from her chair. She saw red. "I'm fine."

The doctor tried to calm her. "It's just for observation. Your behavior is high, then extremely low." He looked at her, hoping she would agree to his request. "There's a clinic on Greenly Street." He stood and walked over to her. "I can phone them right now and have a bed waiting for you."

"No, Doctor Blair," she quickly spoke. "I can manage on my own."

"Are you still having suicidal thoughts?"

"Yes, occasionally. Will you prescribe me something a little stronger? I don't think the medicine I'm taking is working."

"You have to take it for it to work but let me change your prescription to Risperidone." He walked back around to his desk. "Instead of taking one pill a day, you'll take two a day." He scribbled on his pad as he continued to talk. "And I'll prescribe Trazadone for your insomnia."

The sound of the bell alerted Doctor Blair that someone was up front. "I'm sorry." He stood and stepped around his desk, forgetting to turn off the tape recorder. "I'll be right back please have a seat."

In a voice just above a whisper, Niki said, "I have one more person to kill, Wanda Brent. Then my web of murders will be complete and the voices will go away." In Niki's sick way of thinking, if she killed everybody who had hurt her, then maybe the voices would go away. "Wanda Brent will be hearing from me very soon. She's going to pay for what Jet Away Airways and her husband did to me."

Niki had been searching for Wanda for two years, she knew she lived in Dallas and with perseverance she would find her.

Moments later, Dr. Blair returned to his desk. "Those pesky solicitors are always ignoring the sign in the window. Now, where were we?" He checked the recorder, which was still recording. "OK, I'll call the prescriptions in to Eckerd's on Main Street."

"Thank you, Doctor." She gently touched his hand.

"You're welcome. Just remember that it's imperative that you take your medicine—and the voices will go away. You need to find a therapist in Dallas and continue your sessions. That will also help," he said, handing her a list of doctors.

"OK, I will. Thank you, Doctor Blair."

"I wish you would reconsider my suggestion and—"

"Doctor, I can't right now. Maybe in a couple of months."

"Well, I expect to hear from you next month. Call Linda and make an appointment or let me know that you've found a doctor. Good bye and good luck." He patted her on the shoulder as she stood and walked out the door.

Doctor Blair watched Niki through the stained glass window as she hurried to her car. Dialing Eckerd's number, he said, "There goes a sick lady. Those bastards have ruined her life, if I can just keep her on her medication. But that's the problem with schizophrenia patients—some of them refuse to take their medicine."

"Eckerd's Drug. May I help you?"

"Yes, this is Doctor Hank Blair. I'm calling in a couple of prescriptions for one of my patients. She should be there shortly."

Doctor Blair rewound his tape recorder and started documenting his session with Niki, while the pharmacist took the order. Just as he hung up with the pharmacist, his phone rang. He pushed the pause button on the recorder and answered, "Doctor Blair."

"Honey, our flight leaves in three hours and we need to be at the airport in two hours," his wife reminded him.

"I just started documenting my last client's session. I won't be long."

"If you don't come now we are going to miss our flight."

"OK, I'm on my way," he spoke reluctantly, and then hung up the phone. He finished writing his observations while they were fresh in his mind. 'Nicole is a disturbed young lady. Her outbursts are very alarming. I think this individual is capable of committing a diabolical crime. A watchful eye should be kept on her. I told her to continue her counseling and I gave her the names of a couple of colleagues in Dallas that may be able to help her. She's experienced severe trauma as a child and now suffers from schizophrenia disorder.' He continued to write. 'She has panic attacks, trouble sleeping, and hears voices. The voices will subside if she takes her medication as prescribed. Her behavior is the worst that I've seen in the nine years I've counseled her.'

He looked at his watch and decided he would listen to the rest of the tape and finish his documentation next week. Then he reached for his hat and headed home.

****

The sun dropped lazily behind the orange horizon as Niki drove a few miles to pick up her medicine from Eckerd's. Once inside the store she immediately took two pills, followed with some water, then headed back to Sky's house for Sheila's birthday party. Her mind was settled when she arrived at the Winters'.

Aware of the many cars that surrounded the Winters' house, Niki stepped inside the crowded, noisy house, where about thirty family members and friends stood, all laughing and talking while soft music played in the background.

As she stood uncertain in the foyer, she heard a warm voice say, "Hi, Sweetie, you made it back." Niki handed Thelma her keys, then Thelma took her by the arm and led her to the den. "This is Sheila," she said as she placed her hand on her other daughter's shoulder.

"Hi, Niki, I finally get to meet you," Sheila said. Like Sky, she had a warm smile and a friendly presence. She extended her hand.

"It's nice to meet you, too." Niki shook her hand. "Happy birthday and congratulations on your upcoming graduation, that's a big accomplishment." Niki felt the warmth penetrating throughout the house with people smiling and waving at her.

"You're telling me," Sheila said. "Lots of late-night studying, but it paid off."

"Take Niki to meet your dad," Thelma told Sheila, as she looked over at her husband talking to someone in the corner.

Sheila took Niki by the arm. "Come on." They walked over to Reverend Winters, who was talking to another man.

"Excuse me, Daddy; I want to introduce you to Niki, Sky's friend."

The other man graciously excused himself.

"Well, Miss Niki, it's a pleasure meeting you." He covered her hand with both of his, shaking it constantly.

She smiled. "Sky has told me a lot about you."

"Believe only half of what you hear and none of what you see." Reverend Winters laughed at his own joke, his voice filling the den.

"Ya'll come on. Let's have a toast to Sheila," Mrs. Winters yelled from across the room. He took both women by the arm and walked over to Thelma, who was pouring sparkling apple cider into plastic champagne glasses and placing them on the table.

Reverend Winters grabbed one of the glasses from the table and said, "Gather around, everybody, and get a glass of apple cider. I want to make a toast."

Everyone crowded into the medium-size dining room with a drink in hand.

"To Sheila. Happy birthday."

The people cheered.

"We also wish you the best in your endeavors. And remember, always keep God first and you will go far," Reverend Winters said.

Everyone raised their glasses and toasted the birthday girl.

Thelma added, "Reverend Winters will be honored next weekend by the NAACP for his work with the homeless. Let's give him a hand."

Everyone began to clap.

Niki felt a sense of calm, a sense of peace, letting her mind slip away from her recent murders to enjoy the gathering.

Before midnight everyone left and Sky told her mother that she and Niki would take care of getting the dishes done and the food put away. "Mom, go on out on the porch and join Dad. You've had a busy day. We'll take care of things in here."

Niki agreed.

"Thanks, Sky, I was just going to put the food away and then stack the dishes and leave them. I thought I'd get up and do them before church in the morning. If you don't mind cleaning up, I won't have to get up so early." She put the dishes she was holding on the counter, wiped her hands on her apron, grabbed a cup of tea, and went out to join her husband.

"I'll help too," Sheila said as she started to head to the kitchen.

"No you won't. You shouldn't have to clean up after your own party," Niki said. "Go and enjoy what's left of your day."

"You don't have to tell me twice," Sheila said with a laugh as she walked out the door.

Before long, Sky and Niki heard Sky's folks come into the house. Her mom brought the cups to the kitchen. "Thanks again, girls. Sky, your dad and I are going up to bed. Good night."

"Good night, Reverend and Mrs. Winters," Niki said over her shoulder as she finished washing the last of the dishes.

"Night, Mom and Dad," Sky added as she ran to her ringing cell phone. She looked at the LCD screen. "It's David," she said in a raised voice. "Hi David, you missed a good party."

"I'm sorry I couldn't make it."

"That's OK."

"I'm not going to keep you I know it's late, but I'll be there tomorrow afternoon around two."

"I wanted to meet your parents."

"Tomorrow is Sunday and they will be at church all day." David Lied he wasn't ready to be exposed—not that way.

"OK, we'll be ready. Love you."

"Love you too, goodnight."

By the time Sky and Niki had the house in order, it was midnight. "I'm ready to call it a night. How about you?" Sky asked.

"Me, too. It's been a long day," Niki answered.

****

At church on Sunday, Reverend Winters delivered a powerful message of forgiveness. Niki sobbed because she knew that had she forgiven her victims they would be alive today. As long as she took her medication properly, her life would be well balanced. However, Nicole's imbalance behavior would keep her straddling on both sides of the fence—good and evil.

After church on Sunday, the Winters' and Niki went out for brunch before Sky and Niki had to return to Dallas.

"It's been a great weekend having both of our daughters home," Thelma said as they sat around the table enjoying their meal.

"I enjoyed the break, too," Niki said. "You have a great family. Thanks for including me as part of it." Niki had never witnessed such love in a family. She was only familiar with turmoil and drama.

"We were glad to have you. Think of us as family. You're welcome here any time," Reverend Winters told her. "In fact, come back next weekend for the NAACP awards."

"I would love to. Thank you."

After an hour, the waiter brought Reverend Winters the check and he handed the waiter his credit card.

"I guess we should be getting back to the house. David said he'd be by around two this afternoon to pick us up and I still have to throw my clothes into the suitcase," Sky said as the waiter return Reverend Winters' credit card.

"I hate to see you leave, but I know you both have to go to work tomorrow," Thelma said as they stood in a group and headed for the car.

Just as the Winters pulled into the driveway, Sky heard a car horn. She looked around and saw David's car right behind them.

She waved as she got out of the car and walked over to him. "Hi." She leaned in the window and kissed David on the lips. "I didn't think you'd be here until two. Do you want to come in while Niki and I get our things together?"

"That's OK, I'll just wait here," David said. "I've got some new airline rules to look over. Tell your folks I said hello." David was really just being cautious; he didn't know who might stop at the Winters' on Sunday afternoon and he didn't want to take the chance that it would be someone who knew him or his family.

"We'll be out in ten minutes," Sky said as she looked over and saw Niki already going into the house. She turned and walked toward the house. Reverend Winters walked over to David and introduced himself. They stood outside the car and talk until the girls were ready.

Twenty minutes later, the trio were on their way back to Dallas.

Fifteen

*T*he morning after they returned from Houston, Niki sat on the sofa waiting for Sky to pick her up for work, when the phone rang. "Hello."

"Hey, I'm running late," said Sky. "David and I went out for supper last night and then watched a movie. He didn't leave until after one this morning. I'll be there in ten minutes."

"Don't you think you're getting too close to David, too soon?"

"Don't sound so cheerful," Sky replied sarcastically. "I'll be there in a couple of minutes."

Niki's anger billowed. "OK." She hung up the phone and walked past her cherrywood dresser, with its two huge mirrors. She looked at the mirror and screamed, "How can she trust him so soon? She hardly knows him." She slammed her hairbrush on the dresser, walked into the living room, and started pacing. A few moments later, she sat on the sofa, rocking back and forth. She tapped the skinny heels of her shoes on the shiny hardwood floor like the women in an old Baptist church. "Why am I upset? I should be happy for her. But I can't!" she screamed. "I hate men; they can't be trusted." *Nicole, you have to take your medication if you want to get better.* Dr. Blair's words of warning welled in her head. As always, the bottle of pills would rest in the medicine cabinet—untouched.

Her mind went back to that frightful night—even after so many years, she could still feel her rapist's scabby hands trying to cover her mouth as she tried to scream. Niki could hear Mr. Clark whispering in her ear, "Come on, Niki, it won't hurt." She remembered pleading with her foster dad to stop as the sweat dripped from his beet red face. "Please stop! Stop!" she blurted out, as if he were in the room with her, raping her. She remembered the pain and helplessness she had felt afterwards.

The sound of the car horn snapped Niki out of her memories. She grabbed her purse and ran to the door, fumbling in her purse for her keys. She locked the door, once again neglecting to take her medication.

"You're face is pale, are you OK," Sky asked as Niki got into the car.

"I was just thinking about something, I'm fine." She took in a deep breath and let out a big sigh of relief. She buckled her seat belt and Sky pulled out of the apartment complex.

Sky kept up with the flow of the traffic, while listening to K-104's topic of the day, 'Do all men cheat?' Sky shook her head as one caller said, "Yes, all men cheat. Every relationship I've been in, I've caught the man cheating."

Another caller followed. "It's just in their blood to cheat. It's been passed down from generation to generation."

Sky reached into her purse, took out her cell phone, and started calling the radio station. She got a busy signal, hung up, and hit redial. Busy again.

Niki said, "I doubt you'll get through." She watched Sky repeat the action. "What are you going to say if you get in?"

"That I don't think all men cheat. Some men are not willing to risk their relationship and choose to be faithful."

Niki laughed bitterly. "Yeah Right. Where are the faithful ones? I haven't found one yet. All men are dogs; they lie, cheat, and are just plain womanizers. I hate them."

"Niki, you're going to have to trust at some point in your life."

Niki twisted up her lips. "How do you know David isn't cheating on you? You don't even know him that well. You've only been dating him for a few months."

Sky could see that Niki was fuming. "Niki, don't get so

upset. It's just a discussion and you're right—I don't know, but I really trust him; there's something different about this relationship. He wants a commitment just as much as I do, that's what we're working toward."

Niki realized that her emotions were showing and apologized. "I'm sorry. I shouldn't get this upset."

"Girl, that's OK." Suddenly Sky saw a bright red light flashing in her rearview mirror. She signaled and pulled over onto the shoulder.

"Good morning, ladies," the police officer said politely as he approached the car.

"Hello, Officer," Sky replied as she removed her license from her wallet.

"Are you on your way to work?" he asked, looking inside the car.

"Yes, sir." She handed him her license.

"Do you know that you were traveling seventy-eight miles an hour in a sixty-five mile an hour speed zone?"

"No, Officer, I didn't. I was keeping up with the flow of the traffic."

"You know, these BMW 330is are like race horses. Make you feel like you're in the Kentucky Derby."

Sky smirked. "Look at those cars—they're speeding!" she said, pointing out the window as the cars sped down the highway.

The officer turned to glance at the traffic. "That's OK, I'll get them tomorrow. May I see your insurance card?" He said all in one breath.

Damn, I don't need another ticket. "Yes, sir." She looked over at her glove compartment. "Niki, will you hand me my insurance card?" Niki shifted her body toward the door, reached for the insurance card from the glove box, and handed it to Sky, avoiding eye contact with the officer.

The officer stared at Niki as she handed Sky the card. "How are you, ma'am?"

Niki smiled and swiftly turned her body toward the window hoping he didn't notice her face from the surveillance tape. It had been a few months since she killed the passenger in the restroom, at the airport. *If the lady wouldn't have cursed me on the phone, I told her that we were finding her bags, but no, she had to*

call me a bitch and said she would get me and requested my name,
as if I personally lost her bags, Niki thought.

"I'll be right back," he said.

"Did you see how he stared at us?" Sky said, obviously
irritated as she watched the officer walk back to his motorcycle.

Niki didn't hear Sky, her mind was playing tricks on her,
she was in deep thought. *Did he recognize me? Does he know I'm*
the serial killer? Have they found Pebbles's body and linked it to
me? Her hand trembled as she hung onto the door handle. She
knew that if she was recognized, this would be her only chance to
escape. She had already plotted how she would run across the busy
highway.

"I have to slow down. I have a heavy foot," Sky said as
she listened to the sound of cars swooshing by.
Niki continued to be in deep thought as Sky continued to talk.

Sky watched as the officer took a pen out of his shirt
pocket and began writing out a ticket. He walked back to the car
and reached in the open window. "Please sign this," he told Sky,
handing her the ticket along with her license and insurance card.

As he handed Sky her copy of the ticket, he said, "Slow
down and take care of that other ticket before it turns into a
warrant."

"Yes, sir, I sure will." As she pulled back into traffic,
she'd forgotten all about the radio topic of the day. "I'll mail my
check in tomorrow."

****

David stopped by the airport on his way to work, to check
in with Malcolm. He knocked on the door. "It's open," shouted
Malcolm from inside.

David stepped in. "Hey, man, how's it going?"

Malcolm immediately stood. "Hey, what's going on?" He
shook David's hand.

"Just thought I'd check in with you to see how things were
going."

"It's been quiet around here lately."

David tossed a pair of wings onto Malcolm's desk. "The
serial killer is leaving these on all of her victims." He said as he
took his seat.

"What!" said Malcolm as he picked up the pair of wings and walked over to the window to get a better view.

"The wings came from Jet Away, in reservations."

"Jet Away!" he repeated.

"Yeah, the killer is possibly employed there.

"You don't think it's that lunatic Niki, do you?" He said jokingly as he sat at his desk wiggling his jaw thinking about the night she had slapped him."

David laughed, "No, I doubt it, but she does act weird at times."

"I told you man. Something isn't right with her."

David laughed again. "I just stopped to ask you if anything else had turned up here at the airport since the last time we talked.

"No, I thought traffic would slow down once passengers heard the news of the killing, but it's totally the opposite."

"Good. I also wanted you to know that the technicians are trying to clear up the surveillance tape to get a better picture of the woman."

"Nothing new here, thank the Lord. One murder here is enough for a lifetime. I don't know how you detectives deal with this kind of mayhem day in and day out. Do you ever get used to it?"

"Not really, this is probably a good thing. It keeps you from getting careless—and keeps you alive. Getting sloppy is a sure way to put a quick end to your career, or worse yet, your life. You just learn to live with it and try to keep the job from interfering with your personal life."

"Speaking of a personal life, when are you going to tell Sky the truth about your work?"

"There's a lot at stake. I don't want to lose her, but I also don't want to mess up this case and that means not letting anyone at the airline know my identity. Too many people have spent too many hours on it and for me to blow it now would be crucial."

"Keeping your identity from Sky can't be making your life any easier. What if someone recognizes you when you're with Sky? It would be a lot better if she found out the truth from you, not by accident from some stranger."

"I know," he said as he put the wings back in the small

plastic bag. "I have to put in a special code when I call her from the job so the work number doesn't show up on her phone. I have to sneak into the reservation office when I know she's not there. It's too much of an effort to hide it. I plan to tell her the truth tonight. I've put it off long enough. I can trust her not to say anything—It's like a Peyton Place in that office."

"I know, let me know how it goes."

"I will." David stood.

"Tell my uncle hello."

"I will," said David as he walked out of the office.

****

That evening as Sky sat at the kitchen table, she tried to contact Pebbles but her message went immediately to voice mail. She tried her home phone and Pebbles' grandmother answered the phone, "Hello."

"Hello Ms. Stone this is Sky how are you?"

"Hello Sky, I'm doing fine." She said in a tiring voice. "How are you?"

"I'm OK but I've been trying to reach Pebbles for a couple of days now and I can't reach her."

"Neither can I. She told me that she would call me when she got to New York, but I haven't heard from her," said Ms. Stone sounding disturbed.

"Oh she's OK, she'll probably call me later. I'll let you know when I hear from her. Get you a good night sleep."

"I will, good night Sky."

Sky decided to go downtown and pay her speeding ticket after work the next day. She walked into the living room with the phone still in her hand, dropped down on the sofa, and began dialing.

"Hello."

"Hey, Niki, I'm leaving work early tomorrow to pay my speeding tickets. Are you still riding with me?"

"No, I'm going to drive. I need to do some running around after work myself. I thought you were going to mail in your payment?"

"I was, but you remember what happened to Pebbles when they lost her payment."

"Yeah, the police pulled her over."

"Thinking of Pebbles when is she coming back from vacation?" asked Sky. "I tried her cell phone but it immediately went to voicemail. I've been trying to call her for three days now."

Niki spoke quickly, "She had text message me and said she wouldn't be back until the end of the week." Niki lied knowing Sky would never see her best friend again.

"Huh, I wonder why she didn't text message me. Oh well, I'll see you at work tomorrow. Goodnight."

"Goodnight."

Sky lay on the sofa waiting, wondering why she hadn't heard from David. *Must be busy at the airport tonight*, she decided. She fell asleep on the sofa waiting on his call.

Sixteen

Seems like I was just here a couple of hours ago, David thought, as he walked into the Dallas Police Department. Monday flew by like a quarterback throwing a pass and Tuesday came quick to accept it. *The investigation is dragging,* he thought as he sat down at his desk and reached for the phone. He hadn't left the office last night until well after one in the morning and had missed another opportunity to tell Sky the truth.

As he dialed Sky's number, Captain Wineglass walked up to his desk. "Good Morning, Detective Hall."

Damn. "Good Morning, Captain," he said, placing the phone back in the cradle, hating that he'd been interrupted. *He always seems to interrupt me when I'm calling my girl,* he thought.

"How close are we to solving this case?" He looked at David for a definite answer. "I don't see any results."

David stood. "Very close, sir. The wings came from a store downtown Dallas—Jet Away Airways reservation call center had a promotion and distributed the wings in the office during a promotion. I'm ninety percent sure that the killer works or had worked in reservations. I was here late with the detectives; they debriefed me on their findings at the reservation call center. They compiled a list of all left-handed employees. Plus, I'm compiling a list of everyone who has transferred from Houston to Dallas in the past three years. The technician in Houston is working on clearing up the surveillance tape from the airport restroom. I should have received it a couple of days ago." He frowned. "They have some new equipment from Europe that they're testing. I'm going to release the profile to CNN and once it's aired, I'm counting on someone coming forward to identify the killer."

Captain Wineglass took a seat as he continued to listen to David.

David sat. "I'm also working on finding out where the blonde wig was purchased. The hairs found at the crime scenes came from a synthetic wig. Several shops sell wigs like the one the killer wears, I only have a couple left to check out. I also have Malcolm keeping an eye out for signs of any strange activity at the airport, although I doubt the killer would strike twice in the same place; that's not the killer's MO. I stopped by the main office at Jet Away a couple days ago and told the manager it was possible the airline may be a target for sabotage. I explained we had reasons to believe the murders here and in Houston are linked to each other. *Thank God I've been able to get in and out without Sky or her friends seeing me,* David thought. "I'm also checking a list of employees that were fired in the past three years; they may be seeking vengeance against the airline." He took in a breath. "This is a tedious investigation, but I guarantee you—she *will* be caught."

"Good work." The Captain stood. "The sooner you get this solved, the sooner you can get back to your life in Houston."

"Well, sir," he said, clearing his throat. "I wanted to talk to you about that." He stood and walked over closer to the captain. "Do you have a permanent opening?"

"There's always one for you," Captain Wineglass said as he slapped David on the back, and then walked away.

David picked up the phone and dialed Sky's cell phone number; he caught her just before it was time for her to start work.

"Hey, stranger," she said. "What happened to you last night?"

"I worked late again last night." He knew he couldn't continue to keep up this charade.

"Baby, I'll come over tonight and we'll sit and talk. I have something I've wanted to tell you for some time. I've just been waiting for the right time, but I'm not sure there is going to be a right time. There's something about me you need to know."

"David, what is it?" she asked, worried.

"Don't worry; I'm not a fugitive, a criminal, or a married man. It has to do with my job."

"Your job?" she asked with great concern.

"It's really nothing. But I'll tell you tonight."

Pressed for time, she agreed. "OK, I have a couple of errands to run after work. I'll see you around 7 p.m."

"I'll see you then. Love you."

"Love you too." *What could he possibly tell me about his job?* She returned to her desk, plugged her headset into the phone, and took her first phone call of the day.

****

After work, Sky jumped into her BMW and opened the sunroof. "Ooh, that's our song." She turned up the volume as Luther Vandross sang, *Don't you remember you told me you loved...* Twenty minutes later, she pulled up to a parking meter, searched her purse for some change, deposited seventy-five cents into the meter, and ran up the steps.

Sky approached a female police officer at the front desk.

"May I help you?" the officer asked as she turned from the computer to greet Sky.

"Can you tell me where I pay a traffic ticket?" Sky asked, looking around the large open area.

"You're in the wrong building, this is the police department. You need municipal court. If you walk through this breezeway and around the corner," she pointed, "it's the red brick building on the right."

"Thank you," said Sky. She followed the officer's directions and walked around the corner where she saw David talking to a police officer. As she got closer, she could hear the officer addressing David as 'detective'.

She was surprised to see him at the police station but even more surprised to learn that he was a detective. David turned and their eyes locked. "Detective? Is that what he called you?" she asked as the police officer walked off. "Do you work at the airport or not?" she snapped.

He moved closer to her. "Please, let me explain."

"Well, do you?" she asked again, standing with her hand positioned on her hip.

He dropped his head. "No, but I can explain."

"You have nothing to explain, Detective Hall," she exploded. "You've been lying to me."

David put his hand on her shoulder. "You wouldn't have understood. I had to lie. Let me explain," he repeated, staring into her eyes.

She knocked his hands from her shoulder, not caring that people were staring at them. "You had to lie? What kind of an answer is that? How do you know I wouldn't have understood, David?" She frowned. "You didn't even try!"

"Look, Sky," he laughed not thinking it was a big deal. "You're blowing this all out of proportion—I think you're overreacting." David looked into her eyes. *She's pissing me off, it's not that big of a deal,* he thought.

"Overreacting? Overreacting?" She shot him daggers. "How dare you!" Her uncompromising eyes locked on him.

He gently pulled her to the side, into a corner, and whispered, "Sky, quit trippin, it's not a big deal. I've been working on the left-handed serial killer case and couldn't blow my cover. I'm on loan from the Houston Police Department. I was afraid if I told you it would ruin our relationship. That's why I missed a couple of our dates," he explained. "I was going to tell you tonight."

She jerked her arm away. "Houston," she blurted as she looked upside his head. The left-handed serial killer never registered. She continued, "So am I just a pastime until you return back to Houston." Her lips thinned.

"No—girl my feelings for you are real. Please! Trust me."

"Trust you? How can I trust you, knowing our whole relationship is based on a lie?

"I didn't mean to lie, I just didn't want to get you involved. That's all."

"David it's not that you're a cop, it's the principle of it. You lied. I don't ever want to see you again!" she said. She started to leave, then turned and slapped his face.

As she stormed through the breezeway, she felt the tears welling in her eyes.

David looked at her in shock, surprised that she would slap him. "Sky, wait!" He ran after her.

She stopped on the steps outside, saying, "The left-handed serial killer," as it finally registered.

"Yes, I just wanted to protect you. I'm sorry. I never meant to hurt you in any way." He saw the hurt in her eyes as she stared at him without uttering a sound.

"Hell, if you're the detective on the case, you sure have done a lousy job. Why isn't she captured?" She simply turned and walked away, her head held high.

Does he really love me or is he just playing games? She thought as she walked down the steps.

David felt that insult as it hit way below the belt. He walked back into the building when Captain Wineglass stepped out of his office. "Detective Hall," he said, looking David in the eyes.

David wasn't in any mood to explain to the Captain what had just happened. "Yes, sir," he answered reluctantly.

"There's been another murder."

David jumped to attention. "Another what!"

"A woman's body was just found in a dumpster over on Old Sooner Road, next to the old Target building." He whispered, "She had a pair of airplane wings lying next to her body."

"I'm on my way!" He ran to his car.

As David headed to the crime scene, his mind drifted. *I've got to catch this son of a bitch. What beef could she possibly have with the airline? Is she a disgruntled employee or passenger?* "Dammit! Get out of the way, can't you see the flashing lights?" he shouted at the driver who pulled out in front of his police car. David swerved to avoid hitting the car that had pulled into the intersection. Twenty minutes later, he pulled up at the abandoned building where other police officers had congregated around the body.

"Hey Detective Hall," said an officer as David approached him.

"What do we have here, Officer Jackson?" David asked, as he walked toward the body.

"We have a white female appear to be in her late twenties. Her body's swollen and blisters have begun to cover it. Someone brought her here and dumped her as if she was trash." The police shook his head in shame. "She was wrapped in this Oriental rug, along with her car keys and purse."

"Did you say purse?" David asked as he looked around for the purse.

"Yes, that's why we called you. There's a pair of airplane wings next to the body and we have a composite on her. We have her license."

David removed the sheet from the victim's face and immediately his eyes widened and mouth opened. He stood in shock.

"Detective Hall, what's the matter—do you know her?"

"Yes," he spoke slowly as he stared at the partially decomposed body, inhaling in a sharp breath from the foul odor. "Her name is Pebbles Stone." He shook his head in disgust.

The officer looked at the driver license. "Yes, this is Pebbles Stone," then handed it to David. "My guess, she's been here for about six or seven days."

David held the ID tight in his hand. "Pebbles was a close friend of my girlfriend." *This is too close to home.* "They worked together at Jet Away Airways." He placed the sheet back over her face and made a cross symbol over his chest with his finger.

"I don't think we're going to find this killer," said Officer Jackson. "She's as slick as a fox in a chicken coop."

"I beg the differ Jackson," Detective Hall raised one finger as he moved around the body with assurance. "I feel it's *just* a matter of time. I'm so close but not there yet."

After two hours of meticulously investigating the crime scene, he said, "Dust this rug for fingerprints, and comb the area for anything that looks like it doesn't belong here." He spoke in anger, "we got to catch her and NOW." *Sky*, he thought, then ran to his car. *I have to tell Sky, and she may be in danger herself,* he thought to himself. He hollered over his shoulder, "I have a stop to make but I'll meet you back at the station. Thanks guys."

Seventeen

*T*he school bell rang and many students raced in different directions trying to beat the tardy bell. Brittany walked slowly down the hall to her driver's education class. Brittany should have been excited; she had wanted to drive since she turned sixteen last month, but before she could get a driver's license, she needed a copy of her birth certificate. Therein lay the problem. She wondered why her mother had gotten so defensive or angry every time she'd asked for her birth certificate. *Why does she keep brushing me off with these silly excuses?* Thought Brittany.

She flopped down in her seat just as the class started. Coach Reed glanced down at his grade book and then looked up at the class and started pointing. "Brent and Woodfork. This is the second week of class and you still haven't brought me a copy of your birth certificates. I need it by the end of the week if you want to continue in this class."

"Yes, sir," they both replied.

After school, Brittany charged into the house and tore into her mother, once again demanding her birth certificate. "Mama, Coach Reed is going to drop me from the class if I don't have my certificate by Friday." Brittany said angrily. "That will make Friday the thirteenth just perfect!" she added, glaring at her mother.

"I'll do my best to have it by then. I sent off for it; it's coming from Austin. I've told you before, I can't control the mail," she said agitated.

Wanda always had an excuse. Brittany had begun to imagine all sorts of reasons for her mother's reaction. *Is she afraid of me having a wreck? Was I stolen as a baby? What is it?* All kinds of thoughts crossed Brittany's sixteen-year-old mind.

Wanda had told Brittany that she had been born in Houston and they had relocated to Dallas when her father had passed away shortly after her birth, which was partly true.

"What is your problem, Mother? Every time I ask about my birth certificate you freak out." She frowned. "Why?" Then the tears began to pour like Niagara Falls.

Wanda didn't answer. She knew her daughter was right. She planned to tell Brittany some day when she was capable of handling the news. Sixteen was not a good age. *Maybe eighteen or even twenty-one,* she thought.

"Brittany, I'm not angry. It's just that I worry because of the drunken drivers and irresponsible people on the road." She walked away hating to see Brittany cry.

She thought back to when she first adopted Brittany, *What if the mother changes her mind? Will I make a good mother? Is the child going to cause me problems later in life?*

Brittany shattered her thoughts, "Mom," she argued, "I'm very cautious. You've seen me drive. I need this for school— otherwise I going to get kicked out of the class." She followed her mother into the next room.

"It's not you, baby, it's the other drivers."

Brittany infuriated, stormed out of the living room, went straight to her bedroom, and slammed the door. "I hate her. I wish she was dead!" she screamed.

Wanda heard her outburst, and then grabbed her keys from the kitchen counter, dashed out the front door, jumped into her white Mercedes to get away from the pressure. She sat for a moment, getting her emotions in check, then began driving around the neighborhood wondering if she should tell Brittany the truth. She wasn't ready to risk losing her daughter. Brittany was an honor roll student and very well mannered. She's never had a problem out of her. She was mature for her age and very responsible.

But not responsible enough to accept the heartbreaking news, thought Wanda.

Wanda had heard horror stories about children who had become rebellious after finding out they were adopted, and she wasn't ready for the drama. She didn't want anybody to come between her and her daughter. Wanda sat at the stop light thinking back to sixteen years ago, when she had picked up this beautiful baby girl from the agency. She recalled Frances Walters's words when she had called from the Walters Adoption Agency with the good news. "We have a baby girl; she's five days old. Her mother claims she was raped by her foster father and became pregnant," Frances had said.

"I know it's confidential, thanks for telling me this much," Wanda told Frances as she walked into the baby room she had previously painted pink and decorated with matching Barbie sheets and curtains for the day 'her little girl' would come home.

The sound of a car horn snapped her back to the present. She looked up and noticed that the traffic light had turned green.

Still weighing up the issue, she spoke aloud, "I can't tell her this lie that I've been living for sixteen years. She won't understand, she's too young. I know she will think less of me as a woman and as a mother. She won't respect me anymore. More importantly, if I tell her the truth, will she try to find her birth mother?" A tear fell from her eye.

At home, Brittany had heard the door slam as her mother left the house. She wiped her eyes and stomped into her mother's room. "It doesn't take this long to get a birth certificate. And why does she get so mad when I ask? That doesn't make sense." She walked over to the gray file cabinet and yanked on it. "Locked! I should have known." She kicked it.

She searched for the key and finally found it in a purple flower cup on the top shelf of the closet. Brittany unlocked the drawer and rustled through some files behind the letter B. She found nothing. Deciding random searching would be a waste of time, she started at the beginning of the alphabet.

Brittany couldn't believe it when she pulled out the first file in the A section. She screamed, "Adoption! Adoption!"

She immediately took the faded yellow piece of paper from the folder, sat in the middle of the floor, and unlocked the truth. *Baby girl Heather, six pounds and twelve ounces, birthday May 1st. Mother, Nicole no last name. Father unknown.* "What? Mother, Nicole? No! No!" she screamed. "This can't be me," she wept. "She lied! She lied to me. I'm adopted! I'm adopted! This is why she avoided giving me my birth certificate." Teardrops fell on the already discolored paper. "Who is she? Who is my father? My name is Heather. Is this really me?" She asked herself.

Brittany walked from her mother's bedroom to the kitchen as she continued to read. She sat at the kitchen table staring at the document in disbelief and hearing the word 'adopted' repeatedly, as if she was playing a broken record. She laid her head down on her arms and cried. Wanda walked through the front door, past the living room and into the kitchen, where she spotted the adoption papers and birth certificate on the table. She rushed over to her daughter. "Oh, Brittany, I'm so sorry. I never wanted you to find out this way." She reached for her daughter.

"So this is why you were ignoring me. Don't touch me!" Brittany shouted as she shoved her mother's hands away. "You lied to me." She ran into the bathroom, slamming the door in Wanda's face as she ran behind her.

"Brittany, open the door—now," Wanda ordered as she beat on the door.

"Go away. I hate you. You're not my mother."

Tears welled in Wanda's eyes. "Brittany, you open this door—right now," she demanded. "I didn't tell you because I wanted to protect you."

Brittany swung open the door. "Protect me from what? From who? I had a right to know that I was adopted."

"You're right and I was going to tell you, in due time, but—"

"But what? Is this why you couldn't tell me where I got this ugly birthmark under my eye?" She wrinkled her brows. "I hate it. I'm teased everyday at school, but you couldn't tell me anything about it because you don't KNOW." She spoke spiteful.

Wanda slapped Brittany. "Don't you dare talk to me in that tone of voice." She gritted her teeth. "I have taken care of you all your life. You are my daughter and nobody or nothing will ever take that away from me." She spoke sternly, then softened her voice. "Baby, you are my most precious jewel. I love you. Please forgive me, but I felt right now that you're too young to understand."

There was a quiet hush throughout the room; Brittany stared in shock. Wanda had never laid a hand on Brittany before.

"Listen to me." She gently shook Brittany. "I thought if I told you the truth that you would think less of me as a mother. I never meant to hurt you, I was only protecting you. I've heard so many horror stories about what happened when children found out they were adopted."

"Who is my mother?" Brittany's tone softened also.

"Sweetheart, I don't know. I never saw her." Wanda walked her over to the sofa. "All I know is that her name is Nicole and that she was raped when she was thirteen or fourteen. The adoption records are sealed. The adoption papers have only her first name. I was told that she was from one of the foster homes in Houston."

"Which one mama? I want to know who she is!" asked Brittany, absorbing the information like a sponge taking in water.

"I don't know. That information is sealed." Wanda got up and walked to her bedroom, went straight to the file cabinet, and pulled out an envelope with a picture of a young girl holding a baby. She brought it back and handed it to Brittany. She stared at the picture.

"This is you and your real mother. I intended to show you one day, but I didn't think it would be now—not this way."

"Mama, she is so pretty and so young."

"She was just a baby herself." She looked in her daughter's eyes. "I stole that picture out of her file; so one day when you were older, you would have it."

Brittany smiled and began reading the adoption papers. 'Heather, baby girl adopted by Wanda Brent.' Brittany said, "My name is really Heather and Captain Brent isn't my father?"

"Yes, your given name is really Heather."

"No, Baby, I'm afraid not." She smiled and lowered her head. "He was Tia's dad. I'm sorry," said Wanda.

"Who is my father?"

"I don't know, like I said your mother was raped."

Mother and daughter looked at each other with tears in their eyes and pulled each other close.

"It's going to be OK, baby, we'll get through this."

Brittany cried in her mother's arms.

Eighteen

Sky had to confide in someone. She picked up the phone and dialed Pebbles. It immediately went to voicemail. She then called her mother, who answered on the first ring.

"Hello."

"Hello, Mother," she said in her saddest voice.

"Hello, Sky, what's wrong?"

"Mama, has Daddy ever lied to you?"

"What?" she said, surprised she'd been asked that question. "Why do you ask? And yes, he has, but after I got finished with him, he never lied to me again."

"What happened?"

"Well we were in our twenties and in college. We had been dating for three years and your dad was supposed to be at the library studying."

"Was he?"

"Oh yes, he was there, but he wasn't studying books. He was in the corner with another girl. He claimed he was helping her find a book, but it didn't look that way to me."

"What did you do?"

"After I beat him on top of the head with a book, I ignored him and wouldn't talk to him at school, wouldn't take his calls, and pretended I'd found a new boyfriend. One month later, he was in a car accident with his friend. He was unconscious the first day and in the hospital a full week. I realized then how much he meant to me and that I'd been childish refusing to talk to him and pretending I had a new boyfriend. When he regained consciousness, I was at his side. He was so glad to see me that he asked me to marry him. I never did tell him that I didn't really have another boyfriend; the guy was actually cousin Harold. He didn't find that out until a few years later. The important thing was that your dad never lied to me again. What's going on? Why in the world are you asking me about something like that now?"

"Well, David lied to me too."

"About what?"

"He told me that he worked for Jet Away Airways, but he doesn't. He's a detective for the Houston Police Department on loan to the Dallas Police Department. He's been working on the left-handed serial killer case. He deliberately lied."

"I knew I had seen him somewhere before. He was the man on television that morning I called you and told you to turn on the television. Do you remember?"

"I remember that morning, but I don't remember who was talking. I guess I didn't pay that much attention; I was trying to see the picture."

"How did you find out?"

"I went downtown to pay my traffic ticket and inadvertently wandered into the police department. There stood David. I heard the officer call him 'detective'."

"Why hadn't he told you the truth in all these months?"

"He said he couldn't afford to blow his cover and that he was afraid it would ruin our relationship if he told me." She huffed. "I don't want to ever see him again."

"Sky, don't you think you may be overreacting some?"

Overreacting? Sky thought. *Didn't she just hear me say that he lied?*

"But Mama, he lied."

"I know, bless his heart. I think he was just trying to protect you."

"Bless his heart!" She erupted with anger. "Bless my heart, mine is the one that's broken." She frowned.

"Baby sounds like he loves you to me or he wouldn't have gone through such drastic measures to prove how much he cares."

Sky sighed. *He means so much to me.* She flopped down in the kitchen chair. "Maybe I am overreacting."

"I think so baby. Do you love him?"

"Yes, I do. I've only known him for five months but this relationship is so different from any other relationship I've ever had. It has blossomed so quickly. We have so much in common and when I'm with him, I feel like a queen. It's like we belong together." She spoke affectionately.

Thelma could hear the love in her daughter's voice. "Baby, why don't you sleep on it, and call him tomorrow. Let him know how you feel."

"OK, Mom, I guess I will."

"I'm going to bed now. I'll send you my bill," Thelma said, trying to lighten her daughter's mood.

Sky chuckled. "I'll have to take you to lunch when I come home this weekend."

"That'll work, and remember what your dad's sermon was on Sunday."

Forgiveness, she thought, then laughed. "Good night, Mother." She placed the phone back in the cradle and walked into the bedroom to prepare for bed. She stood at the closet, remembering the hurt she had seen in David's eyes when a loud knock on the door interrupted her thoughts. She looked on the top shelf of the closet, focusing on the gun she'd never returned, but instead turned, and walked to the front door. When she looked through the peephole, there stood David. All thoughts about not wanting to talk to him vanished. She opened the door and had to fight the urge to simply fall into his arms.

"I'm sorry, I shouldn't have behaved like that at the police station," she said, not trusting herself to look him in the eyes.

He gently turned her toward him. "Will you forgive me? I made the stupidest mistake ever. I promise I will never lie to you again." He reached out and drew her into his arms as he looked into her eyes. Moments later, he moved into the room and closed the door before speaking again. "I have something to tell you. Let's sit down," he said in a somber voice.

"What is it, David?"

"It's Pebbles." He strained with the words.

"What about her. I've been calling her but she hasn't returned any of my messages."

He lowered his head.

"What is it, David?" she asked, becoming worried.

"She's dead," he blurted softly. "She's dead."

Sky gasped for air. "What!" She said shakingly. Dead!" The tears began to flow. "Oh, my God, she can't be. I just talked to her last week. She took a few vacation days and flew to New York."

David reached out and pulled her into his arms as she shook uncontrollably. "She never made it to New York."

She raised her head, "But how?"

"The left-handed serial killer," he said, clenching his fist so tightly his knuckles turned white.

Sky began to hyperventilate.

"Take a couple of deep breaths," David told her as he quickly removed his arm from around her shoulders helped her to the sofa, and then headed for the kitchen to retrieve a glass of water. He ran back, handing her the glass. "She's been dead for a few days. Last week you spoke with her did she say anything out of the ordinary?"

"No she didn't," Sky managed get out as she sipped her water; her hands were shaking as she tried to digest the horrifying news. "She was on vacation." She kept repeating. "On vacation." Then Sky bolted from the sofa. "I have to tell Niki!" She picked up the phone.

As she dialed Niki's number, her hands continued to shake. "What will I say?" Hearing Niki's voice, Sky broke down again. "I can't do this," she said as she handed David the phone.

"Niki, this is David."

"Hey, David," she said, surprised that he had called her.

"I'm afraid that I have some bad news."

"What is it?" Niki asked, already knowing the answer.

"It's Pebbles." He took a deep breath. "She's dead."

"She's what?" Niki said, trying to sound surprised.

"She's dead—murdered," David repeated.

Niki had just seen the 9 o'clock news; she knew the police had found the body of a white female on Old Sooner Road.

Pebbles should have minded her own business. If only she hadn't been so curious. I told her to leave. I wanted her to leave but she wouldn't! She insisted on snooping and she paid with her life, Niki thought. She had forgotten that David was on the other end of the line.

"Niki, are you OK?" David asked when she didn't respond.

"Yes. Is Sky all right?"

"She's safe but shaken up. I'm calling from her place. She wanted to break the news to you, but after she dialed your number she couldn't bring herself to say the words."

Niki wasn't as concerned about Pebbles as she was about whether someone had seen her dump the body. "Do they have a suspect?" Niki asked, trying to determine if they suspected her.

"Not yet, but she was stabbed. Are you going to be OK?"

"I'll be fine. I'm just shocked. And they didn't mention any suspects?" Niki asked again, hoping she hadn't left any clues.

Sky burst out in a loud cry. "I don't know," he said as he hugged Sky. "Niki, I have to get back to Sky; she's taking this pretty hard. We can talk later."

"OK. Tell Sky I'll call her in the morning. Thanks for calling, good night."

While hanging up the phone David asked, "Do you know how to get in touch with Pebbles's family?"

"Yes, I do, her grandmother lives here in Dallas. I have her phone number. Will you call her for me?" she asked, reaching into her purse. "I don't think I can do it," she added, as tears continued to run down her cheeks.

"Of course, Sky. I'll do it," David said, hating these calls, but knowing he had to do it for Sky. He looked at the number, picked up the phone, and dialed.

When Pebbles's grandmother answered, he said, "Ms. Stone, this is Detective David Hall of the Dallas Police Department. I'm afraid I have some bad news."

"Is it Pebbles?" she asked in a quiet voice.

"Yes it is," he replied.

"The coroner has already contacted me. I'm getting ready to go and identify her body now."

"I'm here with Sky, she's very upset."

"Yes, we all are. Tell her I'm planning a memorial service for Pebbles on Thursday."

"Yes, ma'am. I will."

"Thank you, Detective. Pebbles always said she wanted her ashes scattered in the Gulf. I'll get things moving for the memorial service."

David could tell the woman was crying and he didn't want to intrude so he simply told her good night and hung up.

He told Sky what Pebbles's grandmother had said and then added, "Sky, I really hate to do this to you, but I have to get back to work. Will you be OK alone?"

"Yes, David," Sky whimpered. "Go on, I'll be fine." She knew the gun was in her closet.

He made sure the windows were tightly secured then said, "I'll be back later tonight if it's OK with you."

"I would love that." She said as she walked him to the door.

She reached up and kissed him lightly on the lips. "David, please be careful."

"I will. Lock your door and I will see you in a couple of hours."

Sky was no longer mad at David for lying, but she was frightened for his safety—and hers, with the killer still on the loose.

Nineteen

*T*he early Wednesday morning haze hung in the air as Brittany prepared for driver education class. She was prepared to take her birth certificate to class but that was not a priority anymore. She wanted to find her birth mother, but didn't know where to start. Brittany didn't want to tell Wanda because she was afraid she wouldn't understand, but she knew Wanda had the right to know what she'd decided. As she walked into the kitchen still shaken from last night's shocking news, she looked at the breakfast Wanda had prepared. "Mother, breakfast looks great, but I don't feel like eating, if it's OK with you."

"At least drink your orange juice and get a breakfast bar," she said then smiled.

Brittany walked over to the cabinet with her head down. "I want to find her," she mumbled, reaching up into the cabinet.

"You want to do what?" Wanda asked, hearing the words she'd been dreading.

Brittany hesitated. "I want to find Nicole, my mother."

"Are you sure?" Wanda walked over to Brittany. "Are you ready for this?" She placed a finger under Brittany's chin and tilted her head to see her eyes.

"Yes, I think so."

"Brittany, I don't think you are," Wanda said, trying to dissuade her. "She may not want to meet you or spend time getting to know you." Wanda removed her finger and began pouring a cup of coffee. "The last time I answered the phone it wasn't anyone calling to talk to their lost daughter, and I haven't open mail from some strange lady looking for a child she gave away." Wanda spoke in a sarcastic tone, feeling a touch of jealousy. "You don't know anything about her lifestyle, you might find out something you don't want to know."

"I know, Mama, no disrespect to you, but that's a chance I want to take."

Wanda knew that once Brittany made up her mind to do something, she would stay with it until she had an answer, even if it wasn't the answer she wanted. Deciding it was better to help Brittany than to try to stop her, Wanda told her, "When you get home from school, we'll get on the Internet and see if we can find some help to get you started. It's not going to be easy because the majority of adoption records are sealed."

"Oh, thank you, Mother, I love you." She hugged her mother tight. Wanda wondered if Brittany was ready for what she was about to learn.

****

The news of Pebbles's death spread through the Jet Away staff like a wave rolling onto the beach, leaving the reservation agents in disbelief and shock. Stanley guessed that someone from the police department would probably be around today to talk to those who knew Pebbles. He was right.

Detective Hall arrived early and met with Stanley. He had driven Sky to work. She left him in the lobby and continued to Donna's office before going to the call center.

"Hello, Stanley." David shook his hand. "Hate to be seeing you again under these conditions but I want to speak to some of your employees about the death of Pebbles Stone."

"Yes, follow me, Detective."

Once inside Stanley's office, David asked, "Did you know the young lady?"

"Not personally. I had seen her around the office. Perhaps you can speak to her immediate supervisor, Donna Morris. She should be able to give you more information than I can." He gestured for David to follow him across the hall to Donna's office.

"Donna, this is Detective Hall. He would like to ask you some questions about Miss Stone." Sky looked up and leaped into David's arms.

"I gather you two know each other," commented Donna.

David had returned to Sky's place last night where he held her all night long comforting her as she cried herself to sleep. He realized she was still distraught and bothered by her strong embrace.

"I'm sorry, Ms. Morris, Sky is my girlfriend." He slowly released Sky and shook Donna's hand. "Nice to meet you."

"Yes, we've met over the phone. It's nice to put your face with your voice, Detective." She offered him a seat.

"It's OK if Sky stays." David said as Stanley shut the door and stood with his back to it. "How long had she worked for Jet Away?" David asked.

"For five years." Donna had pulled Pebbles's personnel file, in anticipation of a visit from the detective. The decoys had instructed her to do so.

"Do you know if she had any enemies?"

"No, I don't think so. Her peers liked her. She may have needed a small class in humility, but that's not unusual for her generation. She was a kind person, and lit up a room when she walked in. She was definitely high energy." She wiped the tears from her eyes. "No, she didn't have any enemies. But who would be so cruel?" Sky just sat and listened with the Kleenex to her eyes.

After thirty minutes, David asked to go out on the floor. Donna and Stanley escorted David into the busy call center. Sky stayed behind, trying to get her emotions together.

"Are you here because of Pebbles?" a woman asked as the trio walked by.

"Yes, as a matter of fact I am." David stopped. "How well did you know Pebbles?"

"I didn't know her very well, although we sat in the same cluster of chairs." She pointed to her work area. "She was a flirt, but it was innocent; she wouldn't hurt a flea."

"Is there anything else you can add?"

"No, that's it."

"Thank you," David said. "May I get your name, home address, and phone number in case we need to talk to you again?"

"Sure, Officer. I'm Angela Simpson. My phon—"

"Detective, I can give you the addresses and the phone numbers of everyone who worked with Pebbles when we get done here," Donna said. "That way we won't keep the agents from doing their jobs. As a matter of fact, if Stanley is going to take you around, I'll go back to my office and pull that information right now."

The employee smiled and walked into the break room.

"Of course, Ms. Morris," David answered.

Niki saw David and quickly removed her headset, immediately walking over to him. "David, what are you doing here?" she asked, surprised. "Is Sky all right?"

"Sky is fine. I'm investigating Pebbles's death," he answered.

"Investigating?" she asked, wondering why a skycap was following up on a murder.

"Yes."

"Nicole, this is Detective David Hall," Stanley said.

Her mouth flew open and her eyes were as big as two jack balls as she received the bombshell news. "Detective?" she asked, unable to hide her surprised look.

"Yes, I'm a detective. I'll explain later."

"Do you two know each other?" Stanley asked, looking at both of them as if he had missed something.

"Yes," David answered before turning his attention to the young woman. "Niki, when was the last time you saw Pebbles?"

"It was a week ago when we commuted to work together."

"Did she say anything to you?"

"Uh-uh, no," Niki stuttered.

"Was she in a relationship?"

"No. She wasn't dating anyone." She stammered over her words.

Suddenly David said, "Thanks. I'll talk to you later."

She wondered if her anxiety had begun to show. *Have I alarmed David?* "Ok." She looked stunned as David walked off.

David continued to question employees throughout the morning without gaining much new insight. He decided he needed to know about the connection between Niki and the hotel. He walked back over to Niki who had just finishing up with a customer. "Were you aware of Pebbles being at the Sierra Grand Hotel the night a lady was murdered?"

"Uh-uh, no, I had no idea," she said, wondering if Sky had

mentioned her presence at the hotel to David.

David knew Niki was lying because Sky had told him Pebbles saw her there the night of the murder. He made a mental note. *Why would she lie?*

"Sky said she had talked to Pebbles before she went on vacation. Did you talk to her?"

Should I tell him I spoke to her? Knowing he was waiting for an answer, she spoke quickly. "No, I didn't talk to her before she left."

"How often did you talk to her?" he asked, throwing questions at her like a pitcher on a baseball mound.

Why is he interrogating me? The nerve of him, she thought, and then spoke up. "Everyday; we work together." She pretended to cry and buried her face in her hands.

"I know this is hard, Niki, but it's very important." He placed his hand on her shoulder.

"We commuted to work once a week—Sky, Pebbles, and myself. And of course, we would talk here at the job. Have you spoken to her family?" Niki asked, briefly feeling a tinge of sadness. Still, she needed to know how much David knew.

"Yes, I spoke to her grandmother last night; she's taking care of the funeral arrangements. The wake is tomorrow afternoon; her grandmother is having her body cremated. Are you going?" he asked.

"No. I don't do well at funerals or wakes. The next one I attend will be my own."

David looked at her thinking what a bizarre statement.

If I'm caught, they'll have to kill me, because I'm not going to jail. "How is Sky?"

"She's taking it hard. Maybe you can comfort her. She's in Ms. Morris' office. We're going to catch this killer," David assured Niki.

"Thanks, David," said Niki, as she thought, *I'm not constantly looking over my shoulder, but I know someone who should, if he expects to live—David.*

****

When David returned to his office, Captain Wineglass met him at the door. "May I see you for a minute?"

"Sure, Captain."

They walked a few steps to the captain's office and David shut the door. "What's going on with the investigation—what have you found out?"

"I just left Jet Away Airways."

"Doesn't your girlfriend work at Jet Away?"

"Yes, sir." David looked out the window, wondering if the captain was going to confront him about the incident between him and Sky on yesterday.

"I read your file and understand that the young lady who was found dead was a friend of your girlfriend and she also worked at Jet Away."

"Yes, sir, that's true."

"I hope you won't let your personal relationship get in the way of you doing a good sound investigation. As far as I'm concerned, even your girlfriend is a suspect."

"I'm aware of that, Captain. I have always managed to keep my personal life separate from my profession. So don't concern yourself." He stood with a little attitude. "I've already checked out Sky and her friends. They're clean."

"Good. That's all I wanted to hear," Captain Wineglass said, dismissing David. "Oh, by the way—make sure you air out your dirty laundry at home."

"Yes, sir." David walked out the office. "Asshole," he mumbled. But he knew the captain was right.

Twenty

*A*fter seeing his last client, Doctor Blair began transcribing his notes from the session with Niki the week before. He pulled out the tape recorder and continued to document, midway through his documentation he heard Niki's voice say, "I have one more person to kill, Wanda Brent, and the web of murders will be complete." He quickly rewound the tape, and adjusted the volume for clarity. He heard Niki clearly say, "Wanda Brent will be hearing from me very soon. She's going to pay for what Jet Away Airways and her husband did to me." He replayed the tape again. "One more person to kill—Oh my God! Nicole is killing," he bellowed.

"Brent, Brent," he repeated. "Where have I heard that name?" He pushed out of his chair and rushed over to a wooden cabinet where he pulled out an old Houston Tribune newspaper. He turned to the society page began to read, "The NAACP will host a who's who. Several dignitaries will be honored for their contribution to the community, including Captain Lacy Brent, a pilot on a Jet Away airplane that crashed twenty years ago. Wanda Brent will receive his award posthumously."

Jet Away, the Brents, and Nicole, he whispered. He began to look at Niki's files more closely, flipping the pages back to Nicole's first session. "Her mother was killed in an airplane crash," he said to an empty room. He began counting the years that had past, then checked Niki's age. His whisper became a loud yell. "That's it! Jet Away Airways. I bet Nicole's mother was a passenger on Captain Brent's plane when it crashed." He gasped, as the realization of what was about to happen, struck him. He grabbed the phone and hit the emergency speed dial button.

"911, what's your emergency?" asked the woman dispatcher on the other end of the phone.

"I need the Houston Police Department and make it quick," Doctor Blair said in a voice just below a bellow.

"Let me transfer you."

A couple of seconds past and a deep burly voice answered, "Houston Police Department, Officer Hicks speaking."

"Yes, this is Doctor Blair and I am a therapist here in Houston. My office is loc—"

"Yes, Doctor Blair," interrupted the officer. "I know exactly who you are. How can I help you?"

He took a deep breath, relieved to find out the officer knew of him. He hoped Hicks would believe what he was about to tell him. "Thank you, I need to speak to the detective in charge of the left-handed serial killer case," he said quickly. "I think I have some pertinent information regarding the case."

"I can't get in touch with him this minute, but I can have him contact you, if you give me your phone number."

"Please! You don't understand. It may be too late. I think I know who the left-handed serial killer is. I need to talk to the detective right now!" he shouted. "I think it's one of my patients."

"Just a moment, Doctor, I'll see if someone here has the number; he's working in Dallas." He heard a click and within seconds, Rhonda the clerk answered.

The doctor pushed the button on the speakerphone, then walked around his office as he repeated his story.

"Hold on, Doctor, while I get you the number," Rhonda said when the doctor stopped to get a breath. "The detective's name is David Hall. There are two phone numbers here, I'll give you both. They're to the Dallas Police Department."

"Thank you," the doctor said, relieved as he jotted down the name and numbers, then quickly hung up.

****

David moved around in the kitchen, like a five star chef in culinary school, preparing dinner for Sky, who was attending Pebbles's memorial. He glimpsed at the clock over the sink, knowing any minute she should be there. In spite of what Captain Wineglass said, David knew Sky wasn't the serial killer. He was more concerned about the lie he had been living and hoped she had forgiven him. When the doorbell rang, he walked over, opened the door, and greeted Sky with a hug and a soft kiss on the lips. He handed her a glass of Champagne. "How are you feeling?" he asked as he shut the door behind her.

"I feel better now that I'm with you." She set her glass on the coffee table and hugged him tight, resting her head on his partially exposed hairy chest. A tear fell from her eye as she thought about Pebbles.

"How was the memorial service?"

"It was beautiful. Pebbles would have loved it. It was all about her."

"Are you sure you're OK?"

"I'm OK. Really, I'm fine," she said, looking into his eyes, hoping to convince him.

David lifted her chin with his finger. "Baby, it's going to be OK."

"I know. It's just that everything has happened so quickly." She smiled to cover the hurt that David could see in her eyes. "Can we not talk about this tonight?"

"Sure."

Quickly changing the subject, she said, "The food smells good."

"Are you hungry?" He grabbed her by the hand.

"My appetite vanished two days ago; I haven't really eaten since I found out about Pebbles."

"You need to get some food in that belly." Laughing, he led her into the kitchen where a chef's salad, baked chicken with a white creamy shrimp sauce, scalloped potatoes covered with Rotel, and a bowl of lobster bisque awaited them. "Let's step out on the balcony for a minute and let the food cool." He opened the patio door and Sky eyed the food and breathed in its tantalizing aroma as she walked out the door.

"Baby, I just want to say I'm so sorry for not trusting you

enough to tell you that I was really a detective. I just didn't want to lose you. Mama always said it takes a strong woman to accept the type of work that I do. When I first met you, I said you were special. How could I have doubted you? You're not like the other women I loved and lost. I should have known I could trust you. Now I know how important it is to tell the truth," he said, with a look of shame.

"Shh," she said as she put her finger up to his lips. "I truly understand. Let's not talk about it right now."

"I love you," David said, wrapping his arms around Sky.

She swayed back and forth in his arms, "I love you too."

"Let's make a toast," he released his arms from around her small firm waist.

"OK. And what are we toasting to?" Sky asked they picked up their glasses from the patio table. "To a long and prosperous relationship, and may we have plenty of little ones running around the house."

Her eyes watered. "Why did you make that toast?" she asked somberly.

"Why not? Don't you like kids? Or don't you want my children?"

"I can't have children. I've already had one miscarriage and I've been told I will never be able to carry a baby past four months." She turned her back to him. "I've told you that."

"Where is your faith?" he asked as he took her glass and set it on the patio table. He pulled her close to him, happy to know that she'd forgiven him for being so selfish.

Nothing could spoil his evening. "Where's your faith?" he repeated.

She smiled. "In God."

"That's how I want to hear you talk," he said, releasing her. "Now, never underestimate a Hall. We have strong genes," David said, patting his chest in Tarzan fashion. "Both of my sisters have two each and my brother has two. With all of the modern technology we have today, I don't think you'll have a problem.

She smiled, "Look! There's a falling star. Let's make a wish." She closed her eyes and wished for plenty of children.

"What did you wish for?" He asked.

"I can't tell you, otherwise it won't come true." She began

giving him short pecks on the lips. "I've never kissed a detective before."

"Let me show you how it's really done." He took her in his arms, covering her mouth with his, as he rolled his tongue gently around in her mouth and she moaned softly.

****

Dr. Blair quickly dialed the Dallas Police Department.

"Precinct 211, Sergeant Antonio Carillo speaking."

"I need to speak to Detective Hall."

"He's gone for the evening, may I take a message?"

"Yes, I have some important information regarding the left-handed serial killer. It's imperative that I speak to him tonight."

The department had received hundreds of phone calls regarding the serial killer, but all of them led to a dead-end. "You and every other prank caller," he mumbled under his breath, but not quietly enough.

The doctor heard him. "Listen, this is not a prank call. I am a doctor in Houston. I need to speak to him NOW, before it's too late."

"Give me your name and number and I will have him call you."

"My name is Doctor Hank Blair."

"Right," said the Sergeant, cynicism dripping from his voice.

"And he can reach me at (555) 345-6789."

"Right, Doc. I'll pass the message along," the Sergeant said with unconcern in his voice.

"Thank you," said the doctor, skeptical that the Officer would get the message to Detective Hall, and rightfully so.

Doctor Blair thought aloud, "I know I have doctor-patient confidentiality to protect, but Niki is planning on murdering someone. Let's hope she hasn't done it yet." He dialed the other number given to him as he drummed his fingers on his desk waiting for David to answer. He could still hear Nicole's words "web of murder will be complete." After the second ring he shouted, "Come on, pick up the phone, Detective Hall. Dammit, pick up the phone."

He got the answering machine. "This is David I'm not in at the moment, please leave a message and I'll get back to you."

Doctor Blair cleared his throat and began to speak. "This message is for Detective David Hall. This is Doctor Hank Blair. I am a therapist in Houston and I have some important information that may be pertinent to the left-handed serial killer case. I have a client who is an employee at Jet Away Airways. She has a vendetta against the airline and one of its deceased pilots for killing her mother in a plane crash. Please give me a call at (555) 345-6789. This number rings at my office as well as my home and I don't care what time you return the call just call me. It is very urgent."

Doctor Blair continued listening to the tape on Niki and began to write. "I find this individual is dangerous, and believe that she might be the left-handed serial killer that has been terrorizing Houston and more recently Dallas. I have contacted the Dallas Police Department to inform Detective David Hall that there is a good possibility the serial killer is Nicole Salem. I have an obligation of privacy to my client but she has threatened bodily harm, even murder. That breaks the doctor-client confidentiality. I'm basing my conclusion on her behavior; she has discontinued taking her medication, which has caused her behavior to be bizarre. Her delusions and hallucinations have caused her to be paranoid and suspicious. It is my professional opinion that she MUST be stopped before she kills again."

****

David and Sky were in a passionate kiss when the telephone rang. She tried to pull back but David moved with her. Finally, she gently pushed him away. "Answer the phone."

He held onto her, trying to ignore the phone. "Let the answering machine get it. Now, where were we before Alexander Bell's contraption so rudely interrupted us? Tonight I'm one hundred percent all yours. I'm not going to let anything or anybody come between us; it'll keep until later. Dinner, on the other hand, can't." He opened the patio door and they sat down in the dining room to eat.

"Um, this is delicious. What kind of sauce is this?" she asked, taking a bite of the baked chicken.

"It's a secret, I can't tell," he teased.

She twisted her lip and continued to eat.

They began talking about the day Sky found out David was a detective. "You should have seen your face when you found out that I was a detective. Girl, if looks could kill I would have died that day," David said with a chuckle.

She couldn't help but laugh herself. "I was shocked—I was so surprised to see you. You should have seen your face. You looked like a deer caught in the headlights." She laughed. "How long have you been a detective?"

"I've worked for the Houston Police Department for fifteen years but have been on special assignment in Dallas for over a year. The left-handed serial killer case is a tough case but I'm getting closer and closer everyday."

"I told Mama about how you lied to protect me."

"What?" he said clearly embarrassed. "Now she's going to hate me."

"No, she doesn't. She totally understood and she expects to see us for daddy's appreciation ceremony tomorrow night. You're still coming, aren't you?"

"Yes, if nothing else comes up." He gazed into her eyes. "Listen to me." He placed his hand on top of hers. "I believe the serial killer works in reservations at Jet Away."

"What!" she shouted, and covered her mouth with her hand. "What makes you suspect that?"

"Every time she kills, she leaves a pair of Jet Away airplane wings near the victim. All of the evidence is pointing toward someone in reservations. Don't mention this to anybody, not even Niki. It's confidential until I can find out what's going on." He continued to look in her eyes. "Plus, I want you to be safe."

"But shouldn't I warn Niki?"

"NO," he spoke quickly and sternly. "No one must know, promise me."

"OK, David, I promise." She saw the concerned looked in his eyes.

"There are some police decoys in your department."

"What! This is some creepy shit."

"Just be careful and be aware of your surroundings."

"I will."

After dinner, David turned on the stereo and they slow danced and talked about their relationship. His telephone rang again, but he ignored it. Midnight crept up on them. David was hoping that Sky would spend the night but didn't dare ask. He knew Sky had been celibate for the past three years, but the burning desire was eating at him. He was also worried about her safety and didn't like the idea of her being home alone.

"I didn't mean to keep you out this late," he said. "Let me follow you home." He reached for his keys.

"You'll do no such thing. I'll lock my door and talk to you on my cell phone all the way home."

She picked up her purse and he reluctantly opened the door, but before Sky could make a move to leave, David softly took her in his arms and caressed every part of her body, all the while deepening his kiss. Neither wanted the moment to end.

He couldn't resist any longer. "Don't go Sky," he whispered in her ear. "Please stay."

"I think I'd better not." She said shakingly. A pleasant moan seeped out.

They continued to kiss and her knees weakened, and he shut the door.

"Sky, please stay the night," he begged. He wanted her and she wanted him. When they kissed, he inhaled her soft breath. He could taste her sweet nothings as his hands gently stroked her back moving down to her rounded hips.

"Oh, David, I want to stay, but I...I..."

He began kissing her on the neck and blowing softly in her ear. His kisses were deep and tender. He unbuttoned her blouse and it fell to the floor while covering her perfectly shaped breasts with his gentle hands. His hardness touched her and her resistance fell like the Berlin wall.

"David," she managed to get out. "Yes, I'll stay." The words softly floated out of her mouth.

He gently lifted her in his arms and carried her into his bedroom; candles and several ocean pictures decorated the room. The red light on the answering machine continued to flash but neither of them noticed. He laid her across his neatly made bed and quickly reached for the remote on the stereo, flooding 'the best of Luther' throughout his apartment. He lit the candles and dimmed the lights.

He started singing softly in her ear just above a whisper. *Don't you remember you told me you love me, baby. Said you'll be coming back this way again, baby. Baby, baby, baby, baby, ooh baby.*

She lay there with her eyes closed, enjoying the moment, listening to David's sweet melodious voice.

He tenderly kissed her breasts as he stroked her arms. He raised his head, "I want you—I want to marry you."

She opened her eyes. "You want to what!"

"You heard me. I love you. I want you to be Mrs. David Hall, or Sky Hall if you prefer. I don't want to ever lose you again."

"David, we've only been dating for a few months, but I know that I want you. Yes! Yes! I will marry you." She spoke softly, tears of joy welled in her eyes.

"I promise you I will always be here for you. I'll never let you down. No more lies." He smiled. "Be patient, let me solve this serial killer case and I'm totally yours."

"I love you too," she said as they began to kiss, he held her tight in his arms. Sky remembered that she and Niki were commuting together the next day. She broke the rhythm, "I have to let Niki know I'm not riding with her tomorrow, and of course you know I have to tell her the good news."

David laughed. "Go ahead and tell her."

She picked up the phone and dialed the number, Niki answered groggily. "Hello."

Sky hesitated, remembering that it was after midnight and thinking her excitement so soon after Pebbles's death might be a sign of disrespect. She knew Niki would understand. "Niki, I forgot about the time, sorry I'm calling so late but I wanted to tell you that I won't be commuting tomorrow, and guess where I am?" Before Niki could answer, she said, "At David's. And guess what else? David just asked me to marry him."

"What! That's wonderful. Have you set a date?" Niki spoke with sleep in her voice.

"No, not yet but it may not be long; he's getting closer to solving the left-handed serial killer case."

"He's getting closer?" she asked, not concerned about whether she sounded worried. "How far has he gotten on the case?"

"He said he's getting close and should be making an arrest any day now."

Silence ripped through the phone quick like a lightning bolt. Niki thought, *Any day now? How much does he actually know? How close is he?*

"Niki, are you there?"

"Uh, yes, I was just thinking. I'll see you at work tomorrow. Congratulations."

"Thanks. Goodnight."

David took the phone from her hand and placed it in the cradle. She noticed the light blinking on the answering machine. "You have a message," she whispered, as she lay topless on his bed.

"I'll get it later. Tonight, it's all about you" He said as he turned off the light and gently removed her clothes trailing kisses down her neck and across her silky smooth breasts. The reflection of the blue light from the stereo danced off the wall with the rhythm of the music, creating a romantic atmosphere for the remainder of the night.

Twenty-One

*T*he next morning, taking a risk Niki drove by David's apartment, only to find Sky and David's vehicles still in the parking lot. The anticipation was eating at her like a lion creeping upon an antelope. She had to find out how much he knew and hoped she would find the answers she needed.

Fifteen minutes past and Niki continued to wait in the grocery store parking lot across the street. "Damn, what's taking them so long? Sky should have been gone ten minutes ago. It's seven o'clock." Niki looked at her watch then huffed. Thirty seconds later, she looked at her watch again and slammed the palm of her hand against the steering wheel, seething because she wanted badly to get inside the apartment. At that moment, someone was coming out of the apartment. She quickly grabbed the binoculars and glared through the lens. "It's about time." She watched Sky drive out of the complex. Two minutes later David surfaced and he walked to his car. He immediately turned around and headed back upstairs to his apartment.

"Now what," Niki groaned as she beat the steering wheel in rage.

He was halfway up the stairs when he looked at his watch. Then turned around and walked back to his car. As he got in and pulled out of the lot, Niki slumped down in the driver's seat of the Jeep in case he looked in her direction. She waited five minutes, satisfied David wasn't coming back, and she crossed the street and walked through the breezeway of the apartment complex. She quietly walked down the corridor, making sure no one was watching her. "Here it is, 204." She looked over her shoulder and tried the doorknob; it was locked, "Damn." She took out a tiny tool from her bra and slid it through the keyhole. When the lock clicked, she turned the knob and walked in closing the door behind her.

Niki walked through the spotless living room, into the open kitchen area where she spotted a pile of papers neatly stacked on the counter. She flipped through the papers looking for something related to the serial killer case—nothing was there. She walked down the narrow hallway and stopped at David's tidy bedroom where a sweet cherry fragrance lured her into the room. She saw papers lying on his desk and rambled through them, again she found nothing.

"He has a message," she said to herself after noticing the light on the phone blinking. She hit the play button.

"David, this is your mom, give me a call when you get this message. Love you." After listening to the message Niki sat on the edge of the bed despondent, wishing her mother could leave her a message, but knowing that will never happen.

Then the next message played, "Hello, Detective Hall, this is Doctor Blair. I'm a therapist in Houston." Niki swallowed the lump in her throat, surprised to hear the doctor's voice. After listening to the entire message she sat on the edge of the bed shaking, feeling Doctor Blair was going to betray her. Fear set in as she anticipated the worst. With tears in her eyes and her lip quivering, she said, "Oh no! Oh no! I can't believe he is doing this to me. He promised!" Her emotions rolled over each other as she grabbed her head. "He promised what we talked about was strictly confidential." In rage, she ripped the phone from the wall and tossed it to the floor.

With one swipe of her left hand, she sent his papers tumbling to the floor. "This is why I trust no one. He's going to pay for this," she said, revenge settling in as she stood and wiped the tears from her face. In a split second, she deleted the messages and walked out the bedroom.

Niki paced the living room floor. *What am I going to do?* She was loosing control. She screamed, "Why? Why? Why did you take my parents away? I have been haunted ever since. Help me." She fell to her knees and started beating the floor pleading,

"Help me. Help me. What am I going to do? I'm caught."

Suddenly she was calm. "He's going to pay for what he's done," she stood then hurried out the door back to her apartment. She knew what to do.

****

David was on cloud nine when he arrived at work reminiscing about his exciting and pleasurable evening he had experienced with the woman he loved. He walked over to his desk, picked up the black phone, and began dialing his home phone number to check his answering machine.

Just then, Captain Wineglass came out of his office. "Hey, Detective Hall, have you heard anything else from the lab?"

David didn't get the chance to check his messages. He placed the phone back in the cradle.

"Yes, sir, I got a call from the Houston Crime Lab. The tech there is working quickly to get that surveillance video cleared up. I'm headed to Houston this weekend to retrieve it. We should have an arrest very soon."

"Good," said the Captain before he turned to walked down the hall.

"I'll let you know when I receive the tape," David said, picking up the phone again. He dialed his home number and put in the code but no messages. *Um, that's funny. I know I had a message.* He dialed his number again. Nothing. *The light was blinking. What happened to the message?* He thought.

****

Good morning, Doctor Blair's office, may I help you?" asked the receptionist.

"This is Diamond O'Connell and I want to make an appointment with the doctor as a new patient," Niki said, frantic but trying to disguise her voice.

"I'm sorry, the doctor isn't seeing new patients," the receptionist replied.

"But I need to see him," she demanded.

Doctor Blair overheard the receptionist as he walked out of his office. "Linda, I can see one more."

"One moment, please." Linda looked at the doctor while placing the caller on hold. Doctor Blair was a soft-spoken man who hated to turn anyone away. Linda was overprotective of him. She knew he was swamped with his current patient load. "Are you sure, Doctor Blair?"

The doctor nodded yes.

She glanced in his appointment book. "Well, you do have a cancellation at two this afternoon and the lady sounds urgent." He nodded again. "Doctor Blair, you do remember I'm leaving early today, don't you?" Normally she would have stayed, but she promised she would help with the table decorations for the award ceremony tonight.

"I remember and that's OK. I can handle one patient alone, especially since she's the last patient for the day."

Linda returned to the phone. "How about two o'clock today?"

"Two will be good," Niki answered promptly remembering the awards ceremony is tonight. She had promised Reverend and Mrs. Winters that she would come see Reverend Winters accept his award.

"OK, you're all set for two this afternoon, Ms. O'Connell. Good bye."

"Her voice sounds familiar," Linda said as she turned to the doctor. "She sounded real anxious to see you."

"What's her name?" he asked.

"Diamond O'Connell."

"I don't recall that name, but we'll see," Doctor Blair said as he walked back into his office.

****

Niki had planned to fly to Houston with Sky late that afternoon but Niki couldn't wait that long, she had an appointment to keep with Doctor Blair. She called Sky at work and made an excuse to going to Houston early and she would see her at the NAACP awards that night. She picked up her blonde wig and twirled it around her finger while she dialed Jet Away.

"Jet Away Airways, may I help you," answered the man on the other end of the phone.

"I would like to make a one way reservation to Houston Hobby for this morning, on your next flight. My name is Diamond O'Connell."

"Ms. O'Connell, the next flight departs at twelve noon. May I have your credit card number?"

"I would like to pay cash at the ticket counter please."

"Sure, your flight number is 282 and you can pick up your boarding pass at the ticket counter."

"Thank you replied Niki," As she hung up the phone rushing to her closet. "Dr. Blair, I'll teach you about betraying me. You're going to pay," she said while throwing her clothes into the suitcase.

Ninety minutes later, Niki rushed to the ticket counter like an erupting volcano. She whipped out her ID, still peeved at the doctor for his betrayal phone call. Niki's one fear was the airport recognizing her, but her biggest fear was not getting to Doctor Blair before he left another message for David. She was determined to confront him. She waited in line ten minutes before the next agent waved her to the counter. Niki handed the agent her fake ID and turned away when she saw Malcolm walked by.

"May I help you?" The ticket agent asked, studying Niki's ID, which read Diamond O'Connell.

"I have a reservation on the next flight to Houston." She said breathless as she watched Malcolm walk into the backroom, hoping he wouldn't recognize her from Club Elite.

The ticket agent retrieved the information and asked, "Will that be cash or credit card? Ms. O'Connell."

"Cash," Niki said as she took the money from her wallet and handed it to the agent.

Niki tried to cover her face by brushing the blonde bangs closer to her eyes.

"You look familiar. Have we met before?" the agent asked as she handed Niki her ID and a boarding pass.

"No, I don't think so, thank you." Niki quickly gathered her things and rushed to the gate, expecting airport security to show up at any moment and escort her to jail. She took a seat and watched the passengers as they walked to their various gates. She checked her watch by the minute and kept both eyes on the gate agent.

"Damn, they should make the announcement to board soon," she muttered. Just then, the gate agent announced, "Flight 282 is ready for boarding to Houston Hobby. Please board at gate

42."

Niki pushed out of her seat and stood in line waiting on her turn to board, she handed the gate agent her ID and boarding pass. Within seconds, she had boarded the plane and settled in an aisle seat up front.

When the plane landed, she took the airport shuttle to Auto Rental Car. When she finally got the car, she was already twenty minutes behind schedule. She sped down the freeway, weaving in and out of traffic. She screamed, "Get out of my way!" As she focused on the traffic, she illegally swerved into the HOV lane, not caring that two passengers should have been in the vehicle. Then she swerved back into the regular lane, making a hurried exit off the freeway onto Manning Creek, where she ran into a store and purchased a butcher's knife. She purposely left her knife behind, knowing she wouldn't clear security. She sprinted back to the car and drove a few blocks down, made a right turn into the parking lot and pulled up beside the doctor's office.

Walking briskly, she yanked the door open. A bell sounded, but the doctor didn't immediately come out. She noticed Linda wasn't sitting at her tidy desk. She turned and locked the door.

As she caught her reflection in the wall mirror, she became more enraged. She was fond of the doctor but she knew if she didn't stop him, her quest would be ruined. She stepped a few feet over to the doctor's door placing her ear on it. She could hear the doctor repeatedly requesting to speak to Detective Hall. She rushed in his office and stared.

He swung around to see who had busted in his office without knocking. He placed his hand over the mouthpiece and said, "You must be Ms. O'Connell, I'll be with you in one minute. Please have a seat in the reception area." He gestured to the chair.

Niki walked over to the doctor, snatched the phone from his hand, and slammed it in the cradle. "You won't be calling Detective Hall today or any other day."

"What the hell," he said, looking up at Niki. "Who the hell are you?"

She pulled off her wig and sunglasses then looked with piercing eyes at the doctor.

"Nicole!" he said, surprised by the way she was dressed, but trying hard to keep his voice calm. "Why are you dressed like that?" He could see the craziness in her eyes.

"This is my disguise." She looked at him with rage. "You lied to me," she screamed as she tossed the wig and glasses to the floor. Bitterness raged through her body like a forest fire out of control.

"Nicole, calm down," he raised his hand. "What do you think I lied about?" He squirmed in his seat as concern and fear showed on his face.

"I thought what we discussed was confidential." A few tears fell from her eyes.

"Well, it is," he said as he saw how hurt she was.

"Stop lying to me, Doctor Blair," she screamed. "I heard the message you left Detective Hall."

"What? How—" He looked mystified.

"How did I get the message?" She interrupted then laughed obnoxiously. "You see, Detective Hall's girlfriend and I are very close friends." Niki pulled the large knife from her purse, and then dropped the purse on the floor. "He never got that message. I intercepted it before he got the chance to hear it."

He stared at the knife—his throat tightened. "Nicole, I'm very concerned about you, that's the only reason I called the detective," the doctor said compassionately, trying not to show his uneasiness, but his short frame body was ready to tackle her at any given moment.

"You're trying to get me caught!" she screamed.

"Caught for what?" Her frightened face convinced him that he had indeed done something regrettable.

"Doctor, don't patronize me—you know." She stared into his eyes.

"I know what?" The doctor wanted to hear Nicole admit to her second life.

"You know that I'm the left handed-serial killer!" she snapped as she raised the large shiny blade to his face.

The doctor's eyes grew wide as he rolled back in his chair. "Nicole, let me get you some help." He picked up the handset.

"Put it down! Doctor Blair." She pushed the button on the phone with the tip of the knife and the line went dead. Niki knew she had to get rid of him and quick.

"Let me get you some help. There's still hope," he repeated as he held the phone, staring at the knife. He knew Linda was gone for the rest of the day and he wasn't expecting anyone else. No one was able to hear or help him.

She yelled, "You and I both know there's no hope for me. I have been killing for a few years. But I have only killed the people who have hurt me in some way," she said, trying to justify her actions to the good doctor.

"I understand, but what about Wanda Brent?" The doctor grasped for an out. "On the tape, you said you were planning to kill her. Who is she?" he asked. "What has she done to you?"

Niki, thinking she had nothing to lose, began to divulge the truth. *It's not that he'll be able to tell anyone anyway. I have plans to shut him up,* she thought to herself. "Do you remember when I told you that my mother was killed in an airplane crash?"

"Of course I do Nicole," Doctor Blair said as he discreetly looked around the room for an escape route.

"The pilot killed my mother so I'm going to kill his wife and who knows, maybe the voices will go away." She ran her finger up and down the sharp object and inadvertently cut herself.

She looked at the blood then at the doctor who was still holding the phone in his hand.

"Niki, this is sick thinking." He frowned. "The only way to rid yourself of these voices is by taking your medication. Your mind is the most powerful mechanism in your body. It's like a car—it cannot function without the motor." He tried to reason with her. "A car needs gasoline and oil to help it run. You have to take your medication to help you think logically. Let me get you some help," he repeated as he began to speed dial 911. "Turn yourself in before it's too late."

"No, I can't!" she screamed, then looked at the doctor with a smirk. "Nobody can help me, Doctor Blair. Put down that fucking phone!—please." Her voice escalated like a sound of a wild beast, and in an instant, it purred like a pussycat. Her eyes pierced the doctor. It was time to get rid of him. "Nobody can help me," she repeated. I can't turn myself in."

As she moved closer to the doctor, he placed the phone back in the cradle and spoke softly, hoping to ease the hostility that raged inside his patient. "This can all be over if you turn yourself in." Niki wasn't listening. The doctor began to realize that trying to persuade her to put the knife down or give up her plan for revenge was as hard as asking her to swim the Pacific Ocean. It wasn't happening. "It's never too late." He spoke softly but firmly. Doctor Blair searched for a vulnerable moment to make his move, hoping to reach a weak spot so he could possibly grab the knife. He knew that if he didn't get the knife soon he would be a dead man.

"There's always help." He looked at her with sincere eyes. "I told you that you could trust me and you can." He slowly stood and extended his arms, trying to persuade Nicole to turn herself in. The shadow of his baldhead and short body reflected on the wall. "Come on, let me help you," he said talking to her as if she was a child.

For a fraction of a second, Nicole let her guard down, thinking that the doctor might possibly help her. She wanted help and wanted to be normal. She slowly lowered her arms to the sides of her body. She stood still and quiet wondering if she was doing the right thing. Dr. Blair slowly walked up to her and reached for the knife. The look in her eyes quickly dissipated from fierce and rage to calm and poised as she stood staring hopeless at the doctor. The doctor thought he had won until Niki saw the flicker in his eyes, reminding her that he couldn't be trusted. He hurt her by betraying her trust and now he had to pay. With his hand about to touch the handle of the knife, she raised her hand quickly jabbing the shiny knife in the doctor's chest, then slid the knife across his neck from ear to ear. He staggered, reaching for his throat as blood filled his hands, and he fell hard to the floor. He looked at Nicole in disbelief as she took the knife and stood over him. He lay helpless on the floor, his eyes wide open—then they closed.

She repeated, "Sorry, Doctor Blair, I couldn't let you tell." She stepped over the doctor and placed a set of airplane wings next to his body. She picked up her disguise, and seized the tapes and her files from the file cabinet and placed them in her purse. "Now, if you will excuse me, Doctor," she said in a heartless tone, "I have an engagement to attend." She strutted out of his office, sure that nothing or no one would hinder her on this fearless quest. Murder was usually enormously gratifying at that moment, but tremendous remorse always followed.

As she drove to the hotel to change clothes for the NAACP awards, she tried to convince herself that the doctor deserved what she did to him. "I told him not to tell, but he didn't listen. He was going to tell." She repeated, "He was going to tell." Remorse was beginning to settle in. She wept all the way to the hotel.

Twenty-Two

Dusk slowly crept upon Wanda Brent as she drove into the Houston city limits. The wind was as soft as silk and soft jazz floated from the speakers. She was relaxed and happy. Brittany slept with her head resting against the car window. *If only life could stay as calm and peaceful as it is right now on this nice Friday evening.* The sound of the phone ringing interrupted her sweet thoughts. "Brittany, answer my cell phone."

Brittany squirmed awake and reached for the phone. "Hello." Suddenly she was smiling broadly. "Hi, Uncle Troy!" She sat straight in her seat.

"Hello, my dear. How is my favorite niece?"

"I'm doing fine."

"Where are you? Ya'll should have been here fifteen minutes ago."

She looked around as she saw familiar scenery. "We're here, we just made it."

"Good. Let me speak to your mom for a minute."

Brittany handed her mother the phone.

"Hey, what's up, Troy?" she said, not taking her eyes off the road.

"What's going on? I'm just checking to see where you are. The Awards will be starting in forty-five minutes."

She looked at the clock on the dashboard. "I won't be late. I'm only five minutes away. I'm so excited about receiving this award on Lacy's behalf."

"My brother is well overdue for this humanitarian award. He was a damn good pilot," Troy said proudly.

"Being the first black airline pilot for Jet Away was quite

an accomplishment." A sad smile clouded her face as she thought of her husband. We're pulling into the parking lot of the Radisson now."

"Good. I'll meet you at the front entrance."

Wanda parked her car and she and Brittany got out and walked toward the building. Troy stood next to the pedestal as they approached him.

"How is my favorite sister-in-law?" Troy asked as Wanda and Brittany joined him.

"I'm fine," Wanda answered as they hugged.

He kissed Brittany on the cheek then placed his arms around her and Wanda. The door attendant held the door open and the trio walked into the elaborate hotel.

The ambiance in the lobby delivered a taste of elegance. The room exhibited beautiful pastel blue and white tablecloths on round tables, and candles encased in crystal cut glass rested in the middle of each table. The long blue and white banner draped from the wall read, 'NAACP Awards.' The eight-piece band played soft jazz music while approximately two hundred dignitaries, family, and friends mingled.

Brittany walked over to the oversized flowerpot in the lobby, admiring the beautiful flowers and the gigantic replicas of Picasso's paintings on the wall.

As they walked toward the bar, Troy told Wanda, "They let me see the plaque and it's nice. They left off the years as you requested."

"It doesn't matter now. She knows."

"What!"

"I can't talk right now, we'll talk later."

He nodded. "Oh, I almost forgot... last month a lady called me at home wanting to know if she'd reached Lacy Brent's residence. She was trying to get in touch with you."

"With me?" she asked, surprised that someone would call Troy to locate her. "What did she want?"

"She asked if you still lived in Dallas or did you move back to Houston."

"I told her that Lacy was my brother and that you were in Dallas. That's when she started pressuring me for more information."

"How did she sound?"

"She had a raspy voice. She was very inquisitive."

"Did she say who she was?"

"No, but she started asking a hundred questions, personal questions like where you work, what kind of car you drive, how were you handling your husband's death—"

"How was I handling my husband's death?" Wanda interrupted, looking surprised.

"Yes, that's when it got a little strange so I started asking why she needed that information and she quickly hung up."

"That's strange."

A young man approached Wanda and Troy, interrupting their conversation.

"Evan Rivers!" She grabbed his arm and hugged him. "You made it, I'm so happy to see you."

Evan's black eyes were as dark as the night. His well-groomed hair was short and wavy. He sported a black and gray tuxedo. "I wouldn't have missed this for the world." Standing next to Evan were his wife Kaley, and son Gavin.

"Kaley, you look gorgeous as ever," Wanda said, turning her attention to Evan's wife.

She hugged Wanda and kissed her on the cheek. "Thank you and you look stunning as ever."

Wanda wore an elegant white chiffon sleeveless dress, which flared with ruffles at the hem. Her hair was neatly coiffed in a bun with a couple of curly strands framing her face. Brittany walked over, picked up Gavin, and swung him around.

"I want you to meet my brother-in-law, Troy," Wanda said, then turned to Troy. As Evan extended his hand, Troy frowned and walked away. Wanda apologized. "I am so sorry. He still has issues with Tia's death, our friendship, and this whole ordeal."

"That's OK. I don't expect everybody to forgive me, but as long as I know you have, I'm OK," he said as he watched Troy walk away.

Wanda called out after Troy but he ignored her. "I've arranged to have all of us sit at the same table. I'll see if I can change it."

"No, don't do that," Evan said. "We're going to sit in our

own seats; I don't care if they are next to Troy. We can't keep running away. This situation has haunted me for years, people staring and whispering behind my back. We can't go to the store without someone staring and pointing. But I understand."

"I'm OK with it if you are," Wanda said as she picked up Gavin. "Come on, I'll show you to your seats."

"We've already been to our table," said Kaley. "Evan is right, we can't keep running away."

As they walked toward the family table, Wanda looked at Troy, who was still scowling. *He'll get over it*, she thought.

****

Reverend Gabriel Winters sat at the table with his wife Thelma and his daughters Sky and Sheila. His outstanding work with the homeless had resulted in him receiving an award. He drove a mini bus to pick up the homeless from the shelters on Sundays and cooked breakfast and lunch for them each Sunday. He was responsible for getting about a hundred people off the street and into jobs and houses.

He turned to his family and said, "Thank you for being here to share this great honor with me tonight."

"Daddy, you don't need to thank us for coming. We wanted to be here for you. You mean so much to us," Sky said as she looked at her sister and mother, who nodded in agreement.

"Congratulation Honey. You have done a wonderful job with the homeless," Thelma said, obviously proud of her husband.

"I can't take full credit. You have always been in my corner," he answered as he touched her softly on the hand. "You've been there preparing meals and offering your time. I couldn't have done it without you." He pecked her on the lips.

"Enough, you two, you're making me teary-eyed," Sheila said.

Sky looked past her mother and saw Niki walking through the door. She was stunning in her black, strapless, sequined dress. She glanced around the crowded room, looking for Sky and her family.

Sky stood and waved her hand until she caught Niki's attention. Niki returned the wave and headed to the table. She put Doctor Blair's murder out of her mind.

"I'm sorry I'm late," she said as she pulled out her chair.

"I was about to give up on you," Sky said, as she scooted her chair over, making room for Niki. "They haven't started yet."

"I had a few errands to run."

"Niki, you look beautiful," Thelma told her.

"Thank you, Mrs. Winters. You look glamorous yourself." She turned to Sky, "Where's David?"

"He couldn't make it. Something unexpected came up at the police station."

Niki sat quietly wondering if she should be worried. *Is his police business pertaining to me?*

Niki's thoughts scattered when she saw Sheila hand Evan his napkin that had fallen on the floor. "I believe this is yours," Sheila said to Evan who was sitting at the next table.

"Thank you," Evan said, as he flashed a smile.

Reverend Winters leaned over and whispered to his wife, "He's the young man who killed a little girl in that car accident nearly eleven years ago."

"What? How do you know?" she asked.

"They were in the newspaper. I remember their faces. He's a new member of our church. I can't remember his name."

"I thought his face looked familiar," Mrs. Winters said as she tried not to stare.

"Daddy, it's impolite to whisper at the table, unless you're going to tell everyone," Sky said teasingly.

Reverend Winters leaned over the table. "I was just telling your mother that the young man at the next table is the person who went to prison for driving drunk and killing a little girl. He was only a teenager at the time."

"That's so sad," Thelma said. "Think of the guilt he must be living with."

"I don't know about guilt, but the young man and the dead girl's mother have become very close friends. Now that's what I call a real Christian; she's the one that should have been honored."

"There is no way I would ever forgive someone for killing my child. No way," Niki said emphatically, hiding her anger behind a forced smile.

Reverend Winters got up, walked over to the Brent's table, and introduced himself to Evan. "I just want to tell you that I think this is a unique and wonderful situation. You truly exemplify what being a Christian is really all about."

Evan reached for the preacher's hand. "Thank you Rev. Winters, I appreciate hearing that from my pastor. I've been hurting ever since the accident."

"Everybody deserves a second chance," said Reverend Winters.

"Thank you. This is my wife and son." He gestured, "And Mrs. Wanda Brent, Brittany and her brother-in-law, Troy."

Reverend Winters shook each of their hands, including Gavin's. He turned to Wanda, "Ms. Brent, "You're a remarkable woman. God bless you."

He looked at Evan. "Stop by my study sometime so we can talk."

"Y-eah, yeah, I sure will." Evan smiled as Reverend Winters shook his hand again and returned to his table. Evan was surprised that Reverend Winters would show interest in him, but was very grateful.

Troy turned his back, trying to ignore the heartfelt meeting. He didn't want to admit it, but he was sorry for acting like a jerk earlier. Suddenly he stood and offered his hand to Evan. "This is very hard for me, but I told Wanda I would at least try. I apologize. I just don't want my sister-in-law hurt again. But if she has faith in you, I guess I can try."

Evan took Troy's hand. "Man, this means so much to me, you can't even imagine. I haven't touched a drink since that night. I lecture on drunk driving to teenagers in high school and I speak at AA meetings once a month."

"That's great," Troy said as the two men sat attempting to be acquainted.

Wanda and Kaley looked at each other and smiled.

The orchestra lowered the volume of the music and the honorees began walking toward the platform. "That's my cue," Wanda said, looking at the two men, glad they were reconciling.

"You go on, we'll be here cheering for you," Evan said softly.

"Are you sure?" Wanda asked. She feared the tension between Troy and Evan might flare up again.

Seeing Wanda's hesitation, Troy said, "Girl, go on, we'll

be OK."

She winked and smiled, then proudly walked away satisfied that Troy would behave himself.

A man in his late fifties stood at the podium and began speaking. "Welcome to our Fifteenth Annual NAACP Awards, presented to those who have made outstanding contributions to the Houston community. Without further delay, our first honoree is a woman who has been successful in cleaning up Rosewood Street. She started a treatment center for drug addicts. The center has grown from a ten-bed to a fifty-bed facility and has proven to be ninety-percent successful in keeping drug addicts clean. She also prepares lunch for thirty senior citizens Monday through Friday. Let's welcome Gladys Rodgers."

Wanda watched four honorees cross the stage and accept awards before the emcee called her husband's name.

"Our next honoree spent ten years in the United States Air Force, flying fighter jets, before he joined Jet Away Airways, becoming the first pilot to break the racial barrier. He was never looked at just being a black pilot, but as a great pilot, because of his professionalism and kind heart. Captain Lacy Brent perished in a plane crash."

Niki swallowed the lump in her throat, "Lacy Brent—is that who he just said."

Sky nodded yes, as she continued to listen to the emcee.

He continued, "He perished along with two hundred passengers, when the plane hit wind shears while attempting to land here in Houston."

A silent scream raged inside as Niki thought, *That's right and one of those 200 passengers was my mother,* she wanted to stand and shout.

"He was a proud man who loved to fly. His death was a great loss for all of us."

What about my mother, she was a great loss to me, Niki screamed from inside. She looked on stage for Wanda. *She's here; I can't believe this,* she thought as resentment poisoned the air. Niki took a gulp of water from the crystal glass and began to choke.

"Are you all right?" Sky asked, patting Niki on the back.

"I'm OK," she said as she stared at the women on stage

wondering which heifer was Wanda Brent. She clenched her jaws, trying to control the anger that electrified her body.

The emcee introduced Wanda Brent, "His wife, Wanda, is here to accept the award on his behalf." As the emcee extended his hand and turned the podium over to Wanda, the room erupted with a loud applause. The attention at the table had switched from Wanda to Niki, as Mrs. Winters watched Niki who was now standing ready to attack, but thought better of it and took her seat. *My mother should be standing there, not her,* she thought.

When the crowd quieted, Wanda began to speak. "It is an honor to receive this award on behalf of my late husband, Captain Lacy Brent."

"I'll have the opportunity after the ceremony," Niki mumbled, not realizing that vengeance was flashing from her eyes. "Wanda Brent, you've been under my nose all this time. Yes, you and I will meet tonight," she continued to mumble. "You're going to pay for what your husband did to me."

Mrs. Winters heard the mumbling and glanced across the table. "Niki your lip," she pointed. "It's bleeding."

Niki, unaware she had bitten her lip, dabbed it with the cloth napkin, hoping her malice wasn't penetrating the mask she'd carefully constructed. She didn't know how long this facade would last. She was ready to jump over the table and attack, but the voice in her head was telling her not to, just yet.

Sky looked around, wondering what caused Niki to be so upset. Her peach color skin had turned white as if a vampire had sucked all of the blood from her.

"Niki, what's the matter?" Sky whispered, seeing her face and sensing that something was truly upsetting her friend.

Trying to gain her composure, she said, "I'm fine, really." She was far from fine; her hands shook uncontrollably under the table. "It's nothing," she said seething because there stood Wanda in her elegant gown and her mother was dead.

"Do you know her?" Sky asked as she watched Wanda standing at the podium.

"No, I don't," said Niki, as she continued to focus on Wanda.

Wanda Brent continued to speak. "I know he's looking down and getting a big kick out of this." She lowered her head as a tear dropped. "I said I wasn't going to cry." She smiled then continued her acceptance speech. "He truly had a passion for flying and I know he died doing what he loved best."

You don't know what I'm going through, Mrs. Brent. I have been through pure hell and all because of your husband. You're going to pay, you're going to pay, Niki thought. Revenge blazed in her eyes, her lips trembled, and her heart beat forcefully against her ribcage as she continued to listen.

"I want to thank everyone who had a part in seeing that Lacy was honored with this prestigious award. God bless every one of you. I want to say a special thank you to Troy, Lacy's brother, and my daughter, Brittany." As she held up the plaque, a single tear escaped again and slid down her cheek. "I also want to acknowledge my friend Evan Rivers, and his family." Wanda stared directly at her table. "Keep up the good work." She returned to her seat after delivering a heartfelt message.

You'd think she'd just received an Oscar, Niki thought bitterly as Wanda sat.

Every word Wanda had spoken fueled Niki's rage. Finally, she couldn't take it any longer. She slammed her fist on the table, knocking over a glass of water. She grabbed the napkin from her lap and began dabbing up the water.

People stared at the commotion—and at Niki.

"Are you OK?" Mrs. Winters asked, as she noticed Niki's discomfort and saw the blatant anger in her eyes.

"Yes," Niki answered. Remembering what Doctor Blair had told her—take her medication and the voices would go away—she pulled a bottle out of her purse and popped a pill in her mouth.

Reverend Winters was the last honoree to accept his award and there were several acknowledgements from sponsors. Then the ceremony ended.

While everyone stood around talking, Niki excused herself and wandered off in pursuit of Wanda. She spotted her talking to two other women in a corner. She nonchalantly strolled toward Wanda and stood nearby to eavesdrop on her conversation. She heard Wanda tell the ladies she volunteers at the Boys and Girls Club in Plano. Niki's heart lightened as she realized Plano was just a few miles from her. *I'll just have to pay Wanda Brent a visit when I get back to Dallas.* She turned to Wanda as the ladies walked off.

"Mrs. Brent, how are you?" She spoke quickly. "I'm Nicole Salem and I just wanted to say, I really admired your husband's courage." She cringed inside at the lie. She knew she would attack Wanda and very soon.

Wanda smiled. "Thank you, Nicole, and please call me Wanda." She turned to her daughter. "This is my daughter, Brittany."

"Hi," Brittany said, smiling and locking arms with her mother. Brittany's wavy hair hung past her shoulders as her teased bangs hid her widow's peak, and her birthmark hidden by the makeup.

"Did I hear you say that you work for the Boys and Girls Club?" Niki asked.

"Actually, I volunteer at the club twice a week."

Troy walked over to their small group. "Hello."

"Nicole, this is my brother-in-law, Troy Brent," Wanda said, introducing the newest member of their group.

"Hi," Niki said, hating him for interrupting the moment. "Troy, this is Nicole Salem."

He extended his hand. "Nice to meet you, Nicole," he said, before turning to Wanda. "Are you ready?"

"Yes, it's been an emotional day. I'm a little tired. I need to rest before we make the trip back to Dallas tomorrow."

"It was nice meeting you, Nicole," Wanda said, shaking her hand.

"And you as well." Niki forced a smile because she knew they would meet again. She watched with hatred in her eyes as they walked away, then she followed behind them with an intense gaze as they walked to their cars.

"Evan really isn't a bad person. He's a likeable guy," said Troy.

"I told you. He got caught up with the wrong crowd and it's very unfortunate that Tia had to die. I will never forget he killed her but I will never condemn him again. He has hurt long enough and so have I," she said as Troy opened her car door.

Niki stood eyeing Wanda as she and Brittany got into her Mercedes then she carefully wrote down the license plate number.

Twenty-Three

*D*avid spent part of his shift working with the decoys until late Friday night. As he finished up with them he got a hunch, "This is a long shot," he said to the lady cops. "But get with Donna Morris find out what agent made Leslie Turner's reservation."

"Got it," said the lady cop as she wrote in her notepad.

"Also, I need you to pull Ms. Stone's phone records," He said as he walked around the office with his arms folded. "I need to know the last person she talked with."

"It's the weekend so we probably won't have that information until Monday," spoke the other officer.

"Monday's fine." David said. "And thanks for staying late. I owe both of you." They both stood and walked out the door.

David looked at his watch realizing there was nothing else he could do at one in the morning until he had the surveillance tape. He drove home, placed the key in the lock, and noticed the door was already unlocked. He walked around his apartment with his gun drawn. He checked the patio door and it was locked. He walked into his bedroom surprised to find it in disarray. "What the…" David shouted to himself. "Who was in my apartment and better yet—why?" He picked up the phone sat it on his nightstand and placed the cord back in the phone jack. He picked up the papers and placed it on the once neatly made bed that was now in shambles. He took out his cell phone and called the station within minutes an officer came and dusted for fingerprints. He told David he would have some results for him in a couple of days then left. David notified the apartment and they advised him that someone would be out early in the morning to change the lock.

David lay asleep with one eye opened and his gun on the nightstand. He hadn't rested any that night and got up early to let the maintenance man in, within thirty minutes David had received his new keys and was on the road to Houston to see if he could speed up the process. He was sorry he couldn't make it last night to see Sky's father honored. *She'll have to get used to this kind of thing if she's going to be my wife,* he thought. Five hours later, he pulled up at a Houston wig shop, put the car in park, and followed a few ladies inside. In the past eight months, David had visited thirty wig shops.

"May I help you?" asked the store clerk. There were customers sitting in chairs trying on different wigs and hair stylists styling each customer's wig to their own liking.

David pulled out a surveillance picture of the serial killer, "Have you seen this woman before?" He asked the oriental lady standing behind the counter.

"No, I haven't," answered the clerk as she glanced at the picture. "You buy wig?" She asked.

He showed the clerk the hair strands. "Do you have a wig this color?"

The store clerk laughed. "We have many wigs that color— look around," she said. "We have the falls, which are the long wigs." She pointed. "We have the feathered look, the French cut, the sassy look, there's one with bangs." She continued to point.

"What type is this one?" he asked walking over to the shelf.

"That one is the feathered look—you like?"

He took the wig from the white Styrofoam mannequin and began measuring the length of its hair, which was exactly the same. He felt the texture of the hair.

"What type of hair is this?"

"This is synthetic hair," said the lady feeling the texture. She took a wig from the next shelf, "Now, this one is human hair." David felt the texture.

"Human hair huh, OK, thank you." He pulled a few strands from both wigs and walked out the door.

Fifteen minutes later, he pulled up at the police department. Things weren't moving any faster now with David at the Houston Crime Lab. He walked down to the lab to see if they could help move things along.

"Hey, Detective Hall, how are you?" said Rhonda.

"Tired, disgusted, and impatient," David snapped. Then feeling guilty for taking out his frustration on the innocent clerk, he apologized. "I'm sorry, Rhonda, it's not your fault the lab is so slow. How are you today?"

"I'm doing well." She smiled, and then suddenly remembered that a doctor had called looking for him. "Did you ever get in touch with that doctor who was trying to reach you Thursday night?"

"What doctor?" David asked, giving her his full attention.

She searched her message pad and reported, "Doctor Hank Blair, the therapist that works downtown. He called here asking for you, and I gave him the number to the Police Department in Dallas. He said he had some information regarding the left-handed serial killer."

"He has what!" He moved closer to Rhonda.

"He said he had some important information about the left-handed serial killer that would benefit you."

"I didn't get the message," he said. "Did he say what it was?"

"No, he didn't." She sat down at the desk and looked in the computer. I gave him these two numbers," she said as she looked up at him for confirmation, turning the computer screen toward him.

"The top one is Dallas PD and the bottom number is my home phone, but no one called. When did you say it was?"

David remembered the phone ringing and the light blinking on the answering machine when he left the house Friday morning, but when he tried to retrieve the messages from work they weren't there.

"Whoever broke into my apartment must have listened to my messages and deleted them." He spoke with great concern.

"What?" Rhonda asked.

"Someone knew the doctor called me. But who?" he asked. "Do you have the doctor's number?"

"No I don't, but we can definitely find out." She dialed a few numbers.

"What city, please?" the operator asked from the speaker phone.

"Yes, may I have the phone number for a Doctor Hank Blair located downtown, please?" Rhonda jotted down the number, dialed it, and handed the phone to David.

He would soon know the identity of the serial killer.

A man answered, "Doctor Blair's office."

"Yes, this is Detective Hall, may I speak to the doctor? It's urgent."

"Hey, Detective, this is Detective Eddie Smith. I'm sorry but you won't be speaking to him today, or any other day."

"What do you mean, Smith?" David asked, knowing Detective Smith despised him because the Captain had taken the serial killer case away from him and gave it to David.

"He's lying here dead as a doorknob in a pool of blood."

"He's dead!" David repeated as he rubbed his head in frustration.

"I didn't realize you were in town. Come on over, you need to see this," he said, putting aside their differences.

"Dammit! I'm on my way."

"His office is on Overstreet, 609."

He handed the phone to Rhonda and hurried out the door, forgetting about the surveillance tape. He rushed to his car and made the twenty-five minute drive in fifteen. *Who could have killed him? Was it someone he was seeing? Was it the serial-killer?* Questions tumbled in his mind as he sped down the highway. Putting the car abruptly into park, David jumped out, flashed his badge at the officers standing by the front door, and walked inside the office.

"Hey, Hall," Smith greeted him. "Looks like the trail of the serial killer brought you home."

"Maybe. What happened?"

"We got a call from his receptionist a few hours ago." He shook his head. "She found him lying on his back." He looked over at her. "We can't get any information from her. She's too distraught."

David walked over and flashed his badge at a short

brunette woman in her early sixties sitting at her desk with her head in her hands.

"Hi, I'm Detective Hall. May I ask you a few questions?" he asked gently.

"Yes," she said, trying to control the tears as she held the tissue to her eyes.

"What's your name?"

"Linda," she sniffed. "Linda Wellington."

"Did you see anything or hear anything, Ms. Wellington?"

"No, I left early yesterday. I stopped by this afternoon to catch up on some filing and found him lying in his office." She pointed to the closed door.

"Is the doctor married?" David asked.

"Yes," she said, distracted by investigators rushing in with cameras and forensics kits. "But Mrs. Blair is out of town for the weekend." Her eyes filled with tears.

"We'll notify her," David said. "May I see the doctor's files?" He walked over to the file cabinet.

She stood, took a set of keys from the desk, and followed him to the cabinet. Her hand shook so badly she had trouble getting the drawer unlocked. Her insides churned.

"May I?" David asked, reaching for the keys. His eyes twitched, "Um, it's already unlocked." In seconds, he was flipping through each file. "How many patients was the doctor seeing?" he asked as he meticulously read each name.

"I don't know," she yelled. "They've already asked me these questions." She threw her hands up in the air out of frustration. "Twenty-three or twenty-five, maybe. I can't remember right now."

"I know it's hard," he said. "Do you know anyone who might want to kill the doctor? Did he have any enemies?"

Those acrimonious words hit hard. She felt faint and quickly walked back to her desk and sat down. "No, I don't," she whimpered as she took a sip of water from the paper cup on her desk. "I knew all of his patients, except the lady who was coming in to see him on yesterday at 2 o'clock. I told the doctor her voice sounded familiar."

David walked over to her desk and grabbed the appointment book. He ran his finger down the page, Diamond

O'Connell at two. He flipped through the pages, checking for previous visits. "Had the doctor seen Ms. O'Connell before?"

"No, she was a new patient and was adamant about seeing the doctor yesterday."

"What time did you leave?"

"It was almost noon. His eleven o'clock appointment was leaving and they normally leave five minutes before the hour. He gives each of them 55 minutes. He told me I could leave for the day. I knew I shouldn't have left him alone," she said as she pulled another Kleenex from the box. "Oh my God, who could have been so cruel?"

Then the forensics officer brought David a pair of airplane wings in a plastic evidence bag.

"The left-handed serial killer," David said heavily, hitting the desk with his fist. *She's back and forth between Dallas and Houston. But why?*

"Why would she kill the doctor?" Linda asked.

"Did you know he was trying to contact me the other night?"

She shook her head, no.

"He said it was pertaining to the serial killer. It had to be someone he was seeing."

"I'm sorry, Detective, but I really don't know who it could be."

"If you think of anything, big or small, call me," he said as he handed her his business card. "This number rings at my desk."

"OK," she said as she placed the card in her purse without looking at it as a continuous flow of tears streamed down her cheeks.

"I'll need your home phone number if you don't mind."

"Sure." She picked up a pencil and slowly scribbled her number on the notepad.

"Thank you. You've been a big help." David gently patted her on the back. "You're free to leave. Would you like one of the officers to drive you home?"

She shook her head, no. "I think I can manage." She picked up her purse and walked out the door.

David walked into the doctor's office, lifted the sheet, and looked at the doctor. *What were you trying to tell me—who is she?*

He replaced the sheet over the doctor, and signaled for the coroner to take the body. Eerie echoes whispered in his ear. *She's looking and laughing at you and you can't see her. She's smooth as an eel.* The voice told him.

He walked back into the lobby and dialed the phone number next to Diamond's name; the number was to a Pizza Hut.

He was told that Diamond O'Connell wasn't employed there. How clever he thought then slammed the phone down as he gathered the doctor's files and audio tapes, and headed for his car.

"Thank you, Detective Smith, I'll see you back at the station."

He wondered again about the mysterious missing message. *Who was in my apartment? How?* He chewed his bottom lip. Twenty minutes later, he pulled into the garage parking lot of the Houston Police Department and took the elevator to the third floor. As he walked past the picture window, he saw technicians sitting at tables looking through microscopes. He walked into the room and handed the technician the hair strands from the wig shop so they could compare them with the already collected samples. Then he proceeded to the video room, where the technician met him at the door and escorted him inside. "Hello, Detective Hall," Kyle said.

"Hey, Kyle." David shut the door. "I wasn't sure if you'd still be here," he said.

"They have me working around the clock," Kyle answered, as he popped in the surveillance tape and pulled out a chair for the detective. "Rhonda mentioned that you ran out of here fast like a rocket taking off into space, something about a doctor being murdered." He adjusted the picture.

"Yes, a doctor was murdered and it has something to do with this woman." He touched the screen as he took his seat, eyeing the figure of the killer.

"I was able to get a better view of her face. What do you think?" he asked, proud of his work.

Still studying the picture, David said, "It's definitely better, but that damn baseball cap is partially covering her eyes." He stood and walked over to the phone and began dialing. "I'm going to ask CNN to air it on their late news edition tonight."

"CNN news desk, this is Steven how can I help you?" the

male voice came from the speakerphone.

"Hello, this is Detective Hall from the Houston Police Department. May I speak to Amy Tarnasky?"

"I'm sorry, Detective, she's gone for the evening. Can I help you with something?"

"Yes, I have a surveillance tape of the left-handed serial killer. Amy's been working with me on the case. It's critical that the tape is aired as soon as possible."

"Can you download it and send it to my e-mail?"

Kyle looked at David and nodded yes.

"We sure can," David quickly answered.

"Production won't be done with it until late tonight. It won't start airing until early tomorrow morning around seven. Is that OK?"

"Yes, perfect. What is your e-mail address?"

"sqmajors@cnn.com."

David jotted down the address. "Thank you, Steven, we'll get this out to you ASAP and tell Amy that I'll be in touch."

"You bet. Have a good day, Detective." The call disconnected.

"Yes!" David shouted, thrusting his right fist into the air. "Kyle, make it happen. She must be stopped."

"You got it, Detective."

David picked up the tape and left the room headed to his parents' house for the evening, before driving back to Dallas later that night. He talked to Sky briefly who was out with her mother.

****

After a few restful hours with the family and several failed attempts by them to persuade David to stay and leave for Dallas early Sunday morning, David drove back around midnight. He was anxious to get through the files he had retrieved from the doctor's office. He arrived back at the office after four in the morning. He knew that once CNN had aired the tape things would get crazy around the station.

"Hey, Detective Hall," one of the other detectives said when he saw David enter the police station. "I heard you found another body in Houston. Same MO?"

"Hey," David replied as he dropped the crate of files on

his desk. "Yes and yes. But I did get one break—the lab got the taped cleared up. CNN will run it on the morning news and ask for the public's help in identifying the woman."

"Oh boy! Watch the switchboard light up then. Guess I'd better go home and get some shuteye. It's going to be a long day. You know how all the would-be detectives crawl out of everywhere when we put out that kind of information."

"Yeah," David said, "that's why I stopped by tonight. I wanted to give everybody a heads-up for this morning. As soon as I check my messages, I'm outta here, too. I just got back from Houston and I will never do that again."

"Do what?"

"Drive to Houston and back in the same day."

"I'm beat." He sat down quickly checking his messages then got up, pushed his chair under his desk, and headed for the door.

"I'll see you in a couple of hours." He told the detective.

"OK, drive safe."

Twenty-Four

*D*avid had just snuggled under his cover good when the alarm clock sounded at 8:30 a.m. on Sunday. He knew he'd better get to the station even if he only had three hours of sleep. Once CNN air that tape, the station would start hopping.

He grabbed a quick shower, thought about fixing breakfast, and decided he'd grab something on the way to work. *One good thing about being up this early is I shouldn't have to wait forever in line at one of those drive-through places,* he thought as he grabbed his jacket, locked the door, and headed for his car.

As soon as he walked into the station, it was evident that the tape had aired. Phones were ringing everywhere. David put his breakfast sandwich on his desk, shrugged out of his jacket, and dropped into his chair. Just as he was about to take a bite out of the egg, double bacon, and cheese sandwich, his phone rang. "Darn, guess I should have eaten at home," he mumbled, reaching for the phone. Callers continued to swamp the switchboard all morning. Two hours after answering calls David finally found time to eat his very cold breakfast. He took the first file from the crate and meticulously went through the files. "Nothing out of the ordinary here—marriage problems." He slipped in the patient's audio tape. He pulled out another file and slipped in another tape. He had also simultaneously popped in the video tape of the serial killer. As he watched the tape he paused, fast-forwarded, and rewound it, trying to identify more of the woman's features. There was something familiar about the mysterious woman. *Are you Diamond O'Connell?* He thought.

He ran her name in the system and two names popped up from Houston. One was a forty-eight-year-old lady. The other one had been dead for five years. He jotted down the information on both then picked up the telephone. "Hey, Detective Smith, this is Hall. Will you do me a favor?"

"Sure, what do you need?" he asked, glad to be part of the investigation.

"Will you check out these two people, same name—Diamond O'Connell? One is possibly deceased. Get back with it as soon as possible—Oh while you're at it get me some information on Nicole Salem she lived in Houston and moved to Dallas a couple of years ago. Nothing came up when I check initially. But I need to dig a little further."

"OK, I'll get back to you. Goodbye."

"Goodbye." David went back to studying each file.

"Hall, I have thirty messages from people who said they know the killer," the police clerk interrupted.

"Thanks." David took the names, scanned each of them, and then added them to a list already piling up on his desk.

After five hours of working, David stopped only long enough to grab something to eat from the vending machine. He thought about calling Sky, but she didn't expect to get back until late Sunday night. The calls were no longer coming into the station as fast; the other detectives were able to handle them, so he went back to the tapes. At 10 p.m., he decided he'd had enough for one day. He tried to call Sky. He got her voicemail. Maybe he would stay one more hour. "Hey, baby, I'll be leaving the station in another hour, headed home, call me when you get in so I'll know you made it back safely from Houston."

After an hour he headed home, his mind reverted to the video. There was something about the woman in that picture. Her body—he knew he'd seen that body, but where? He let himself into his apartment, searching the refrigerator for something quick to eat, and headed for bed. He'd only slept seventeen hours out of the last forty-eight. He was exhausted and crashed out.

****

Aunt Cindy reached for the remote and turned on the television to catch the late edition of the Sunday night news. Once again, the nurses had ignored Sky's request to keep her aunt from watching the news. When the picture of the left-handed serial killer appeared on the screen, Aunt Cindy began to choke. "She was here with Sky! I know that's her. She can't fool me with that wig on. She's the devil!" Aunt Cindy said wildly, before calling for the nurse. "Nurse, I got to get out of here, Nurse," she called as she pressed the call button and started to crawl out of bed. "I can see it in her eyes."

"Miss Winters, what's the problem?" the nurse asked, as she rushed into Aunt Cindy's room. "It's almost midnight. What are you still doing up?" The nurse turned off the television, straightened the covers and tucked Aunt Cindy back into bed.

Aunt Cindy wasn't about to give up that easily. "I got to get out of here. My daughter is in trouble." She attempted to get out of bed again but the nurse stopped her.

"Miss Winters, you don't have a daughter," the nurse told her.

"Yes, I do! Get me out of here," she insisted. Her body shook like a cocoon ready to open and let out a butterfly.

"Miss Winters, let me get you something to help you sleep. I'll be right back." The nurse left and headed for the medicine cabinet.

"I don't need anything to sleep," she screamed. "I need to get out of here before it's too late." Aunt Cindy slowly moved out of bed, carefully walked to the closet, and grabbed her coat. "People think I'm crazy but they are fools," she said as she placed her arm in the sleeve of the coat just as the nurse returned.

"Miss Winters, where are you going?" the nurse asked politely, as she took off Aunt Cindy's coat, which she didn't need in eighty degree weather, and hung it back in the closet. "Come back to bed and in the morning I'll let you talk to your daughter." She winked at the head nurse who had just walked into the room to assist her.

"But she's in trouble right now," Aunt Cindy shouted with emphasis then stomped her feet. "I'm not crazy! I have to save her now. Tomorrow will be too late," she insisted, as she jerked her arm away from the nurse.

"Try to get some sleep and we'll call her first thing in the morning," the nurse told her as she handed her a sleeping pill and a glass of water.

"I don't need medication," Aunt Cindy told the nurse, as she reluctantly took the pill, put it in her mouth, and washed it down with a few sips of water. She sat on the edge of the bed as the nurses observed, not leaving until the medicine took effect. "The left hand," Aunt Cindy said, as her words began to slur. "The left hand," she gurgled.

The head nurse looked at her patient's hand. "There's nothing wrong with your hand." She rubbed it. "Now lie down and try to sleep." She pulled back the covers, gently swung Aunt Cindy's legs into the middle of the bed, and tucked in her sluggish body.

"The phone." Aunt Cindy softly spoke then drifted off to sleep. The nurse put the phone in a dresser drawer.

"She's delusional," the head nurse whispered as they left the room. "Poor lady, sometimes she's here and other times she just isn't."

"It's awful having dementia. She loses concentration very easily, poor lady. Yesterday she couldn't remember how to get out of the bathtub; now this," the floor nurse said sadly.

"She thinks someone is after the daughter she doesn't have," the head nurse said. "For some reason she always thinks she has to save her niece or her daughter." She looked back at Aunt Cindy's room. "Watch her. She's slipped away from here before," she said, before heading back to her office.

"She won't get past me. Anyway, that sedative will have her out for the rest of the night."

****

With rain in the forecast, Sky pulled her umbrella from the closet and placed it next to the living room door as she got her things together for the following day. She had returned from her weekend trip to Houston at around midnight and had turned on the television to catch the weather. She didn't pay much attention until she heard the newscaster say, "Up next, do you know this killer?" Curious, she turned around in time to see the killer's face plastered on the screen just as the station went to commercial break. The picture was hazy but Sky thought she saw a slight resemblance to Niki.

Not at all sure about her first impression from the teaser, Sky crossed the room to the television and sat directly in front of it. As the commercial droned on, she thought that she had seen a cap like the one she'd given Niki for Christmas on the woman's head; but again, she wasn't sure.

"It can't be Niki," Sky said as she waited impatiently. "The picture resembles Niki, but it can't be her. Niki's taller than the woman on the screen. Or is she? Oh, it can't be. I'm imagining things. Niki is so sweet and kind, she would never hurt anyone."

When the news returned, Sky concentrated on the woman's picture. Shocked at the resemblance between Niki and the woman, she picked up the phone. The answering machine came on. "Hey, honey, I know you told me you're working late but when you get this message, please give me a call. It's very important. It's Niki." David sound asleep, as if he was in a coma had missed the phone call.

Sky turned off the television and lay on her white satin sheets thinking, a*ll the heartache that Niki's been through she deserves to be happy. It can't be her. It can't! I'm imagining things.* As she drifted off to sleep suspicion spinned around in her head like a whirlpool, she tossed and turned as the images from the newscast relentlessly played in her head. She dreamt that Niki attacked her with a switchblade and left her lying in a pool of blood. The dream seemed so real. She awoke drenched in sweat then sat up and looked around. "It's just an awful nightmare," she said aloud, trying to shake the feeling of impending doom. Sky lay down again, but had trouble falling asleep because she couldn't ignore the eerie resemblance between Niki and the killer. "Niki is right handed," she said as she took a bottle of sleeping pills from the nightstand drawer and popped one in her mouth, then chased it with a drink of water.

The clock flashed 2 a.m. and no call from David. She tried his cell phone, but no answer. She called the home phone again and after the third ring, she hung up. She decided to set a trap for Niki and dialed her number.

"Hello," Niki answered in a groggy voice.

"Hey, Niki, sorry to call so late but can I borrow your

black blouse tomorrow? The one with the white stripes?"

"You're getting to make this a habit calling late at night. What time is it?" she asked, agitated.

"It's two, I'm sorry. I didn't mean to wake you."

"Sure, I'll bring it. I'll be there around seven-forty-five," she said as she cleared the sleep from her throat.

I have a few questions to ask you, when you get here, Sky thought. "Ok thanks, goodnight."

"I have to do something to get her to use her left-hand and if she does—she's the serial killer." Sky told herself as she lay in bed.

When the sleeping pill started to take effect, Sky drifted into a deep sleep—a sleep so deep that she didn't hear her phone ring when David returned her call.

"Hey Sky, I'm returning your call. I see on caller ID. that you've called. My answering machine isn't working, I'll explain later." When Niki threw down the phone, she broke the answering machine.

"I'll call you in the morning before you go to work. Love you."

Twenty-Five

*T*he thick clouds covered the sun as Sky lay lethargically in bed still under the effect of the sleeping pill. Niki rang the doorbell—no answer. Then she beat on door after three minutes Sky slowly walked to the door.

"Here's the blouse," Niki said as she walked into the living room.

"Thank you," Sky reached for the blouse.

"No problem." Niki handed the blouse to Sky with her right hand. "You better put a little pep in your step if you want to get to work on time."

Sky didn't reply. "Did you know that CNN profiled the serial killer and showed a picture of her last night?" Sky asked, watching Niki closely for any reaction.

"They did?" Niki asked, looking surprised. She had fallen asleep on the sofa and missed the news. *Just my luck. The one night I miss the news, they air something I've been dreading.*

"Yes," Sky answered, staring at Niki. "This sounds so silly, but the woman in the picture has a striking resemblance to you."

"Resembles me?" Niki laughed. "That's crazy." Her 'what if's' now started to surface. *What if David's getting close to finding out? What if he knows it's me? What if he's setting a trap?*

"That's what I said," Sky said as she threw the hairbrush to Niki, catching her off guard.

Niki quickly caught it with her left hand, she grinned, "That was clever."

Sky was stunned. *Niki must be the killer,* she thought. *Oh, I wish David had called me back last night.* Her shock showed on her face.

A sick, twisted smile crossed Niki's face. "You figured me out." Niki threw the brush to the floor and quickly took the switchblade from her purse, dropping the purse on the floor.

Sky stood frozen, then bolted to the closet and pulled down the cardboard box, forgetting her earlier unwillingness to touch it. Afraid, heart fluttering, Sky grabbed the gun, but in the haste dropped the clip, bullets went rolling across the floor. Before she could grab them, Niki came at her like a bowling ball and knocked her to the floor—strike.

"Niki, what are you doing?" Sky screamed, keeping an eye on the knife and trying desperately to reach the bullets. The sleeping pill she had taken the night before wasn't helping; its effects hadn't yet worn off. *Why did I try to do this alone?* she asked herself as she twisted and squirmed, trying to get a loose. Even when she was fully awake, she couldn't match Niki's strength.

Niki held the knife at Sky's throat. "Sorry, Sky, I never wanted it to get to this point. I had just started trusting you. I won't hurt you, if you do what I say." Niki helped Sky up, and led her to the bed. Sky looked at her in disbelief.

"How did you know?" Niki asked as she leaned forward, picked up her purse and removed a roll of duct tape. "I always come prepared." She looked down at Sky.

The ringing of the phone made both of them jump. "It's David," Sky said. "He knows I'm home and if I don't answer the phone, he will be here in a matter of minutes."

Niki sneered at Sky, jerked the cord from the wall, and threw it to the floor. "Here," she said as she handed Sky the tape, "Tape your feet together." She tossed the phone to the floor. "You won't be talking to him this morning."

Sky began wrapping the tape around her ankles, not uttering a sound for fear of alarming Niki even more. She didn't know what to expect next; she had never suspected such a side to Niki, this mad woman.

"How did you know?" Niki repeated as she checked the tape for tightness, then cut it loose from the roll. "You see, I never leave home without my blade." She twirled it in the air, a murderous grin on her face. Sky sat stunned.

If I wasn't seeing this with my own eyes, I'd never believe it, Sky thought. She looked up and spoke slowly and deliberately. "I didn't know until I saw the profile on the news last night, and I wasn't sure then. But why?" she cried. "Why did you do it, Niki?"

Niki thought, *If they showed my picture on television, my time is up. I'll have to deal with Wanda Brent today—now.* "The killings were revenge," she said. "I've never killed without a reason."

"Niki, what are you doing?" Sky looked up at her. "Killing is wrong. Please, let me help you."

"Sky, you can't help me." She took the tape from Sky and quietly told her, "Put your hands behind your back."

"Niki, please don't," Sky begged, looking up at her.

"Put your hands behind your back," Niki repeated, a sharp edge to her voice this time.

Sky slowly placed her hands behind her back.

Niki pulled a long strip of tape from the roll, cut it with the knife, and slipped the roll into her purse. "It's too late, Sky. Was it wrong for Charles to rape me?" she asked, her voice growing louder as she taped Sky's hands.

"Who?" Sky asked.

"Charles, the man at Club Elite, yes, I killed him too."

Sky sat still, shocked. "Oh, Niki, please tell me you didn't." She twisted her body trying to free herself.

Niki ignored her. "His name was Charles Scott. He was the boy that molested me when I was a young girl," she said. "That night at Club Elite, while you were dancing with Mr. Jet Away, he stumbled over to our table. He had the nerve to ask me if I knew him. His words were slurred and his breath smelled like a cesspool. He was stumbling over me with a drink in his hand. I told him, no, and to get away from my table. He screamed over the music, 'Yes you do. You're the girl that used to live with us.' He reached for my waist. I told him not to touch me." She flinched as if he was there touching her right then. "He asked me to go outside with him." Sky sat quietly watching her friend's transformation, becoming more frightened with every word Niki uttered. "I looked around and saw you and Pebbles still dancing. I decided to teach him a lesson about touching young girls. I agreed to go outside with him and I helped him inside his car. When he started tugging on my clothes, the memory of being raped flooded back and I lost it. I pretended to pull off my blouse as he began to unbutton his shirt and his pants."

"Oh, Niki—no."

A tear rolled down Niki's cheek. "I snatched my switchblade out of my purse and hid it between the seats. Then I told him to lie back while I took care of him. With his head on the headrest, I slid the knife across his neck then slipped out of his car and returned to the club before you knew I had even gone outside."

Sky could only hope this was a dream. She shut her eyes tight, taking deep breaths and slowly releasing the air. She opened her eyes, hoping Niki was gone, but Niki stood there looking at Sky as if she were seeking her approval. "Sky, I had a rough life growing up. You don't know anything about that; you had it made. You came from a loving family."

"Niki, both of your parents loved you. You will always have those memories. No one can rob you of that."

"Captain Brent did," she said as she stormed over to the window. "They were short memories."

"Captain Brent," Sky repeated softly. *I've heard that name before,* she thought as she discreetly eyed the gun lying on a pile of shoes on the closet floor, wondering how she could reach it.

"Yes, Captain Brent, the pilot." Resentment swelled inside her. She waved her knife in the air. "He was the pilot that was honored at the NAACP Awards Banquet." Malice flashed in her eyes.

Sky stared directly into Niki's face. "What does Captain Brent have to do with you?"

"My mother was on that plane that crashed twenty years ago that Captain Brent was piloting." She hung her head.

Sky gasped. "Niki, I'm so sorry. I didn't know. You never said how your mother died. So that's why you were acting strange at the ceremony. Please untie me and let me help you." Sky saw her grief.

Niki ignored her. "She was on the plane with the two hundred passengers that perished. It makes me sick just thinking about it. I never mentioned it because it was too painful. I vowed to get even with the pilot for ruining my life. That's why I started working for Jet Away."

Sky remembered Wanda Brent saying wind shear was responsible for the accident. "Niki, that was an accident, it wasn't intentional." She began to tremble, realizing how disturbed her friend really was.

"He could have turned the plane around if he wanted to," Niki replied, her voice as hard as steel. "He had to have known." Tears rolled down her face. "He had to."

"They couldn't measure wind shears back then like they do today. He couldn't have known until it was too late."

"I don't give a damn what they can do now, they should have done it then. He could have done something. He could have." Niki's eyes widened as she visualized her mother's last minutes on earth, screaming, crying, and begging God for her life. Something she often played relentlessly in her head as a child that spilled over into adulthood.

"Please release me so I can help," Sky begged as she continued to squirm, trying to free herself. "I'm begging you. I just want to get you some help."

"You can't help me now," she said, shaken out of that dreadful vision. "I have to finish what I set out to do. I have to get rid of these voices. You'll see, they'll leave." She spoke in a child's voice, believing it was true.

"What voices?" Sky asked, confused.

"Can't you hear them?" Niki turned around, her head tilted as though she were listening to something or someone.

"Yes, Niki, I hear the voices, too. Let me get you some help." Sky would say anything at this point to get her friend to release her.

"Pebbles said the same thing." Niki walked around in circles. "But she wanted to get me in trouble. She was going to turn me in."

"Oh no!" Sky's eyes locked on Niki; her heart began to flutter. "Please tell me you didn't." She could feel her eyes fill with tears that threatened to overflow. Her panic was quickly turning to hysteria. *She has lost her mind. If I can only get that gun*, she thought as she eyed the gun again. Sky's fear had begun to show, but she tried valiantly to hide it. "Why, Niki? Pebbles never hurt anybody."

"The voices told me to kill her. I couldn't control them. I tried to get Pebbles to leave but she wouldn't and before I knew it, I had stabbed her. I didn't want to." She broke down crying. "But when she saw me at the hotel, I knew she was going to be a problem." She sat on the edge of the bed with her head down, full of guilt.

"Hotel," Sky's mouth trembled as she listened to Niki's tortured life unfold. Hoping that Niki hadn't killed the woman at the hotel, she had to ask, "You didn't kill the woman at—"

"Sierra Grand," Niki finished her sentence. "Yes, I killed her, too. She was so hateful to me when I made her reservation. She also abused her foster children." Niki stood and shut the closet door.

"Oh no, Niki, you've killed passengers too?"

"Only four," she said. "Two here and two in Houston, they were all so nasty to me."

"But, Niki, how did you know she was abusive? You didn't know her."

"I knew," Niki said. "I heard her yell and curse at her kids while I was making her reservation," she said, waving the knife in the air. "I was treated the same way, slapped, cursed at, and physically abused." She clenched her fist tight. "I can spot an abuser anywhere."

"I know you had an unfortunate life. I really understand." Sky tried to reason with her. "But you can't go around killing people because of your past. Let me help you before you get hurt or killed," Sky said, feeling genuine pity for her because of her horrible abuse.

"I told you, it's too late."

Sky stared in silence, taking deep breaths and trying to get rid of the lump in her throat.

With fire in her eyes, Niki pulled a crumpled piece of paper from her pants pocket and walked into the living room, removed the phone from the cradle and walked back into Sky's bedroom. She jabbed at the numbers so hard she had trouble holding the handset. "Wanda Brent has to pay for what her husband did to my family." Tossing the paper to the floor, she waited for someone to answer.

"Niki, please let—"

"Is Wanda Brent working today?" Niki asked, cutting Sky off in mid-sentence. Sky cried out, "Help!" hoping someone could hear her in the background but Niki quickly ended the call.

"Sky, I'm sorry," she said. "I never wanted it to end like this. I never wanted you to find out that I was the killer. I tried to get help but nothing seemed to work."

"That's bullshit Niki." Sky shook like a volcano on the verge of an eruption, "Let me go," she shouted. "It doesn't have to end this way."

"I'll call David after it's over and let him know that you're here," she said, looking at her reflection on the knife.

"Niki, please, stop!"

"Sky, stay out of it. This doesn't have anything to do with you. I'm going to kill Wanda Brent today." She stomped her feet. "I have to do this, and then the voices will end." She was adamant. "See, when I'm in disguise with my blonde hair and black attire I become Diamond O'Connell. Her voice and others in my head tell me to kill," she said, glad she had revealed this to Sky. "See, the voices are back, they are telling me to hurt you. Do you hear them?" Niki walked over to Sky, took out the tape, and covered Sky's mouth. She emptied Sky's purse and retrieved her cell phone. "You won't need this." Niki put it in her purse along with both phone cords. She removed the tape when she heard Sky trying to speak.

"You did a hell of a job hiding your emotions." Sky said disappointedly as she shook again trying to free herself.

"I had many years of practice, unfortunately." Niki replaced the tape over her mouth and ran out the door, knocking over the coffee table and chair in the living room.

Twenty-Six

*T*he sound of the food cart awakened Aunt Cindy on Monday morning, but because of the sedative she had been given the night before, she was still groggy. She tried to sit up but could only manage to rest her head against the headboard. She lay there like a zombie until the dietitian knocked on her door and pushed a cart into the room.

"Miss Winters, you missed breakfast today," she said.

"Can you help me sit up, please?" Aunt Cindy's voice shook as she attempted to raise her body.

"Sure." The dietitian, who was making a second attempt to get people to eat breakfast, took Aunt Cindy by the hand, lifted her to the side of the bed, and rolled the table closer to her. "I brought you bacon and grits along with a glass of orange juice."

Aunt Cindy lifted the plastic top off the plate and took in the aroma. "This smells good. Thank you."

"Enjoy," said the dietitian, then turned to leave.

Aunt Cindy looked around for the phone, but didn't see it. "Before you leave, will you dial this number for me?"

The dietitian walked around the bed and followed the phone cord inside the dresser drawer. "What's the number?"

"214-666..." She paused, unable to remember. "Now I know her number, it was Aunt Cindy's phone number that she had for over fifteen years." She looked around the room as if the number would appear on the wall.

"Who are you calling, Miss Winters?"

"My niece, Sky." Aunt Cindy pointed to the nightstand. "Will you get that black book and find Sky Winters?"

The dietitian reached into the drawer and retrieved a small address book. She flipped a few pages before she started dialing the number. "I'm sorry, Miss Winters, no answer."

"Try it again! She's got to be there." Aunt Cindy took a sip of her juice.

The dietitian redialed with the same results, "Sorry, but I still can't get through."

"She's in trouble! My daughter is in trouble! I know she is."

"What kind of trouble?" the dietitian asked.

"The serial killer is her friend and if I don't get out of here she'll be dead."

"I see," the dietitian said. She was sure that Aunt Cindy didn't know what she was talking about but went along with her to keep her calm. "I'll try later for you," she said as she jotted down the number on a slip of paper, stuck it in her pocket, and left the room.

Certain that Sky's friend who had come to the nursing home was the woman on the news, Aunt Cindy formulated a plan. She took a couple of bites from her bacon and finished her orange juice, then pushed away the table. She stood and slowly moved to the closet, reaching for a dress.

When the staff and patients were going about their daily routine, Aunt Cindy, fully dressed, walked out the door, and down the hallway toward the entrance. She could see a taxi in front of the nursing home. She walked with celerity over to the fire alarm, pulled the handle, waited for other patients to head for the door and rushed out with them. The staff was busy evacuating the chaotic home and didn't see Aunt Cindy walk over to the taxi.

The driver, who had just dropped off a nurse, heard the alarm and looked over just in time to see a woman walk toward the car. Aunt Cindy handed him her black address book. "Please take me there," she demanded as she got in the backseat. "And make it quick. My daughter is in trouble."

"You bet, ma'am," said the driver still sitting and watching as the people hurled out of the building.

She hit the back of the driver's seat for emphasis. "Hurry

my daughter is in trouble." He pulled out of the circular driveway when Aunt Cindy screamed.

"What kind of trouble?" the taxi driver asked.

"I don't know. I just can sense that she's in trouble, please hurry," she said as they flew by the fire truck.

The taxi driver sped in and out of traffic, trying to get Aunt Cindy to Dallas as quickly as possible. Thirty-five minutes later, he pulled up at Sky's house.

Aunt Cindy opened the car door and moved swiftly up the walk as fast as she possibly could and banged on the door. "Sky, are you in there?" She tried the doorknob and finding the door unlocked, she walked in. Aunt Cindy looked around the living room and noticed a coffee table upside down, and a chair flipped over. She walked into the kitchen but saw no sign of Sky. "Sky, are you in here?" she called again. Aunt Cindy cautiously entered the bedroom, looked around, and found Sky gagged and bound on the bed, squirming like a worm. Aunt Cindy bent over her niece and removed the tape from her mouth.

"Aunt Cindy!" Sky shouted, catching her breath. "I'm so happy to see you. I wasn't expecting to see you of all people. Quick, take the tape off my wrists," she said as she wiggled her fingers to get circulation. "You tried to warn me but I thought you didn't know what you were talking about." She shook her head. "I'm so sorry." Sky let out a sigh.

"Baby, you didn't know," said Aunt Cindy, trying to console her while removing the tape from around her wrist. "It's you're friend, isn't it?"

"Yes, how did you know something was wrong?"

"I may be forgetful, but I'm not crazy. Your mother's no fool." She looked Sky in the eyes. "There was something suspicious about that girl. I could see it in her eyes," she said, sucking on her bottom lip as if she was sucking on snuff. "Then I saw that woman's face on the news last night. I knew it was her, that same look was in her eyes."

"You're right; she's the left-handed serial killer," Sky said, quickly removing the tape from around her ankles. "She's killed a couple of people in Houston and Dallas. I can't believe it." She shook her head in disbelief. "I would have never known had I not seen her picture on television last night too." She stood and hugged her aunt. "How did you get here?"

Before Aunt Cindy could answer, they heard a loud knock on the door. "The taxi—I forgot to pay him." Aunt Cindy felt around in the pocket of her coat for some money.

As the taxi driver stepped through door, he called out. "Hello. Is somebody going to pay me?" Then, looking around and seeing things tossed around in the living room, he yelled, "Hey lady is everything all right?"

Sky called out, "Everything is fine. I'll be right out."

"I should have seen the warning signs," Sky said as she grabbed some money from the dresser.

"That's OK, you probably wouldn't have known; she wore that disguise. But I could tell it was her even with that hat on—she's the devil."

Sky handed her aunt the money, "Go pay the taxi." Then she rushed over to the closet, picked up the gun and clip, and quickly tucked them into her purse.

Aunt Cindy's eyes widened. "Girl, what are you doing with that gun?" She moved slowly out of the way, holding her chest as she went to pay the taxi driver.

Sky shouted to her, "It's for protection."

As Aunt Cindy walked back into the bedroom she saw Sky pick up the wrinkled paper from the floor, and jot down the address and phone number. "Please give this to my boyfriend, Detective David Hall. Remember I told you about David, he's very tall, and should be here soon. Tell him to meet me at this address. Don't forget Aunt Cindy give him this piece of paper."

"Sky, you don't want to get involved. Let your boyfriend take care of it," Aunt Cindy said, taking the paper and still eyeing Sky's purse.

"I can't. It may be too late, I have to stop her." She was glad that she hadn't returned the weapon. "I just hope I get there in time," she said aloud as she rushed out the door.

****

Wanda Brent placed the paddle on the ping-pong table when she heard her name over the intercom. She walked into the office, brushing the curls back from her face.

"What's up?" Wanda asked Jayson, the seventeen-year-old with an attitude. It had been a busy morning; kids were out of school for the summer. She had volunteered to be at the Boys and Girls Club by 7 a.m. on Monday, inspite of her busy weekend. She and Brittany had made it back to Dallas late last night.

"Do you have any enemies out there?" Jayson asked, obviously pissed someone just hung up on him.

"What?" she asked in surprise. "What are you talking about? Do I have any enemies?" she repeated.

"You got the strangest call a second ago," Jayson said, still looking slightly alarmed.

"I did?" Her eyebrows rose. "Here?" She was surprised because no one ever called her at the club.

"Yeah, a lady called and asked if you were working today. When I answered yes, she had the audacity to hang up."

"Huh," Wanda said, wondering if the caller was the same person who had called Troy. "Did she say anything else?"

"No." Then, thinking back, Jayson revised his answer. "Wait a minute. She cursed then slammed the phone in my ear."

"What did her voice sound like?"

"She had a raspy voice," he said. "I tried to get her name."

"OK, Jayson, thanks. It's probably nothing."

"Be careful, Ms. Brent, you know that lady serial killer is still on the loose," he said, gazing at her intently.

"The serial killer," she began laughing. "Boy, you're letting your mind run away with you. That is crazy. Why would she call me? Thanks, Jayson." Wanda walked slowly back to the ping-pong table, thinking back to the night of the awards ceremony. "Troy did tell me that someone had called and inquired about me. That was strange, and now I'm getting calls here. Maybe I'll mention it to Officer Wallace," she mumbled. Wallace was a retired police officer who handled part of the security duties at the club. He'd been employed at the Dallas police department for thirty-five years before retiring two years ago.

Marcus, her ping-pong opponent shouted, "Ms. Brent, you're up."

Wanda just stood there deep in thought.

Marcus repeated more loudly, "It's your turn, Ms. Brent."

Wanda picked up the paddle but was still considering the fact that maybe the phone calls were worth mentioning to someone. "I'll be right back, Marcus," she said as she headed toward a thin man.

"Hello, Officer Wallace," Ms. Brent said as she approached the officer.

"Hi, Ms. Brent. How is it going?" He tipped his hat.

"It's going well but can I talk to you for a moment?"

"Yes, what's the problem?" he asked, looking around the center at the children playing.

"Well someone called here inquiring about me and when Jayson told her I was here she quickly hung up the phone in his face."

"Was it intentional?"

"Yes, I think so."

He furrowed his brow. "Do you have any idea who it may be? Do you have any enemies?"

"Enemies? Why would I have enemies?"

"I had to ask," he said as he bent down and picked up the basketball that had rolled his way.

"No, not that I'm aware of but my brother-in-law told me that a lady called him last month asking a lot of questions about me—where did I lived. Had I remarried? Did I have any children? What type of car did I drive?" She frowned.

"Do you think the same person might be calling you here?"

"Maybe," she said. "I'm not scared, but it's bothering me, a little. This happened to me twenty years ago when my husband died. He was the pilot of a plane that crashed, killing everyone onboard and a couple of angry family members wanted revenge.

"You can't take this too lightly. I'll drive through your neighborhood once in the morning and again in the evening if that will make you feel more secure."

She brushed off his suggestion. "Oh, this is so silly. I'm just overreacting, forget I even said anything. My neighborhood is gated."

"On the contrary, I don't think it's silly at all, Ms. Brent. I can tell that this is bothering you. With that serial killer running around, you can't be too careful. Consider it done."

"OK thanks, I appreciate it. I'll give you my address and code before I leave today," she said relieved.

Wanda returned to her game. "OK, Marcus, where were we?" She hit the ball and sent it sailing past Marcus.

"Sixteen to seventeen," Marcus yelled, as he chased the ball.

Waiting for him to return, Wanda started thinking again about the mysterious phone call. *Why would someone call me and especially here? Why not at home?* When the game ended, she walked over to Officer Wallace and handed him a business card with her home address on the back and the handwritten security code to the gate.

As the officer studied the card he said, "I know this area quite well." Then he flipped the card over, "Hey, this is a nice picture of you," he commented before slipping the business card in his uniform pocket.

She smiled. "Thank you, Officer Wallace."

"No problem, I'll start late tonight."

Twenty-Seven

*D*avid was back in the office in the pre-dawn hours of Monday morning. He called Sky around 7:30 a.m. but got no answer. He assumed she was at work. He would call her on her first break. David had started to go through the files again when the phones started to light up all around the office. CNN had run the tape again early Monday morning, starting a new round of calls.

As the sun climbed high in the Dallas sky, David realized it was already 9 a.m. wondering, w*here had the time gone*? He'd been working steadily, simultaneously going over files, reviewing the video, and helping handle the calls about the mysterious woman on the videotape. So far, the department had about a couple hundred leads; only a few of them sounded promising, many were clearly pranks. There was nothing out of the ordinary regarding the doctor's files.

"It has to be here," David said with frustration in his voice. "The answer's got to be in these files." He started looking back through the files again. *Maybe I can't find what I'm looking for because it's not here.* He stopped, picked up the phone, and dialed a few numbers.

A woman answered, "Hello."

"Hello, Ms. Wellington, this is Detective Hall."

"Hello, Detective. How are thing going. Have you received more information pertaining to the doctor?"

"Not yet, but I was wondering if you could help me with something."

"Sure. I want his murderer caught."

"If I read you the list of names, do you think you can tell me all of the doctor's patients?"

"That shouldn't be a problem; there were only a couple dozen. But I know it's this Diamond lady."

David started reading until he ran out of names. "OK, that's twenty-four. Is that it?"

"Somebody's missing. Could you go over the names again?"

"Brewer, Springer, Hernandez, Foster—"

"You didn't call Nicole." She paused for a moment, before adding, "Doctor Blair saw her for about eight years. He told me Nicole couldn't cope with her mother's tragic death. Her mother died in a plane crash some years ago."

"Plane crash!" His voice elevated.

"What's her last name?"

"Her last name was Slum, Solam, Salem. That's it! Nicole Salem's file is missing. I shouldn't have but I read her file." She said, embarrassed. "She's schizophrenia; he was also treating her for deep depression."

"Nicole Salem," he repeated with surprise.

The way he repeated her name, made Linda think that he might know her. "Do you know her?"

"I don't know if she's the same person," he said, anxious to find out. "Does she have shoulder-length bleached blonde hair?"

"She has shoulder-length hair, but it's black."

"The Nicole that I know is right handed," he said, wondering if they could be the same person.

"Nicole Salem is left handed," she told him.

"Are you sure?"

"Yes. I know because I watched her write her checks many times."

"What does she look like?"

"She's very attractive with peachy-colored skin, hazel eyes, about five-feet, eight-inches tall."

"That's Niki," he said, not wanting to believe what he heard. "You mentioned she was schizophrenia." David fell silent as he thought, *Plane crash, depression, schizophrenia; we can't be talking about the same person.* He had never seen Niki in that state.

"Hello, Detective Hall—are you still there?"

"Yes, sorry." He paused, then quickly asked, "Do you have a fax machine?"

"Yes. Detective, do you think she murdered the doctor?" Linda asked worriedly.

"I don't know. I'm going to send you a picture of Niki. Would you look at it and tell me if we're talking about the same woman?"

"Yes," she eagerly replied.

David reached into his wallet, pulled out the picture of them at the club, and then faxed it to Linda. He heard the machine printing in the background and then a sharp intake of breath from Linda. "Ms. Wellington, are you there?" No answer. "Are you there? Ms. Wellington?" he repeated.

"I'm OK. Seeing the picture shook me up a bit. Your Niki, is the doctor's Nicole."

David bolted from his chair like a pilot ejecting from a fighter jet. "Thank you. I've got to go." He ended the conversation quickly and ran out the door. "Niki's the killer. Dammit, she's ambidextrous." He slammed the car door. "Her motive was her mother's death in a plane crash." He dialed Sky's cell phone but the call immediately went to voicemail. "Hello, Sky, I hope you're at work. I have something very important to tell you about Niki. Please don't mention to her that I've called and stay far away from her—she's dangerous. I'll see you in fifteen minutes." *She's trying to get back at Jet Away. I bet those victims she killed were passengers on the plane.* As he drove to Jet Away, he thought about his interactions with Niki. He remembered how she looked the first time they'd all gone to Houston; she had appeared to be somewhat out of it. How she lied about being at the hotel.

"How could I have missed the warning signs? Stevie Wonder could have seen that. Now I find out Doctor Blair was treating her for schizophrenia." He beat the steering wheel with his fist. His cell phone rang and he quickly answered it, "Hall speaking."

"Detective, this Officer Olivia Brown at the reservation

center."

"Yes Officer Brown."

"I wanted to let you know that the person that made Ms. Turner's reservation, was Nicole Salem."

"She's the killer, but don't try to apprehend her, I'm ten minutes away."

"Ok Detective, we'll wait on you."

Ten minutes later David pulled up in front of Jet Away and dashed out of his car, into the lobby, just as Donna walked through.

"Detective Hall, nice to see you again," Donna said. "Where is Sky she didn't show up for work today and that's unusual, she hasn't missed a day with the company in five years. Plus she hasn't called in."

"What! Is Nicole Salem here today?" he asked alarmed, walking toward the call center.

"No, she didn't show up either."

David quickly turned and sprinted to the door.

"Is everything all right?" Donna asked, but the detective was already out the door.

He jumped into the unmarked patrol car and triggered the radio mic. "This is Detective Hall. I need back up dispatched to 321 Michigan Lane, immediately. I'll meet the officer there."

David continued to call Sky's numbers but repeatedly got the voicemail on her cell and home phone.

David had just arrived at Sky's place when the officer pulled up. He filled the officer in on the situation as they walked up onto the wooden porch. He looked around for Sky's car as he knocked on the door and called her name. He was surprised when Aunt Cindy answered the door. "Aunt Cindy, where's Sky?" He remembered her face from the pictures on the wall.

She jumped back with her hands high in the air when she saw David and the officer with their guns pulled.

"Please don't shoot me."

"I'm not going to shoot you, where is Sky?"

"She's left already." She looked at him with terrified eyes. "You're her boyfriend, Larry, right?"

"It's David, Aunt Cindy. Where is she?"

"Now I'm supposed to give you something." She said

looking confused as she felt around in her pocket. Then she remembered and removed the paper from her dress pocket. "She told me to tell you to meet her at this address."

He opened the paper and read, "Wanda Brent—328 Willow lane, Plano."

"Her friend is the serial killer. Hurry! Sky has a gun."

"A gun!" He jumped from the porch and ran to his car, with the officer right behind him.

Twenty-Eight

*W*anda, still shaken by the mysterious phone call, took her purse and umbrella from behind the desk and walked to the door. Just as she approached the door, the director called her name. She looked over her shoulder and noticed the director walking toward her.

"Yes, Steve" she said with her hand relaxing on the door handle.

"I want to thank you for coming in early this morning. We're always understaffed in the summer. You're a big help."

"You're welcome, Steve. Wish I could stay longer than four hours but I want to get home before the rain starts, and before Brittany gets out of driver's ed class. I also have a couple of errands to run." She looked out of the glass door at the gloomy dark clouds that had started billowing across the sky. The rain would start any minute.

"Thanks again," Steve said as he opened the door for her.

Wanda waved goodbye and ran to her Mercedes, getting in her car just as the rain started to pound down. She pulled out of the parking lot with Niki right behind her. As she turned onto the street, the rain got heavier.

If I didn't need milk and a few other items, I sure wouldn't stop in this heavy rain, she thought as she pulled up at the grocery store. She opened her umbrella, dashed out of the car, shopped quickly, and was back in the car in less than fifteen minutes. Wanda decided to take an alternate route to avoid the heavy traffic and the fender benders that slowed traffic on the highway. Her mind was occupied with the phone calls; she didn't notice the vehicle behind her followed every turn she made. As she drove, she kept wondering about the calls. *Who keeps calling and inquiring about me?*

Ten minutes later, Wanda pulled up to the security gate, keyed in her code, waited for the black wrought-iron gate to open, then wheeled her Mercedes into the circular driveway, and shifted the gear into park.

Niki drove slowly past the gated community and pulled into a neighborhood park about an eighth of a mile away. She reached into the glove compartment, pulled out the blonde feathered wig, and positioned it onto her head. "Wanda Brent we're going to meet right now," she muttered with gritted teeth. Her twenty years of suffering and resentments were about to be vindicated. She slammed the car door and walked purposely, but cautiously, through the rain toward the beautiful $500,000 homes, secured behind the eight-foot, wrought-iron fence.

Niki looked around to see if anyone was watching, then quickly scaled the fence, and landed quietly on the ground just inside the gate. As her eyes slowly scaled the elaborate homes around her, her anger grew with each step taken into the well-to-do neighborhood. *She's living like a queen and all my life I've had to be subjected to hell holes,* Niki thought as she crept closer to Wanda's house.

Wanda had just started to take off her coat when she thought about the pharmacy a half a block away. She'd completely forgotten about it. "Well, I'm already wet, I might as well go back and get that prescription," she said as she headed for the door.

Niki spotted the white Mercedes and quickly stepped behind a bush as the house door opened and Wanda came out, got into her car, and drove off. She waited until she heard the iron gate open and close and then started checking the windows. Locked. She moved to the back patio door, removed the switchblade from her pocket, and picked the lock on the beautifully carved white French door. She walked into a large master bedroom.

Niki, so focused on revenge, failed to appreciate the understated elegance. Beautiful dark purple and white custom draperies covered the windows, giving the room an air of elegance as if it were out of a *House and Garden* magazine. A four-post mahogany bed with long, carved poles and a matching twelve-drawer dresser with ornate gold handles lined one wall. A matching armoire, overflowing with custom-made jewelry, stood next to the dresser.

The vaulted ceiling and plush white carpet seemed to absorb and muffle her steps as she trailed muddy footsteps through the bedroom and down the long hallway. Then, suddenly, there he was, a large portrait of a man in uniform glaring down at her. Still holding the knife, she briskly grabbed the frame and ripped the portrait from the wall. Niki pressed the button and the sharp blade flipped out. She began to slash, each swing stronger than the last as her anger mounted until the portrait lay in shreds on the floor. "You're going to pay for what you did," she whispered, vengeance boiling in her eyes. "You're going to pay."

Niki continued down the hall into a large kitchen, where her fingers trailed gently along the beautiful marble counters and wooden cabinets, feeling the texture, admiring the beauty. *All this should be mine for taking my mother away,* she thought as she paused in the middle of the room. She turned suddenly when the living room door opened and slid to the side of the refrigerator, holding the switchblade tightly in her left hand.

Moments later, Wanda walked into the kitchen, dropped a small bag on the counter, shrugged out of her wet coat, and started to go to the closet.

Niki stepped out of her hiding place, grabbed Wanda, and pressed the knife up to her neck. Driven by self-preservation, Wanda broke free and darted for the telephone. The younger and more agile Niki caught Wanda from behind, grabbed her by the hair, and placed the knife against her neck again, knocking the phone out of her hand.

"Please don't kill me," Wanda begged, her voice cracking and her big black eyes filling with fear as she tried to pull away. "I have money in my purse—please take my car, there's the keys, just don't hurt me."

"I don't want your damn car," Niki snapped as she escorted Wanda to the living room, shoved her onto a wooden chair, and took the duct tape out of her pocket. "Put your hands behind you."

"Please let me go," Wanda pleaded.

Niki pressed the knife tighter against Wanda's neck. "I said put your hands behind your back." Growing impatient, Niki grabbed Wanda's hands, forced them behind her back, and taped her wrists.

"Do I know you?" Wanda asked, her voice shaking.

"Does the name Salem ring a bell?"

"Salem, Salem. No it doesn't. Should I know that name?"

Niki ignored Wanda and began taping her feet to the chair.

"You're the one who's been calling me, aren't you? I've reported the calls to the police. Please let me go, Wanda pleaded as Niki continued to bind her feet. "I promise I won't say anything. Please let me go."

"Shut up! Shut up!" Niki screamed, her face beet red with rage, as she tore the tape with her teeth and threw the roll on the floor. Revenge was at hand and Niki was enjoying every minute of it. "You're going to get exactly what you deserve! Twenty years ago, my mother, Debra Salem, was on a flight from Los Angeles to Houston. She never made it. The plane crashed during landing. I have never forgiven the airline or the pilot. I vowed that I would get everyone responsible for her death. And that includes your husband."

Wanda sat in disbelief. She thought her husband's ordeal was behind her, now it had resurfaced after twenty years. "Oh no," Wanda said as she squirmed on her chair, trying to get free. She knew by the look in Niki's eyes that if she didn't free herself she would die.

Niki walked to the window and stared at the rain beating against the pane, and then walked back to Wanda, pure hatred radiating from her very being.

"Lady, please, let me go!" Wanda begged, fear evident in her eyes and voice.

Ignoring Wanda, Niki continued, "When I saw you at the awards ceremony—"

"That's where I saw you," Wanda interrupted. "You're...you're..." she said, stumbling over her words as she tried to remember Niki's name, "Nicole."

"Shut up, bitch!" Niki screamed belligerently and slapped Wanda hard across the face. "I could have killed you that night."

Wanda closed her eyes, feeling the pain. A woman with a reputation for helping and saving others bowed her head, wondering if she would be able to save herself. She tried again to reason with Niki. "Lacy didn't kill your mother on purpose. It was an accident."

Niki bent down in front of Wanda and looked her in the eyes. "You're his wife and since your husband killed my mother, I'm going to kill you." The tears began to roll down Niki's face. "That's only fair—Right?"

This is insane, thought Wanda. "But it was an accident, Nicole," Wanda pleaded. "You're not thinking logically."

"I didn't get to spend any time with my mother. I didn't get to know my mother because your husband took her away from me when I was only seven."

Wanda could truly see the pain in Niki's eyes and for a split second empathized with her. She knew so well the hurt and pain of losing a loved one.

Niki walked around, running her hand over the well-polished furniture. "All of my years growing up, going to school, I wanted so badly for my mother to be there with me. I was shuttled from foster home to foster home, molested by my foster dad and foster brother. I had no one to save me." As Wanda looked at Niki, she saw a child in a twenty-nine-year-old body. Wanda could definitely feel her pain. She sat staring, as Niki's emotional scars surfaced. "I cried out for help, day after day, and no one came to my rescue. If I reported the abuse, they would just send me to some place worse."

"Nicole, I'm very sorry. I know many lives were affected."

Niki stared at Wanda and continued to talk. "I had to fight for my survival to the point that I had to kill a few times, so I won't have a problem killing you." Niki stared hard into Wanda's eyes, and then snatched off her wig. "I'm the left-handed serial killer, but I can justify every murder. It was revenge, only revenge!" she said, without remorse.

Wanda sat shocked knowing she was in serious trouble; she looked around for a way to escape. *Maybe if I share my loss and forgiveness of Evan that may reach her,* she thought. "I've known personal loss and agony, too. A drunk driver killed my daughter. He was only a teenager himself. I forgave him. In fact, he comes around on holidays and spends time with me and my daughter, Brittany," Wanda said, trying to keep panic out of her voice.

"There's no such thing as forgiveness, only revenge!" Niki snapped. She remembered seeing how happy Wanda and Evan were at the awards ceremony. Niki walked around the room as she continued to talk. "My first brush with murder was when I tried to murder Mr. Clark after he raped me. I made coffee for him and slipped in some rat poison. He drank the coffee, but I guess I didn't use enough poison because it didn't kill him, just made him sick as hell. A month after he raped me, I started getting sick every morning. Eight months later, I faced a dilemma a fourteen-year-old should never have to experience. And you expect me to forgive someone like that?"

"Hell, no I don't; I doubt if I could either, but you have to understand, there's a difference between what that man did to you and what happened to the airplane. That man deliberately hurt you; the crash was an accident. I know it's hard to forgive someone who has taken someone precious from you, something that can never be replaced. It took years for me to forgive the young boy that killed my daughter." Wanda spoke softly, trying to diffuse Niki's anger.

She thought she might be getting to Niki because she put the knife down, sat on the sofa, and appeared to be listening to Wanda. "I feel so sorry for you. Please let me help you." She looked at Niki with genuine compassion.

Niki jumped up from the sofa, grabbed the knife again, and danced the point of it around Wanda's face. "I don't want your sympathy. It's all your husband's fault. I blame him." Niki wanted to be the victim she'd been conditioned to be.

Wanda turned her head away from the knife, flinching when the sharp blade touched her skin. *How can I get out of this?*

"You have this big luxury home. I don't see you hurting for anything," Niki spat, contempt in her voice and vengeance in her eyes, as she looked around the beautiful living room.

Wanda glanced at the clock on the wall and tears welled in her eyes. "My daughter will be home in fifteen minutes. Please leave," she begged. "I promise I won't say a word."

"And miss the opportunity of seeing your lovely daughter again? I don't think so." There was no way Wanda wanted Brittany caught up in this—she couldn't afford to lose another daughter. She tried to reason with Niki. "I've been hurting for twenty years, too. I've had to learn to live without my husband and daughter. After my husband died, I cried myself to sleep many nights." Wanda looked toward the front door, knowing that at any moment Brittany would walk in.

"I told you to shut up. At least you have family. I have no one. My father died of cancer shortly after Mom's death. I tried to be strong and bounce back, but I couldn't. My losses have haunted me all my life."

"Niki, do you think if you keep killing people, this hurt and rage will go away? It won't. Please put the knife down."

Niki walked over to Wanda, picked up the wig, and re-positioned it on her head. "Mrs. Brent, this is what your husband has created."

Wanda's heart raced when she heard a key turn in the lock.

Niki heard the sound too and quickly moved over to the door. "Don't you utter a sound—if you do, she's dead." The look on Niki's face left no doubt she was serious.

****

"Come on get out of my way!" Sky screamed, as if the drivers could hear her as she rushed along the slick streets. She looked at the crumbled paper then started reading the numbers on the building. She pulled up in the parking lot to find that it was the Boys and Girls Club. She rushed out of the car and hurried inside. Children were playing ping-pong, basketball, and video games. She looked around in search of Wanda Brent, trying to remember her face. She proceeded to the office after three minutes of searching.

Jayson sat at the front desk. "Are you here to pick up your child?" he asked Sky as she approached the window.

"No, actually, I'm trying to catch Wanda Brent." Her heart was racing. "Does she work here?" she asked, looking around the busy recreation center.

"Hey, are you the lady that called here for her and hung

up?"

"No, but she could be in serious trouble," she advised the seventeen year old. "Her life is in danger."

"For real!" Jayson sat in disbelief. "How do I know you're telling the truth?"

"Listen, every second I stand here with you is a second off her life."

Jayson became worried and called the officer over the intercom, "Officer Wallace, you're needed in the office and hurry."

Officer Wallace hurried to the window and stood next to Sky. "Hey Jayson, what's so urgent?"

"She's requesting to see Wanda Brent," Jayson said as he pointed to Sky.

"What business do you have with her?" The officer turned to Sky.

"Her life is in danger, and if I don't get to her in the next minute she could be dead."

"Dead! Let me see some ID?" asked the officer.

"Sure." She reached into her purse and he immediately saw the gun.

"Hold it right there, ma'am. Do you have a permit to carry that gun?"

"No, but I can explain."

"Weapons are not permitted on the premises." He looked at her. "You can explain at the police station."

"No, you don't understand. Wanda Brent is in trouble," Sky said as the officer turned to apprehend her. She shoved the thin man, knocking him to the floor, and Wanda's business card slid onto the waxed floor in front of her feet. Sky noticed Wanda's picture on the card and quickly picked it up. She flipped it over. There was the address.

"I'm sorry, Officer. My fiancé is Detective David Hall. He works for the Dallas Police Department. Call him and give him Wanda's address before it's too late," she said all in one breath, as she ran out the door. She knew David would be at the club soon if Aunt Cindy gave him the note.

"Wow, this is like being at the movies!" Jayson said. "Everything happened so quickly. Are you OK?" He asked Officer

Wallace who was up and on his phone confirming Sky's story.

****

Fear gripped Wanda and she felt hopeless because she was afraid she couldn't save her daughter. Wanda's hands were tied, literally, but she knew she had to try something. She couldn't let this crazed woman kill her daughter. As the door opened Wanda screamed, "Brittany, get out of here—fast!"

It was too late. Brittany walked into the room and Niki jumped in front of her, shoved the knife under her chin, grabbed her by the arm, and swung her to the floor. Her papers scattered in all directions. Brittany gave her mother a scared and confused look. *Who is this woman and why is she holding my mother hostage?* she wondered, as she lay still on the floor, afraid that if she moved, this mad woman would slash her throat.

"Please don't hurt her," Wanda pleaded, seeing the fear in her daughter's eyes. "She doesn't have anything to do with this." Wanda strained against the tape on her hands and ankles as she looked at her daughter cowering at her feet.

Niki walked up to Wanda, "I told you to shut up. If you scream again, you're dead." Niki put pressure on the knife, piercing the side of Wanda's face to prove she was serious. A thin line of blood slowly rolled down her face.

"What's going on, Mother?" Brittany whispered when Niki walked across the room.

"Don't say anything," Wanda softly mouthed.

Niki turned her attention to Brittany. "Get up and sit on that chair next to your mother." She threw the duct tape to Brittany. "Start taping your legs, and don't say a word."

Once Brittany finished taping her legs, Niki snatched the tape from her and started taping her wrists. Brittany stared expressionless at a picture on the wall; her tension increased with every breath, until she could no longer hold back the tears. "Why? Why are you doing this to us?" she cried.

"Revenge. That's why. Your dad killed my mother and I'm going to kill both of you." She placed the tape on the table.

Brittany sat stunned, shocked by what she had heard. She turned to her mother with a look of confusion, then back to Niki. "We haven't done anything. Please just let us go," Brittany pleaded as she continued to cry. Her body shook with fear.

Wanda looked at Brittany. She wanted to comfort her but the tape held her tight. She whispered, "Shh, don't cry." She tried again to reason with Niki. "Please, revenge is not the final answer," Wanda said. "You'll suffer in the end."

"You just don't get it, do you lady?" Niki replied. "I've been suffering all my life. This is the end."

Before Wanda had a chance to respond, the living room door flew open and Sky hurried in with her gun in hand. She stared at Niki, hoping she hadn't done anything foolish. "Niki," Sky said, "please put the knife down."

Niki moved closer to Sky until she saw the gun, "I thought I took care of you at your place. How did you get away?" Niki looked around, wondering if David was going to burst through the door next. Had he untied Sky?

"Niki, don't make me use this thing. Put the knife down," Sky shouted as she aimed at Niki's head, closing the door with her foot.

Niki, taken by surprise at Sky's assertiveness, took a step back. "Sky, this doesn't have anything to do with you. It's about me and them." She pointed the knife toward the Brents, who sat looking in disbelief.

Sky's heart fluttered as she remembered seeing Wanda and Brittany at the awards ceremony. *Niki has literally lost her mind*, she thought.

"Mother, what's going on?" Brittany whispered, also remembering seeing both Niki and Sky at the awards ceremony. She sat there in disbelief, thinking, w*here are the cameras because this is definitely made for a movie.*

"I don't know," she answered, trying again to free her hands. "But we have to get out of here."

"Niki, you're sick. Let me get you some help," Sky pleaded. "I promise you, I'll be with you all the way." Even though, knowing Niki was the killer, Sky still wanted to help her because of her abused life as a child—Niki was like a sister to her.

Niki ignored her and stood gripping the knife tight, calculating, and plotting.

Sky walked closer to Niki, pointing the gun at her face. "Put the knife down!" Sky told her emphatically. "Don't make me use this." She shook the gun with great force to let Niki know she was serious.

"Please help me." Niki faked a cry and walked slowly toward Sky, lowering the knife to her side. "I'm sorry, Sky," Niki said, pretending to show remorse. *It worked on Dr. Blair*, she remembered.

Sky let out a big sigh, relieved that Niki decided to give in. "I told you Niki I'm here for you all the way." She smiled and reached for the knife then Niki forcefully pushed her friend to the floor, sending the gun sailing in the air. As the gun hit the floor, it discharged sending a bullet into Brittany's shoulder.

Brittany let out an agonizing cry. Wanda squirmed and tried to get to her daughter, but the only thing she could do was watch the blood slowly seep through the sleeve of Brittany's blouse. "You shot her!" Wanda said in complete shock before turning her attention to her daughter. "Brittany, are you all right?"

Brittany took a deep breath. "Yes, I guess so," she said, looking down at her arm. "The bullet just grazed me. It's stinging Mom but I'm OK," she assured Wanda.

Niki and Sky fought for the gun, then Sky knocked Niki to the floor with her fist. Niki amazingly landed right next to the gun and quickly grabbed it. "If you move another inch, you're dead," Niki said as she lay on her back pointing the weapon in Sky's face.

"Please don't hurt her," Wanda pleaded. "Look at my daughter; she's bleeding. She needs to go to the hospital," she said, hoping to find a way to get Brittany out of the house.

"Move real slowly and walk over to the chair." Niki told Sky as she stood, still pointing the gun at her. Niki picked up the tape from the coffee table, "Now slowly, wrap the tape around your ankles, I told you to stay out of this. It wasn't any of your concern, but you wouldn't listen." She snatched the tape from Sky and began taping her hands as she held the gun tight. "You won't get away this time," Niki said as she tightened the tape around Sky's ankles. "Now I have to kill you too; you've left me no other choice."

"Niki, you won't get away—David knows."

But Niki ignored Sky and slid the gun into the corner of the room. She walked over to Brittany and toyed with her, sliding the knife around her neck.

Sky screamed at Niki, trying to distract her. "Niki, look at me! I'm Sky, your friend. We work together—we've gone out together." Niki ignored Sky. "You've met my family." Niki stopped sliding the knife around Brittany's neck as she looked at Sky thinking about the love she had received from Sky's parent. Then she went back to tormenting Brittany running the knife up and down her face.

Sky shifted her eyes from Niki to Wanda to Brittany and back to her disturbed friend. "Niki, you're scaring her," Sky said, watching the tears fall from Brittany's face. She hoped to reason with Niki.

"That's the plan. I want her to feel the way my mother felt the last minutes of her life—SCARED."

"Shh, don't cry, Baby. Everything will be OK," Wanda told her daughter as a plan began to take shape in her mind.

"How old are you?" Niki asked Brittany, putting the knife to the tip of her nose.

Brittany stared straight ahead without uttering a sound. She tried to be brave for her mother's sake, but when Niki ran the knife around her ear, she screamed. "I'm sixteen!" Her bottom lip quivered from fright.

"Look at me! Look at what your father created!" Niki snarled, staring into Brittany's coal-black eyes.

"My dad didn't kill your mother," Brittany screamed bravely. "I don't know my father. I'm adopted." The tears continued to pour.

Niki looked like she'd been gut punched.

"I told you she doesn't have anything to do with this. Please at least let her go and keep me," Wanda cried.

Brittany continued. "I was adopted sixteen years ago. He couldn't have possibly been my dad. I don't know my parents."

Niki stepped away and caught her reflection in the oval wall mirror. She saw a confused woman and began to slowly back away as the unwanted voices resurfaced. With Sky begging her to put the knife down, Wanda pleading for her daughter's release and Brittany crying. Niki became discombulated, covering her ears, she screaming, "Everybody keep quiet!" She quickly swiped the knife across Wanda's face, leaving a long thin cut from her temple to her chin enough to scare her quiet.

Wanda's red eyes widened as she continued looking at Niki in shock.

Brittany started to cry hysterically when she saw the blood on her mother's face. "Please leave her alone."

Niki turned her attention back to Brittany, taking small pokes at her neck and arm.

Brittany cried out, each scream louder than the last.

Wanda screamed, "Oh my God, you're hurting her. Please, God, help us!"

"You don't know what you're doing, Niki. Please stop," Sky shouted, hoping to draw Niki's attention away from Brittany.

Niki turned. "Oh, I don't?" she challenged her co-worker. She leaned forward and slid the sharp knife around Sky's neck at an agonizingly slow pace until blood began to seep from the side of her neck. Satisfied that would keep Sky quiet for the time being, she turned her attention back to Brittany. In a less-than-human voice Niki said, "It's your time."

Wanda screamed, "No!" in a monumental explosion of energy she managed to stand with the chair still taped to her body and swung the chair around, sending Niki and herself crashing to the floor.

Niki's vicious smile broadened as she crawled over to the knife that had fallen on the floor. She grabbed the knife and stood over Brittany, raising the knife to her neck.

"No!" Wanda and Sky bawled.

Brittany squinted her eyes and dropped her head, trembling like a leaf.

Then Niki suddenly froze and stumbled backward as she looked down at the floor.

"Where did you get this?" She picked up a picture.

Twenty-Nine

*W*ho in blazes pulled that alarm?" the head nurse asked once they got all the residents back into their respective rooms and settled down. "See if anyone is missing," she told the other nurses. The nurses methodically checked the rooms, finding everyone exactly where he or she should be until they reached Aunt Cindy's room. Empty.

They continued to check rooms, thinking she might be visiting someone else or trying to find a television she could turn on to watch the news. Still nothing.

The head nurse was about to call security to check the grounds when the dietitian walked up to her. "Do you remember how insistent Miss Winters was about talking to her niece or daughter or whatever she is? Someone named Sky?"

"Yes, but I told her we'd call in the morning. She immediately fell asleep after we gave her that sedative," the floor nurse said.

"She was still worried about this Sky person this morning when I stopped to try and get her to eat some of her breakfast," the dietitian said. "She wanted me to call her. I had to track the phone down. I guess she put it in the drawer."

"No, I put it there so she wouldn't see it when I was trying to calm her," the floor nurse explained.

"Well, anyway, she asked me to call Sky. I tried a couple of times, but I didn't get through so I told Miss Winters I would try again. Shortly after that the alarm went off and I forgot all about it."

"Do you happen to remember the number or the address?"

the head nurse asked.

"As a matter of fact, I jotted down the phone number so I wouldn't have to look it up again when I tried to call later." She reached into her uniform pocket and pulled out a neatly folded note. "Here it is. Do you think she pulled the alarm just so she could get out and find this Sky?"

"It's a good bet," the head nurse said. "It wouldn't be the first time she has managed to walk out of here. One night she left in just her pajamas and we didn't miss her until Sky brought her back the next morning. We still don't know how she got from here to Sky's place. Give me that number; I'll see if Sky has seen her." She dialed the number and after three rings her voicemail came on. She tried again with the same results. "I have her cell phone and work number in the office. Let me get it." She called the cell phone with the same results—straight to voicemail. Then she dialed her work phone number and was advised that she wasn't in. After the nurse explained the reason for the call, Donna, Sky's supervisor advised her that Sky hadn't called in and that she had never missed work before. *I guess we need to send someone over there just in case*, the nurse thought, as she called security, and told them her problem. The head nurse would meet someone at the front door.

Forty-five minutes later when the head nurse knocked on Sky's door, Aunt Cindy answered. "About time you got here. Where have you been? I'm not supposed to be here. I'm supposed to be in that awful nursing home," she said. "I even had time to clean this place up while I waited for you. Where were you, anyway? Don't you know you shouldn't leave a sick lady like me alone?"

"I'm sorry, Miss Winters, we didn't realize you were gone. Someone pulled the fire alarm and panicked the whole place," the nurse told her, ignoring the comment about the 'awful nursing home'. She found Aunt Cindy's coat hanging neatly in the closet, took it out, and folded it over her arm. "OK, let's get you back where you belong."

"And hurry. I want to watch the news and see if they caught that serial killer," Aunt Cindy said as the nurse walked her to the car and helped her get in. "It was that friend that Sky brought to the nursing home. I tried to tell Sky that her friend was the devil, but she wouldn't listen to me. She was glad to see me today when I got here, though. I came to warn her, but she'd already figured it out only she couldn't do anything about it. She was all wrapped up in tape and her phones were missing. After I got all the tape off she grabbed a gun from the closet, scribbled an address on a piece of paper, and told me to give it to a man. Then she flew out of here without even closing the door. I don't know what's wrong with that girl. She should know better than to leave her door open with a killer on the loose."

The nurse chuckled softly to herself as the car pulled away. Miss Winters obviously wasn't any worse because of her little escapade. She was running true to form. One minute she was imagining things and the next she seemed perfectly OK.

Thirty

*N*iki stood in a trance as she held the picture tight, "Where did you get this?" she repeated.

Brittany opened her squinting eyes and saw Niki holding the picture that her mother had given her a few days ago. "My mother gave it to me." Brittany's tears had washed away her makeup, revealing the discolored birthmark; the same one the day that Heather was born, the one Niki said she would never forget when she saw her daughter.

Niki turned to Wanda. "Where did you get it?"

"From the adoption agency, the day I picked up Brittany."

Niki gasped and then leaned forward, gazing directly into Brittany's eyes. She placed her hand underneath Brittany's chin and gently tilted her head, brushing her bangs back from her forehead to look for the second identifying mark—the widow's peak that extended her hairline. Sure enough, it was there.

Niki began to tremble, letting the switchblade drop to the floor. She reached out and softly touched Brittany's face, "Your mark…your face, it's…it's..." She stuttered over her words.

"It's what, Niki?" asked Wanda, shifting her gaze between Brittany and Niki.

Niki tried to speak but soundless words floated from her open mouth. Confused silence filled the room. Then, finally, she whispered, "What agency?"

"Walters Adoption Agency," Wanda replied.

That was the agency that had approached me demanding that I give up my daughter, thought Niki.

"My daughter…Heather…this is me. This is us," she said

pointing to the faces on the picture. "But Heather's dead."

Brittany and Wanda's eyes met in disbelief.

"Niki, when was your daughter born?" Wanda asked.

Niki didn't answer. Her mind had traveled to the past.

Wanda asked more forcibly, "Niki, what day was your daughter born?"

"She died," Niki answered in a dazed voice as she continued to look from the picture to Brittany. "She died a few days after she was born."

"Niki, her birth mother named her Heather," Wanda told her. She was born May 5th; she's Heather, your daughter," Wanda said again.

"She can't be," Niki looked at Brittany, confused. "She died years ago."

"Mama, is she…" Brittany started to ask and stopped to gather her courage. "Is she my mother?"

Wanda nodded. "Yes, Niki, she's Heather, she's your daughter," she said through her tears. "Niki, she's Heather—your daughter," she repeated. "She's been with me all this time."

"How?" she paused. "They told me you were dead." Niki continued to stare at Brittany. "I believed them. I believed them," Niki cried. Her hard edges instantly softened. "I'm sorry, Heather. I never meant to hurt you. I'm so sorry." She stumbled to the floor and with trembling hands started freeing Brittany's feet.

They all stared mesmerized as they watched Niki, the once bitter woman, change her hatred to remorse.

"If I had known you were alive, I would have looked for you." Once she removed the tape from around Brittany's hands, she rested her head on Brittany's lap and wept. Brittany, confused, slowly began to stroke Niki's hair.

Niki raised her head and repeated, "This is us," she said with an ill smile. "The nurse snapped a picture of us a couple of days after you were born. I was having second thoughts about giving you up—but I knew I couldn't take care of you, that's when the nurse told me that you had died. I was sick and couldn't attend the burial."

Sky looked at Wanda. "But how?" Her bottom lip trembled.

Wanda swallowed hard. "I was called by this adoption

agency that I thought was reputable." She continued, "However, the courts closed the agency about two years later for fraud. They were stealing babies; so I was afraid to report it, fearing the court would come and take my precious child." Wanda felt ashamed. "So the hospital told you that your baby had died—and sold her to me. It had to have been an inside job—several people went to jail."

"I didn't know," Niki told her baby. "I never meant to hurt you. I thought if I killed Lacy Brent's widow, all of my troubles would disappear. I never knew that she had adopted you. I never would have—"

"It's OK," Wanda interrupted. "We want to help you." She smiled. "When I heard that you were raised in a foster home and had been raped, I wanted to help you."

"You wanted to help me," Niki said. "I never imagined that someone would be interested in me."

Sky stared in amazement at Niki's contrite behavior. She was definitely sorry for her wrongdoings.

"Yes, I did," Wanda replied thinking how ironic all of this was becoming.

"You don't know my mother, she's kind like that."

"I'm so sorry Wanda."

"It's OK, Niki. But we need to get you some help."

Niki pulled her jumpsuit off her shoulder and showed a mark on her shoulder blade.

"I have one too. That's your birthmark," Niki whimpered as she rubbed Brittany's face. "It came from my mom—your grandmother."

Wanda smiled as her daughter received some history on her biological family. "Niki, we need help, our wounds need to be cleaned.

"I only tried to protect myself, that's the only reason why I killed," Niki confessed.

"We understand, Niki, but you have to call 911," Wanda said, concerned.

Niki got up, went to the phone, and dialed 911. Just as she finished giving the address, David and the Officer dashed through the door with their guns drawn.

Niki quickly scrambled back to her knife and picked it up,

throwing the phone to the floor. "Put the knife down, Niki," David said as he walked toward her. When Niki ignored him, he repeated, "Put the knife down I know everything."

"No! David—don't," the ladies screamed in unison.

David and the Officer stood in confusion, wondering why they didn't want him to harm Niki, despite her heinous acts of murder. Before David could ask, Brittany groaned and grabbed his arm.

"Are you OK?" he asked as he checked out her shoulder.

Through her tears, Brittany said, "Niki called 911. The ambulance is on their way." David stood surprised by Niki's act of kindness as he glared at her. He repeated, "Put the knife down Niki." She tossed the knife to David and sat on the floor next to Brittany. The Officer moved toward Wanda and began removing the tape. Sky shouted for David to untie her, David moved toward Sky and began removing the tape while wiping the blood from her face. With everyone in the room preoccupied with the chaos— Niki saw an easy opportunity to escape. She slowly stood to her feet, with her finger to her lips, "Shh," she gently whispered to Brittany and like a feline she eased by her, gently touching her. Brittany sat wondering what she should do—should she alert David or let her newfound mother get away. She sat quiet as Niki dashed down the hall and out the French doors. As Niki ran from the house, she stumbled over a ceramic flowerpot, sending it crashing to the ground. "Damn!" Niki said under her breath, hoping no one inside heard the noise.

David heard something break outside. He looked around the room noticing Niki had left. He ran to the window and peered out, just in time to see a figure skirt the bushes and climb over the eight-foot fence. "Damn! She's getting away. I need to stop her," he said as he reached for his radio.

"Stop, David, don't do anything that will hurt Niki. She needs your help, not someone hunting her down like a scared animal. Find her, David, but don't kill her," Sky pleaded.

"Sky don't let appearances fool you. Though she may look innocuous, she is a vicious killer."

"Please don't kill her," Brittany begged. "She's my mom."

"What!"

"I'll explain it to you later David," Sky said. "Find her

before someone else does. Go, David. Niki is the one who needs your help, go." Assured they would be OK until the paramedics arrived, David sprinted to the security gates and saw Niki's Jeep disappear around the corner.

"When I told you I wanted to find my biological mother, I never dreamed it would be this soon, and like this."

"Neither did I, Baby, neither did I." Wanda stood with a shiver of relief. "Maybe if I could have found her right after I adopted you, her life would have been different."

"Now, I don't know anything about my mother. She's gone. I may never see her again."

Sky walked over to Brittany and put her arms around her, "I can tell you all about her."

****

Niki sped down the street, running two stop signs, which caused two vehicles to collide, as she whizzed onto the highway, weaving in and out of traffic. Her whole world was caving in around her. She stomped the accelerator to escape from the David.

David caught up with her and followed behind her closely. He picked up his radio and called for backup. "This is Detective Hall. I'm traveling eastbound on Interstate 35. I'm getting ready to pass the Royal Lane exit. I'm following the left-handed serial killer. She's traveling in a black 2004 Jeep Cherokee. She is not armed. I repeat, the suspect is not armed. If there are any units in the area, please try to intercept her, but don't shoot. I repeat, do not shoot. Just detain her until I get there."

Within minutes, two police cruisers had pulled onto the highway, setting up a makeshift roadblock. As Niki drove a hundred miles per hour around the curve, she suddenly saw flashing police lights and panic. She quickly stomped her breaks on the rain-slick highway causing the Jeep to flip twice and coming to a rest on top of the guardrail.

David grabbed his radio. "There's been an accident on Interstate 35 near Marsh Lane, please send paramedics NOW." He jumped out of his car, and ran over to Niki whose car was teetering on the guardrail. As he got closer, he could hear the metal squeaking and knew at any moment it could collapse. Then he heard Niki's voice.

"David, please help me, please help," she moaned. "I'm so

sorry. I never meant to hurt anybody." Blood was covering part of her face.

"Niki stay calm and don't move. I'll get you out," he said, trying to help her through the door, which had jarred partway open on impact. As he glanced inside, and saw airplane wings, they reminded him that he was about to save a serial killer.

"David I'm afraid, get me out of here." She took a deep breath. "Please help me."

"Shh....Don't try to talk, Niki," David said as he attempted to force the door open far enough to pull her out. The movement caused the Jeep to rock precariously and tumble down the forty-foot muddy embankment with Niki still inside. "Niki!" David hollered as he watched the Jeep slam into a tree and burst into flames. "Oh my God!" he hollered. The momentum had sent Niki sailing out of the broken window and into the bushes. Within minutes, a fire truck and rescue team arrived on the scene. Minutes after the fire was out, the paramedics lost no time getting down to the vehicle.

One of the rescue workers radioed up to David who was pacing back and forth. "I thought you said there was a lady in the vehicle."

"There is," he said adamantly, looking down at the still-smoldering remains.

"You mean there was."

"No. I mean there is," David shouted.

"This Jeep is empty."

She'd vanished.

Epilogue
(18 Month Later)

David wheeled Sky and their new eight-pound bundle of joy wrapped in a beautiful pink blanket toward the hospital door. After the Niki saga, Sky and David were married in a small ceremony conducted by Sky's dad, Reverend Gabriel Winters, in Houston. Sky had quickly become pregnant.

Sky smiled as she watched her precious daughter open her eyes. When she looked outside, she sat straight up in the chair; someone was sitting in David's car. "Who's in the car?" she asked and then broke into a big smile when she saw who got out.

David stopped on the passenger side, locked the wheels on the wheelchair, took the baby, turned, and handed her to Aunt Cindy.

Sky got up slowly. "Hello, Aunt Cindy." She kissed her on each cheek.

"Well, hello, Mommy," Aunt Cindy replied as she began unwrapping the blanket to get a peek at little Pebbles. Sky never wanted to forget her dear friend, who had been in the wrong place at the wrong time and had paid with her life.

"David, thank you."

He blushed. "For what, Mrs. Hall?" he asked, admiring his wife's figure, which had already started to return to its pre-pregnancy shape.

Aunt Cindy secured the baby in the car seat and made sure the straps were tight, but not too tight, then crawled in beside her in the back seat and buckled her own seatbelt.

"Come on, ladies, let's ride." David slid in behind the wheel and started singing in the tune of Sister Sledge, 'We are family, I got all my *ladies* with me'.

Sky slid over next to David in the front seat and poked him in the side. "I know we talked about her coming, but I didn't want you to feel pressured. Especially since we've only been married a little over a year."

As David listened to Sky, he watched the nurse come get the wheelchair and wave goodbye to them.

"After Aunt Cindy visited you yesterday, I couldn't take her back to that nursing home, especially since they found out that she was the one who pulled the lever on the fire alarm."

Aunt Cindy had managed to keep her secret for more than a year and then one day when she had aggravated one of the nurses, she'd told her, "I'll pull that alarm again and walk out the next time your back is turned."

Sky snickered as she remembered Aunt Cindy's devious way of getting out, and then she became solemn thinking how Aunt Cindy came to her rescue.

David's cell phone rang and he looked down to see who was calling. He was on vacation, so it had better not be the police department. Then he saw it was a friend. "Hey, Malcolm, how is Jet Away going?"

"Much better, thanks," he said. "It took the people in reservations a while to forget about what happened, but it's pretty much behind them now. The board members are thrilled that the vendetta is over, or at least they assume it is. It's been dull around here since that lady serial killer vanished. I knew something wasn't right with that girl when she slapped me at the club that night."

"Yeah, she had a lot of issues, some stemming from her childhood. She had a raw deal growing up. I just hope that wherever she is, she's finally getting the help she needs," David said.

"Did you ever figure out what happened at that accident scene?"

"Not a clue," David said. "Unless she starts to kill again, the captain said the case is closed and will probably never be solved."

"Well, at least she hasn't surfaced around here," Malcolm said. "But, hey, that's not why I called. I just heard you're a new daddy. Congratulations. A little girl, right? What did you name her?"

"Pebbles, after Sky's friend," David said, looking over at his wife.

"Congratulations to all of you. How is Sky and the little one?"

"Thanks, man. Mommy and baby are doing fine."

"If it's OK, I'll stop by some time next week."

"Love to see you. Talk to you later."

"Later, man."

****

Another season had come and gone and Wanda, Troy, Evan, and his family gathered around the dining room table to bless their Thanksgiving dinner. Wanda was relieved that her secret was finally out. The lie she'd carried around for years had stopped echoing in her mind. She still felt guilty that Brittany had found out about the adoption the way she had and that she had found and then lost her birth mother in a matter of hours. Seeing a counselor had helped them get their lives back in order. Wanda was at peace and Brittany was happy because she'd had a chance to meet her real mother and hear her stories from Sky. Brittany was now driving and hoped one day she would see her mother again.

Brittany stopped in the doorway and surveyed the table before she walked into the dining room and headed for her seat.

Wanda turned and admired her daughter, who had decided not to wear makeup to hide the discolored beauty mark. It was her way of remembering her biological mother; they had a unique bond.

"Come on, sit down," Troy said as he pulled out Brittany's chair. After Wanda's ordeal with Niki, he had decided to put the past in the past and live for the future. He had begun to accept Evan. He was pleased to have dinner with him and his family. In fact, they all flew from Houston to Dallas together for the holiday on Evan's airline pass.

"Evan, is Skyline hiring?" Brittany asked as she helped herself to the food.

"We're doing a mass of hiring, but you're still in school."

"I was just thinking ahead, maybe I could work there for the summer before school start in the fall."

"Come see me this summer, you definitely have a job," Evan told her.

****

A week later, Evan was sitting in his office, glad it was Friday. He was ready to go home to his wife and son. He had one last applicant to interview before his workday ended. He picked up the application, scanned it, and told the receptionist to send in the woman.

A woman with extremely short, curly, jet black hair stepped through the door. Her sharp dark eyes zeroed in on Evan as she took a seat across from him.

He extended his hand. "Miss O'Connell, your resume is very impressive."

"Just call me Diamond."

BOOK CLUB GUIDE

1. What do you think influenced ████ to become a Serial Killer?

2. If apprehended, what do you think ██████ punishment should be?

3. What age do you feel is appropriate to tell an adopted child that he or she is adopted?

4. Could you forgive a drunk driver if he/she killed your child?

5. Who do you feel was the real hero in the book?

6. Do you think Sky waited long enough before having sex with David? How long should you wait?